TA

THE King's Obsession

THE COMPANION SERIES

4

For Luke.

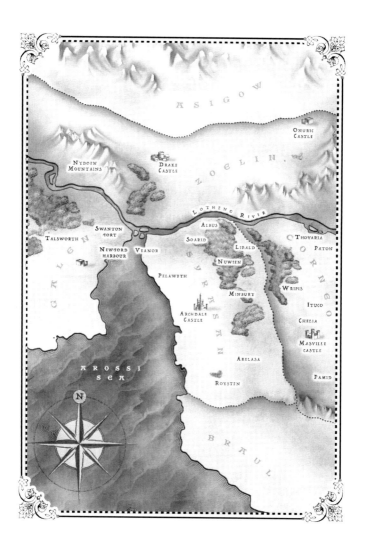

PROLOGUE

She felt his absence before she opened her eyes. Petra blinked, drowsy and nauseous as she took in her surroundings. She slid a hand over the cold patch of linen next to her and looked to the window to gauge the time. The harsh angle of the sun told her it was late in the afternoon.

'Drink this,' came a voice. Not the soothing tone of the midwife, but the firm voice of the physician.

She turned, trying to focus on the tall figure looming over her. 'My son,' she said, her own voice hoarse.

He lifted her head and pressed a cup to her mouth. She recoiled at the overwhelming smell of sage and something unfamiliar.

'Drink,' he repeated, tipping the cup so she had no choice but to swallow.

She closed her eyes against the foul taste. 'Where is he?' she asked, the moment the cup left her lips. Her breasts tightened and she felt a release of milk. Her hands went to her engorged and painful chest. How long had she slept? Babies needed frequent feeding, and she needed the relief.

Her eyes sank shut. So tired. The effort of staying awake…

*

'Milk fever, you say?'

It was the king's voice, and she flinched at the sound. Forcing her eyes open, she focused on the lantern casting soft light over the enormous bed. Was it really night already? She tried to focus on the king and failed.

'I will send the midwife to remove some of the milk.' That was the physician. 'I suggest it is done regularly until her supply dries up.'

Dries up? Her eyes sank shut again, her hands like lead over her empty belly.

'Drink this,' the physician urged.

There was that smell again. What was it?

'That's it,' he said as she swallowed the liquid.

It came to her then. Mandragora. They were sedating her…

*

She felt the sun on her but could not open her eyes to see it. Her throat was on fire and her head pounded. She shivered despite the blankets piled on top of her.

'Where is he?' she whispered to the empty room.

It should have come as no surprise that her son had been handed over to a wet nurse. The king could hardly have the castle's mentor off feeding an infant when there were women to be groomed.

She wanted to wake up, to search for him…

*

'Petra' came a familiar female voice.

The sound startled her awake, and this time she was able to open her eyes. The king's Companion sat by the bed, both hands wrapping hers and an expression of pity on her face.

'Where is Xander?' Petra whispered. Her mouth was so dry that she struggled to speak. 'Where is my son?'

Marden shook her head. 'I do not know.'

The girl was incapable of lying, so she knew it to be the truth. Propping herself up on her elbows with great effort, Petra studied her clean nightgown and the expensive linen covering her legs. The blankets were gone. Her hands went to her breasts, finding them soft.

'You had milk fever,' Marden said, letting go of her hand and standing to fix the pillows behind her. 'You must have been very sick. The physician came every day. I was not even allowed to see you.'

Petra was trying to wade through the mental fog. 'Every day?' She turned her head to the window. It was morning. 'How many days?'

'Today is day nine.'

Petra's gaze shifted to the Companion, searching her face. '*Nine?*'

Marden swallowed. 'There was an abscess.'

She knew letting the baby feed frequently could have prevented it from progressing that far. She struggled to sit. 'I need to speak with the king.'

Marden glanced at the door. 'You are not supposed to leave this room.'

Petra pressed her palms against her eyes. 'What? I have not seen my son in nine days. Take me to him.'

A firm hand held Petra's leg. 'I will fetch the midwife.'

She pushed the hand away, her effort feeble. 'I am fine. I just need to see my baby.'

Before she had a chance to stand, the midwife swanned into the room carrying a basin of water and a washcloth.

'Oh, there she is, awake at last. Fever broke last night, so I knew it would not be much longer. How are you feeling?' She placed the water on the table next to the bed and dunked the cloth, wringing it out before bringing it to the mentor's face.

Petra drew back from the hand. She did not want to be touched, she wanted to see Xander. Giddy, she focused on the colourful tapestry hanging on the wall. The women in it wore pastel dresses and carried baskets of food across a green lawn. Not a child in sight. 'I want my son brought to me.' She fought the relentless urge to lie down and go back to sleep.

The midwife straightened, her confused expression melting into something far worse—sympathy. 'The baby was healthy and strong. I cleared him for the journey five days ago.'

The entire room seemed to spin, and Petra held on to her knees for balance. For a moment, she could do nothing but stare up at the woman who looked back at her with pity. She repeated the words in her mind, trying to decipher their meaning. 'What journey?'

The midwife glanced at Marden, who wore the same unsure expression. 'The infant has already been placed with his new family.'

There was no conscious reaction to that statement, only reflex. The realisation that the king had taken her son broke something inside of her. She swung her heavy legs over the edge of the bed, praying they would hold her weight.

'What are you doing?' Marden asked, visibly alarmed.

Petra was done talking with them; she was going straight to the king for answers. The midwife grabbed hold of her arm, a firm, authoritative grip. It was the same grip Petra had used on Companions for years. She shoved the woman away with both hands, surprised by the sudden burst of strength. 'Do not touch me!'

The woman tumbled backwards into the wall, and Petra heard the air leave her lungs. She did not have the capacity to care. If anyone else tried to stop her, she was certain she would claw their eyes out with whatever strength she had left.

'You cannot walk about the castle in your nightgown!' Marden called to her back, her pitch a few octaves higher than normal.

Ignoring the Companion, Petra stepped out into the corridor, dizzy and struggling to think clearly. She stumbled down the gloomy passageway while confused servants moved aside to watch her pass. He would likely be in the throne room. *Which way?* Her mind fought to get its bearings. Finally, she rounded the corner of the west wing and staggered straight into a guard. He caught her arm, his grip like a vice.

'Where is the king?' she screamed at him, surprising even herself.

The guard took a small step back while keeping hold of her. 'Best you return to your quarters.'

'No!' She looked past him to where another guard stood in front of the throne room. 'Is he in there?' she called.

He glanced at the closed door behind him before walking over to where they were standing and taking her other arm.

As the men began leading her away, she screamed, 'King Nilos! Where is my son? Come out here, you cowardly bastard!' Her legs failed her at that moment, but the men just kept walking, dragging her bare feet along the marble floor.

The door to the throne room swung open and the king stepped out, looking both ways down the corridor before his gaze settled on her. She tried to turn her body to him.

'Where is he?' Petra pleaded. 'Where is my baby?'

Prince Felipe joined his father in the corridor, scowling with disapproval.

How dare he judge me? How many times had his Companions returned to her bloodied or bruised? How many times had she patched them up and sent them back to his bed?

The king leaned in and whispered something to his son. Felipe nodded before walking off in her direction.

'Please,' she called to the king as he turned away from her. 'I will do anything! Just tell me where he is.'

The door seemed to whine in protest as it swung shut behind him. Petra faced forwards, her hands going over her face. 'Please,' she sobbed. 'I want my baby.'

The prince's footsteps closed in behind her.

CHAPTER 1

*P*etra sat on her bed in the darkened room she shared with the other women. A piece of folded parchment hung from her limp hand. She had waited for the Companions to be requested before reading it, the words burning holes in her pocket all day.

He was not there. I am so sorry.
A

He was not there.

She was so sorry.

It was the first proper lead in over a year, and they had not found him. If not there, then where? Someone had him. That someone had had him for five years. Her hand went to her stomach, but before she had a chance to drown in her disappointment, Golda appeared in the doorway.

Petra jumped, then stood. 'Why are you not with the king?'

The Companion appeared ashamed, resentful even.

Petra buried the letter in her pocket as she studied the girl. 'What is it?'

'It is always the same. He cannot… finish.'

A feeling of dread climbed the mentor's spine. 'I see.'

'He has asked for you.'

No surprises there.

They stared at one another for a moment.

'Are you all right?' Petra asked.

Golda looked away. 'He does not want me as his Companion.'

'Did he say that?'

'He does not have to.'

Petra brought her hands together in front of her. 'Go and bathe, and then get some rest.'

She waited for the Companion to leave before sinking down on the bed. In a moment she would have to get up and go to him. She would not bother to change her dress, fix her hair or paint her face; the king was long past caring about those things when it came to her. He would immediately strip her bare, breathe her in, his coarse beard destroying her face and leaving the skin on her neck and breasts raw.

She pushed down on her fingernails, a habit formed over the years, which seemed to be getting worse the longer she remained at Masville Castle.

Press, press, press.

Even in the dark, she could see the purple bruises beneath her nails. It should have been enough to make her stop, but it was not. She could not help but marvel at how her nails matched the bruises on her wrists. Her hands worked as though she were playing a lute, fingers moving swiftly.

Press, press, press.

When she arrived at the king's quarters, the doors swung open and the guard immediately waved her through. King

Nilos stepped around his large bed, his trousers removed after his Companion's failed effort. She felt so cheap in that moment, sent to finish the job. She kept her eyes up, forced to meet his gaze.

'You asked to see me, Your Majesty?'

He nodded and had the decency to look ashamed. 'Come here.'

The door creaked shut behind her. It was the softest clicking noise, but it still made her jump. She did as she was told, staring at the floor while his fat fingers moved over the buttons of her gown. She shut him out as best she could. How else could she survive?

The following morning, Petra stood looking out the large window in the south wing, her arms crossed against the cold. The sun never reached that part of the castle, passing directly overhead so she was forced to live in shadows. She had been watching the supply carts arrive, unload and leave again. The drivers took it for granted that the gates opened and closed for them, that they were free to return to their villages, their families. Did they ever think about the people locked inside?

Her gaze went beyond the wall, where she could see the tops of the trees in the distance. She struggled to remember what lay between the wall and the forest, because she had not left the castle in years.

She did not normally allow herself to wallow in self-pity, but it was the day of her son's birth. He was five years old, and she needed time and space to imagine him at such a bold age. She remembered her younger brother at five, stocky legs thumping around the house with a voice too loud for the small space. He was always on the move, running and tumbling about with a permanent smile on his inquisitive face. He had woken each day armed with questions about the world and did not stop until he was finally wrestled into bed at the end of the day. Nothing could wake him then. Perhaps Xander was the same. Or maybe he was different, reserved and cautious—like she was.

'My lady.'

Petra jumped at the sound of Nyla's voice behind her, then turned.

'Sorry,' the Companion laughed. 'I spoke three times before you heard me.'

'What is it?' She tried to keep the abruptness from her tone and failed.

The smile fell from Nyla's face. 'Prince Felipe is waiting for you outside our quarters.'

Just what she needed.

'Tell him I am on my way.'

The meeting was no doubt due to the fact that Petra had declared his new Companion unfit to socialise despite having been with them for nearly four months. She waited for Nyla to turn the corner before following after her, preferring to make the short walk alone. A few minutes later, she arrived at the Companions' quarters, where she found Felipe pacing in front of the door. He did not like to be kept waiting.

'Good morning, my lord,' she called, back straight and shoulders down. She laced her bruised fingers in front of her. 'How can I help you?'

He stilled, his expression far from friendly. 'What is this I hear about Orla not being available for tomorrow's feast? It is her job to be available.'

Petra stopped a polite distance in front of him. 'I understand it is inconvenient, but she is not ready.'

His eyes narrowed at her. 'Why not? You told me she is an exceptional dancer.'

The girl *was* an exceptional dancer, but she was also prone to fits of tears that sometimes lasted hours. 'Her social skills are lacking.'

'So fix them,' he said through clenched teeth.

Petra lifted her chin. 'She is young, and she is still missing her family a great deal. The smallest trigger can reduce her to tears. Given the important guests that will be attending, including King Jayr of Zoelin, I think it best she remains behind.'

Felipe crossed his arms. 'If I had known she was so weak, I would have selected another as my Companion at the tournament.' He shook his head. 'Perhaps it is more a reflection of the job you do with these women.'

'Prince Kyril has been satisfied with his Companion for a number of years now.' She should have let it go, but he had picked the wrong day to attack her.

He shook his head. 'My brother has the only compliant Companion within these walls.'

Petra squeezed her fingers together to stop them from going at her nails. 'Again, I apologise for the inconvenience, my lord, but Orla needs more time.'

'Fine,' Felipe said, already walking away. 'Have it your way.'

My way? She was stuck inside a revolving nightmare, beginning each day with a tearful prayer that she would survive just long enough to see her son one more time.

She should have gone straight in and told Orla to stop crying, that she had been spared a few more days. Instead, she turned and walked off down the corridor, desperate to be alone once more.

She had just turned the corner when she heard Nyla calling her.

'My lady!'

Petra winced at the sound. Whenever she tried to find a

few moments of solitude, someone always came to her. Was it too late to sink into the shadows of the corridor and pretend she had not heard? Perhaps Felipe had returned to their quarters to have another go at her. It was not unusual for him.

'My lady!'

Much closer this time. Definitely too late.

When Petra turned, she was surprised to see Nyla *running* towards her. 'Companions do not run,' she said, resenting the words she was forced to speak. Nyla did not slow down, which was unsettling, because the girl thrived on rules. 'Whatever is the matter?'

Nyla stopped in front of her mentor, out of breath as she let the skirt of her dress fall to the stone floor. 'She is bleeding everywhere, and I cannot wake her.'

'Who?' It came out as a whisper, because she already knew the answer.

'Orla.'

What a sight, two of Corneo's most refined women sprinting along the corridor towards the Companions' quarters. By the time she reached the main room, Petra was panting. But she pushed on, past the lively fire sucking all the air from the room, through the door on the other side, and down the walkway that led to the bathing room.

She stopped in the doorway to take in the sight before her. Nyla pushed past, collapsing in the pool of blood beside the lifeless Companion. She had wrapped both wrists, no doubt hoping to stop the bleeding. Whatever colour the fabric had been, it was now a vivid shade of red. Petra's gaze travelled up to Orla's eyes, which were still open.

'Help me!' Nyla sobbed.

Petra blinked and stepped into the room. Kneeling on the floor, the skirt of her dress soaking up the bloody water, she lowered her head to Orla's chest, listening for a heartbeat or any other sign of life, but all she could hear was the pounding of her own heart. She tried to feel for a pulse, but touching the icy skin only confirmed what she already knew—Orla was dead.

The mentor pushed herself back and grabbed the edge of the wooden tub while nausea rose and fell within her. 'Fetch the physician,' she said to Nyla. 'And send word to Prince Felipe.'

Nyla shook her head, staring down at the corpse. 'Can the physician do anything?'

'No.' Petra pulled herself up. 'But we still have to send for him.'

Nyla's hands went over her mouth, stifling a sob. Petra leaned forwards to help her to her feet while keeping hold of the tub.

'Go,' she whispered. She watched Nyla flee the room. There were so many things that needed to be done in that moment, and it was Petra's role to implement everything instilled by her own mentor, including remaining calm and in control of the situation. Instead, she turned and vomited into the tub while her legs shook beneath her.

'I am sorry.' The apology was aimed at Orla, but she could not bring herself to look at the girl.

She should have begun cleaning up: herself, the dead Companion at her feet, the room. She should have washed away the fact that a young girl had chosen to take her own life rather than spend one more day in this prison. But she needed air. If she could just get some clean air, she might be able to think clearly.

Stumbling through the door, she made her way through their quarters and out into the corridor. She had planned to stop there, stand by the window and regroup, but she kept walking. Her feet squelched in her shoes and her wet skirt chafed her legs, leaving a red smudge on the ground behind her. A bloody trail. She descended the stairs and passed the laundry before exiting through the small door that led outside.

Air. She needed to breathe clean air and rid her nostrils of the metallic smell of blood.

The cold morning air was like a slap to the face. It was exactly what she needed at that moment. Gulping greedily, she glanced across the lawn. It was still too cold for people to be loitering outside unnecessarily. Just a few moments and she would return upstairs.

But when she looked down at her filthy hands and dress, she realised she could not do it. She could not go back and face that girl and the prince responsible for her death.

How would the king react? It would put ideas in his head, make him fret, and drive his paranoia. Later he would call her to his bed, needing her to reassure him. And perhaps every day after.

Her eyes went to the wall then, recalling the Companion who had escaped over it. Petra had turned a blind eye and let her flee, along with her prince. She had promised to find Petra's son. That was the reason she had let Aldara go. Not the entire reason though. The girl had figured a way out, and who was she to deny someone an out? Now that Companion wrote to her regularly, always with the same disappointing news.

'He was not there. I am so sorry.'

Perhaps she should go over the wall, but she did not have an elaborate plan. The narrow steps along the wall would only lead her to the top, where she would be forced to jump and likely die on the rocks below. Was that better than what awaited her inside?

'My lady?'

She gasped and turned, surprised to find Velma, the young laundry maid who delivered her private letters, standing there. The maid's gaze moved down her dress, eyes widening.

'Are you all right?' she asked, shifting nervously. 'Are you hurt?'

Petra had come outside to get some air, so why could she not breathe? 'No.'

Velma watched her for a moment. 'Whose blood is that?'

It was all of theirs—every Companion who suffered before and after her.

She held out her bloodstained hands, staring down at them. When she did not answer, Velma asked, 'Should I fetch someone for you?'

Should she? No. Petra did not want to return inside. 'I need to get out of here,' she breathed.

Velma glanced behind her at the empty doorway before asking, 'Do you mean out of the castle or… outside its walls?'

Petra blinked as she processed the question. She should have dismissed it and returned inside—calm, composed and ready to deal with the practicalities of what had just taken place. She should have scolded the girl for even asking such a question. Swallowing, she replied, 'Outside its walls.'

CHAPTER 2

*P*erhaps Velma was waiting for Petra to snatch the words back, laugh them off and say it was all a big joke, because she looked very unsure in that moment. Petra opened her mouth to speak and then closed it again. Did she want to take them back? It was not too late.

'If you're sure, I might know a way,' Velma said, watching the mentor closely.

Petra swallowed, mind racing. She was not even sure if the girl was capable of helping her without getting them both in a lot of trouble.

'Are you prepared to leave right now? With nothing but the clothes on your back?'

If she said no, she would have to return upstairs. She knew she would lose her nerve if she had time to think it through. 'Yes.'

Velma looked torn for a moment, then, as though making up her mind about something, stepped past her. 'Follow me.'

She did not know why she obeyed so blindly, but Petra turned and followed.

They walked along the stone wall, through the courtyard,

which would soon be full of maids carrying baskets of laundry to be hung, until they reached the west wall. The ground was covered in mud and ice, so they kept to the narrow path that led all the way to the stables. It was the perfect opportunity for Petra to stop and question the maid, to take back some control over what she was about to do, but she did not have it in her. If Velma could be trusted to deliver and receive letters on her behalf, perhaps she could be trusted to get her out of the castle.

The whinny of a horse reached them from the mounting yard, and Petra jumped at the noise. Velma glanced over her shoulder but said nothing. When they were close to the stables, the maid held up a hand and they both stopped walking. A few grooms stood with horses, chatting as they brushed the animals down. Velma pointed to the cart outside the stalls, where a lanky boy stood shovelling straw into a wheelbarrow.

'That's Hugon. I'm going to marry him one day,' Velma announced.

Petra closed her eyes for a moment. 'I see.' She glanced about at the trees around them, wondering why on earth she had followed this naive girl.

'He'll leave here shortly,' Velma continued. 'Soon as the cart's loaded.'

Petra's gaze returned to the boy. 'You mean *unloaded?*'

Velma shook her head. 'The old straw has to be taken away.' Seeing that Petra was confused, she added, 'The guards never check the cart because of the smell.'

The mentor's hand went over her mouth as she digested the proposal. 'You want me to leave here in a pile of horse manure?'

'You'll have to cover yourself with it.'

Press, press, press.

She raised a hand to her forehead as she tried to think

past the panic and grief twisting inside her. A few moments earlier, she had been considering leaping off the top of the wall to be free of this place. Now, presented with a much safer out, she was having second thoughts about the entire thing. Where would she go if she made it through the gate? She could never return to her family. That life was over, and she would only bring danger to them.

Her hands fell to her sides. 'Why are you helping me? Do you understand what might happen if the king finds out?'

Velma pressed her lips together before replying. 'I wash enough linen to know what happens behind closed doors in this place.' She glanced down at Petra's blood-soaked dress. 'Were you with child again?'

Again. A fair question given her long history. Petra looked down at her bloodied dress and noticed she was shivering. 'It is not my blood.' Orla's face flashed in her mind, and she closed her eyes against the image. When she found the strength to open them again, she whispered, 'I will do it.'

Velma nodded. 'Wait here.'

Petra watched from the trees as Velma made her way to the stalls to speak with Hugon. The other grooms looked up but, seeing who it was, returned to their work. Obviously the maid's presence at the stables was not too out of the ordinary.

Hugon stopped his work and leaned on the pitchfork, watching as Velma came towards him. As they spoke in hushed tones, Hugon glanced over in her direction, shaking his head. Understandable. There was great risk, and he did not even know her. Velma moved closer to him, speaking for another minute before he finally nodded.

Oh God. What am I doing?

Velma turned away from the boy and made her way back to Petra, twisting her apron in her hands the whole time. 'He'll stop on the track, just down there,' she said, pointing to the spot. 'Be ready to climb in. He can take you north, but only as far as Chelia.' She frowned up at Petra. 'Do you have somewhere to go?'

Petra swallowed. 'I will figure it out.'

'Do you have any coin?'

She glanced down at the jewels on her wrists and fingers. 'I have items to trade.'

Velma shifted her weight. 'I told Hugon you would pay him.'

Of course she had. Why else would he risk his life for her? Petra reached for the large gem hanging from a chain around her neck. 'Good thing I am overdressed for the occasion.'

A crow flew overhead, its shadow passing over them.

'How long until King Nilos comes looking for you?' Velma asked.

Petra shook her head, thinking. 'I do not know. It might take him some time to figure out I am not here.'

'Then he'll come for you. He loves you. More than the queen, they say.'

It was not love, but the easiest response was a nod. He would come for her because she belonged to him, and he would turn the kingdom upside down until he found her.

'I need you.'

It was always the same. 'You do not need me.'

'I do. If you were to leave—'

'I cannot leave.'

He kissed her stomach. 'Because you love me?'

'Because you will not let me go.'

She would need to get out of Corneo. Perhaps she could go to Lord Belen's manor in Wripis and ask Aldara to help her come up with an actual plan. The princess owed her that much. If anyone learned of her part in their escape, she would be labelled a traitor. But she had been rendered powerless the moment the Companion promised to help track down her son.

'I think the less you know, the better.'

Velma nodded. 'I have to get back.' She hesitated before reaching out and giving Petra's hand a brief squeeze. 'I really hope I don't see you back here.'

'Thank you,' Petra whispered.

Velma began to leave, then looked back. 'And I hope you find your son.' She turned and hurried back up the path towards the castle.

It seemed everyone remembered the one pregnancy that had not been terminated.

Blood had dried on Petra's hands, and her skin felt like paper. She wiped them on the skirt of her dress, but it did not help.

She looked over at Hugon to gauge his progress. He had just returned to the cart with a wheelbarrow full of old straw and was now shovelling it in. Slipping between the trees, she made her way down to the waiting spot Velma had pointed out. With her back resting against a trunk, she looked about, expecting the guards to come for her at any moment. At one point she thought she heard shouting and worried they were already looking for her, but it was just the grooms' conversations carried on the breeze.

The more time that passed, the faster her heart raced. Her mouth went dry, and she was no longer aware of the cold air as she sweated beneath her gown. No cloak, no water, no food. It was not too late to return to the castle, to explain her absence, to prepare the dead Companion for her burial. But then what? She would have to welcome another, train her, and hand her over to Prince Felipe. As much as she liked to think of herself as strong, she knew she did not have it in her to ruin another life.

Ten minutes later, she heard a cart approaching. Pushing off the tree, she peered between the trunks as Hugon made his way towards her. The reins were relaxed in his hands while he whistled a tune, no doubt to warn her of his approach.

Only once the cart was directly in front of her did she dare step out onto the road. The horse stopped, and for a moment she worried she might not have the courage to climb in. There was a good chance she would be found, maybe even executed. He continued to whistle while gesturing for her to get in. She sucked in a breath, then moved to the back of the cart and climbed up.

The overwhelming smell of urine and manure made her throat close and her stomach heave, but she lay down and began pushing large handfuls of the filthy straw over herself. Hugon jumped down and walked around to help, whistling the entire time. He used the pitchfork to push the straw over her until she was fully covered. When her stomach heaved again, she wormed a hand up to cover her nose and mouth. The cart lurched forwards, and she worried the straw would shift as they swung side to side over the bumpy surface.

The screech and crunch of the portcullis rising made her heart squeeze. As predicted, no guard came to check the cart. No words were exchanged. A moment later, they rocked into motion and she heard the portcullis lower behind them. One more gate and then they would be outside the walls. She listened for the noise in front, but the only sound was that of footsteps approaching.

'You'll have to wait' came a voice much too close to her.

Petra held her breath.

'What's the problem?' Hugon asked, his tone easy-going.

Footsteps moved around the cart. 'No one in, no one out,'

replied the guard.

'Why is that?'

'A death in the castle.'

Petra's lips pressed tightly together. At least there was no mention of her.

'How long will the wait be, do you think?' Hugon asked.

The guard paused at the back of the cart. 'As long as it takes. I just follow orders.'

'Sorry about the stench,' Hugon said.

The guard coughed as the smell took over the air.

'Corneo's finest horse shit,' Hugon said before resuming whistling.

The footsteps moved on, quicker that time. Petra heard another guard complain of the smell, but no one let them pass. The horse became restless, taking a few steps back.

'Easy, boy,' Hugon called.

More waiting.

Petra wondered how much longer she could keep still. The guards on the wall above could see straight into the cart. Finally, a guard appeared behind them and shouted through the gate. 'Suicide. Let him through.'

Suicide.

One word that conjured images of Orla's naked form, lifeless on the floor. She finally exhaled at the sound of the gate lifting. She felt dizzy from holding her breath, and with the prospect of being outside the walls that had held her captive for so long. The cart rolled forwards, and although she could not see past the straw covering her, she noticed a change in light as the sky opened above her.

They descended a gentle slope down to the main road, and a few minutes later Hugon reached back and pushed the straw off her head, his face appearing above her.

'Thought you might like some air,' he said. 'Best keep the rest of you covered though, just to be safe.'

She nodded, her lungs expanding, taking in the clean air. She tried not to look at the straw because the smell was bad enough. Instead, she watched the sky. Grey clouds stretched in all directions, the cold season's final attempt to hold on. She tried to remember how far was it from Chelia to Wripis, where Lord Belen's manor was located. Everything she knew about geography had been learned from lessons and books. Prior to that, she had never travelled far from Pamid, a village in the south of Corneo where she had grown up. Aside from weeds and a few sturdy animals, nothing really survived that far south. Her family had done what most families did, learning to live with the little they had and hoping they had a daughter pretty enough to capture the attention of the royal men.

A few hours later, the roads grew noisy, and Hugon turned in his seat to cover her properly once more. He was kind enough to try and pick some of the cleaner parts of hay. She heard the laughter of children as they entered the village. The sound made her breath catch. How long had it been since she had heard that noise? Years. So many years.

Hugon greeted a few people as he passed them. It reminded her of her childhood. Villages were enormous families in many ways, yet she realised with sadness that she would be long forgotten in those parts now.

A few minutes later, the cart turned off the main road, and the sound of bleating sheep and children faded. When they finally came to a stop, Petra lay still, listening.

'Up you get,' Hugon said, jumping down onto the road.

Petra broke through the straw and sat up, pins and needles in every limb. Hugon walked around the back of the cart, waiting for her. She gave her cramping neck a stretch as she looked around. They were not at a house, just pulled up on the side of the road. She turned to him, frowning.

'Where are we?'

'Just west of Chelia.' He gave her an apologetic look. 'This is as far as I can take you. If I'm caught—'

'I understand,' she said, crawling over the top of the straw to him. He took her by the arm and helped her down.

'You got somewhere to go?' he asked.

She nodded.

Pointing behind her, he said, 'There's a well behind those trees. Usually has water.'

She squinted in that direction. It had been a long time since she had drawn water from a well. 'Thank you.'

He cleared his throat, not moving.

'Oh,' she said, looking down at her necklace. She unclasped it and dropped it into his hand.

He nodded his thanks, then turned and walked back to the front of the cart. Climbing up into the seat, he picked up the reins. 'If you get caught—'

'You will not be implicated in any way.'

Another nod. 'Good luck,' he called over his shoulder. Then with a click of his tongue, the cart lurched forwards.

Taking in her unfamiliar surroundings, Petra felt a sudden surge of panic. 'Which way is north?' she called to his back.

He raised a hand, pointing. She looked out over the bare paddocks, knowing she would need to keep an eye on the sun to prevent getting lost. She knew Wripis was north-west from Chelia. She also knew she would never be able to walk that distance before nightfall.

A breeze blew from the north and she shuddered. It was tempting to fall apart, to just collapse in a heap on the side of the road and wait to be found by someone, probably King Nilos's men. How long could he really stay angry at her? She had ways of earning his forgiveness. Instead, her eyes went in the direction of the well. Drawing a long breath, she headed for water.

CHAPTER 3

*P*rince Tyron's voice reached him through the thick canvas. 'Leksi, get out here.'

The knight leapt from his cot and snatched up the dress that lay in a pile on the ground, tossing it to the woman in his bed before grabbing his own clothes. She was lying on her stomach wearing nothing but a coy smile.

'Get dressed,' Leksi pleaded.

'Leksi!' The prince was losing patience.

God dammit. There was a reason he had not entered—he knew.

Lord Belen's eldest daughter stretched luxuriously, making no effort to cover up. One look at her flushed cheeks would confirm the prince's suspicions.

'I will need my underthings if I am to return to the house and face my father.' Her smile was mischievous.

He looked around, trying to recall where he might have flung them earlier. She had just shown up, unannounced, coming into his tent without an invitation. All right, without a *recent* invitation. He had promised the prince he would stay away. What was he supposed to do when a woman showed up wearing nothing beneath her dress?

He stopped searching and narrowed his eyes at the girl. 'You weren't wearing any undergarments.'

She laughed, thoroughly enjoying herself.

'Leksi,' Tyron called.

He had really done it this time. 'One moment.' He fell to his knees beside the bed. 'Please get dressed.'

She leaned in to kiss him. 'Can I visit again tomorrow?'

He glanced at the entrance to the tent. 'Absolutely not.'

She pouted. 'What do you mean, "absolutely not"?'

He reached down and tapped her bare bottom. 'There is a good chance I won't be alive tomorrow thanks to you.'

She reluctantly sat up and slipped her dress over her head while Leksi straightened his clothes. He smoothed down his hair, which she had been clutching with both hands for the previous two hours, and slipped through the flap of the tent wearing his most relaxed expression.

Tyron stood with his arms crossed in front of him, wearing royal attire and a scowl. Leksi closed the distance between them.

'You off, then?' he asked, trying to sound casual.

Tyron looked past him to the tent. 'Lord Belen is going to cut your throat in your sleep when he finds out.'

Leksi took a few steps, hoping Tyron would follow. 'No idea what you're talking about.'

The prince shook his head, feet anchored. 'I must leave. Unfortunately, that means you are in charge until I return.'

Leksi feigned offence. 'What do you mean *unfortunately*? I say lucky men.'

The flap of the tent went back and Lord Belen's daughter strode out. The neat braid she had arrived with had dissolved into a mess of curls that hung about her face and neck. She had that unmistakable satisfied glow he had come to recognise in women over the years.

'You couldn't wait five minutes?' he said between closed teeth.

She winked at him. 'Until tomorrow, Sir Leksi.' She stepped past the men and walked off down the path that divided two rows of tents.

Leksi closed his eyes, feeling Tyron's disapproving stare on him.

'What is happening tomorrow?' the prince asked.

Leksi opened his eyes. 'To be clear, I said no to tomorrow.'

'But yes to today?'

Leksi rubbed at the stubble on his face. 'Actually, I said no, initially.'

Tyron shook his head and began walking. 'How did that go?'

Falling into step with him, Leksi's gaze went to the swaying hips a few yards ahead of them. 'Not great, as you've probably figured out. She was rather persuasive.'

Their feet slushed on the worn path that wound through the canvas-covered lawn. Clusters of men sat on upturned crates playing dice, standing to attention when the men passed.

'Just try to behave while we're gone,' Tyron said, not looking at him. 'Time spent with my family is stressful enough without worrying about what is happening here.'

They passed a roped-off behourd where six men trained with axes.

'I hear Queen Cora is making the journey,' Leksi said once they were past the noise.

'Any excuse to escape her husband.'

'Don't blame her.' A man approached from the other direction carrying a pig carcass on a hook. He moved off the path and waited for them to pass. 'The whole family, together again.'

'Not the whole family.' Tyron nodded at the man. 'Stamitos and Sapphira remain in Galen.'

'Still? Probably having the time of their lives. Nothing but vineyard tours and tournaments.'

Another shake of the head. 'Something like that.'

As they emerged from the maze of tents, Leksi spotted the royal wagon. Tyron's squire stood beside it, holding the prince's horse. Mako stuck his head through the door and called to Leksi. 'You coming with us?'

Princess Aldara leaned forwards to grab hold of him to prevent him falling out of the carriage.

Leksi smiled. 'Not this time. Someone has to keep West Corneo secure while your father takes his leisure trips.'

Tyron took the reins from his squire. 'I should have offered to go to Galen in Stamitos's place.'

'Ignore him,' Aldara said, wrestling Mako back into the wagon. Princess Zelia sat comfortably in her lap, watching her brother in awe. 'He is in a mood.' She gave Leksi a knowing smile.

Tyron mounted his horse and gathered the reins. 'A month with Pandarus has that effect on me.'

'On most people,' Leksi added.

Aldara's gaze travelled past him to the woman climbing the path back up to the large house, then returned to him. 'He finally caught you, then?'

'You knew?' Tyron asked, riding up beside the window.

'I suspected. There is a difference.'

'Can I ride with you, Father?' Mako asked, bursting through the window again and startling the horse.

'It's safer in there with your mother,' Tyron replied.

Aldara laughed. 'Hardly. His sister likes to get a good handful of his hair and never let go.'

Leksi opened the wagon door. 'Come on,' he said, holding his hands out to the boy. Mako leapt into his arms, fearless as always. 'Up you go.' He handed Mako to his father.

Tyron settled the boy in front of him, then looked at Leksi. 'Behave yourself, and keep hold of the West. That is all I ask.'

'Is that all?' Leksi stepped back to let the horse pass. 'Have you forgotten that you promised me an actual house?'

'Have you forgotten that you promised to keep your hands to yourself?' Tyron called over his shoulder.

Leksi shook his head and turned to Aldara, bowing. 'Give my regards to the family.'

'Keep well, Sir Leksi,' she said with a knowing smile.

He winked at her. 'My lady.'

The driver flicked the reins and the wagon rolled away. Leksi remained where he was, watching the family and their entourage of mounted guards until they were swallowed up by the trees that lined the west side of the manor.

'There you are, sir.' Leksi turned to see Charis running towards him, out of breath. 'Did Prince Tyron find you?'

Leksi crossed his arms and glared at his squire. 'He sure did.' In his fifteenth year, Charis was far from the sharpest lad Leksi had ever trained. 'Next time, you come and tell me he is looking for me.'

'I was going to, but you had company, and when I informed the prince of the fact, he insisted on going himself.'

Leksi rolled his eyes. 'Well, I could have done with the warning.' He stepped past the confused boy. 'Fetch my horse, would you?'

'Where are you going?'

'Boundary check.'

Charis turned and ran to catch up to him. 'Do you need some men to escort you?'

'You can come if you want.'

The boy's chest expanded to twice its usual size. 'Yes, sir.' He took off at a jog towards the yards where the horses were kept.

It was mid-morning by the time they reached the western boundary. Their horses plodded slowly between the trees while Charis told a story Leksi could not follow. He was fond of the boy, but he had learned very early on to shut out the incessant noise that came from him.

A low fog lingered, typical for that time of year, when the cold season hung on too long for everyone's liking.

'What's that?' Charis asked, stopping his horse.

Leksi sighed and looked to where his squire was pointing, expecting to see a spotted mushroom or a large frog. The boy had the mind of a child at times. Instead, he saw a pile of pale green fabric on the forest floor. He pulled up his horse, peering through the fog.

'What is that?' Charis asked again, leaning sideways on his horse to get a better look.

Leksi brought a finger to his mouth and listened. He was not one to step into traps. Some might take the bait and immediately rush over to investigate, but he would ensure they were alone first.

'I think it's a body,' Charis said loudly.

Leksi turned to him. 'For the love of god, boy, shut up.' He turned back and listened. Nothing but the buzz of insects and creaking of trees. He signalled for Charis to keep watch, then drew his sword, dismounted and approached what indeed looked like a body. Keeping an eye on his surroundings, he listened for the crack of a twig or shuffle of hooves. Silence.

His gaze returned to the body at his feet, and he was surprised to discover a woman curled into a tight ball. Blue lips were visible through the hair covering her face. Probably dead. He crouched, still holding his sword, and checked for a pulse. She twitched as his warm fingers touched her neck. She was alive, but cold.

'Dead?' Charis called to him.

Leksi shook his head. He would have to remind the boy later about the meaning of quiet.

He searched the trees around him one more time before turning his full attention to the woman. She was filthy, covered in blood and mud. At least, he assumed it was mud; it smelled more like manure. His gaze landed on her jewelled hand, and he reached out and kneaded the fabric of her dress between his fingers. Over the years he had acquired the ability to categorise a woman within a few moments, and her dress was of high quality. She was not common.

Leaves crunched behind him, and he swung his body, sword raised. Charis froze, hands up in a gesture of surrender.

'You are supposed to be keeping watch,' Leksi said, turning back to the woman.

The squire peered over his shoulder. 'Is she breathing?'

'Yes.'

'Sleeping, then?'

Leksi pushed the brown hair from her face, his fingertips brushing her soft skin. She was definitely the indoor type. He watched as her eyelids fluttered. 'Miss,' he said, loud enough to wake her properly.

Her eyes snapped open and she turned her head with a small gasp. Blazing amber eyes stared up at him. She went to speak but swallowed instead. He pulled her up into a seated position, preparing to interrogate her.

'What is your name?' he asked.

Her eyes went to the red *S* on the sleeve of his tunic before answering. 'Petra,' she said. Her voice was hoarse, and she was shivering.

Leksi hesitated before putting his sword away and

removing his tunic. She studied him as he wrapped it around her shoulders, equally as suspicious.

'What are you doing out here half-dressed in these temperatures?' he asked.

'I got a little lost in the dark.'

Even in her current state, she sat with a straight back and hands folded in her lap. She was definitely of the privileged variety. She also had a very distinct Corneon accent.

Leksi looked around. 'So then, my next question is, which way were you walking?'

She lifted her chin. 'West.'

He nodded. 'I see.'

'What do you see?' Charis asked. The art of subtle conversation was lost on him.

Leksi glanced down at her wrists, noticing faint bruises beneath the bloodstains. 'You running from someone?'

She followed his line of sight, then pushed the sleeves of her dress farther down her arms. 'Actually, I am looking for someone.'

Leksi studied her. 'Who would that be?'

'Princess Aldara.'

She was searching his face, no doubt watching for his reaction to that name. He gave nothing away. 'Why?'

Her confidence seemed to falter. She looked past him to the boy, as though hesitant to speak in front of him. 'Because… because she is the only person who might be able to help me.'

As Leksi processed the information, it dawned on him why the name seemed familiar. 'You're the mentor.' She looked taken aback by the fact that he knew of her, but then her shoulders fell as she relaxed a little. 'You let them escape.'

'A wise move, it turns out.'

He shook his head. 'I imagine your king is looking for you.'

She shuddered. 'Probably.'

'Definitely. You're the muse, the one who ruined him for all future Companions.' He stood and linked his hands on top of his head, stepping away to think for a moment. Petra pulled the tunic tighter around her as she watched him. 'What am I supposed to do with you now?'

Charis stepped up to Leksi and, speaking in a very loud whisper, said, 'Send her back. If King Nilos gets word that we have her, he'll send an army.'

That was the sensible thing to do, given he was in charge, but he also knew Aldara would likely frown on him tossing her back over the border and wiping his hands of the mess. Though as far as he was aware, they had promised to help track her son, not provide her a safe house if she was crazy enough to escape.

He turned to her, staring at her dress. 'Are you injured?'

She shook her head. 'No.'

'Did you kill someone?'

Her face collapsed. 'No.'

He sighed. 'When was the last time you ate? Had something to drink?'

'Yesterday morning.'

He continued to watch her as he thought. He could take her back to the manor discreetly, then send a messenger to Tyron and let him make the decision. He could hardly leave her out in the woods. 'Can you stand?'

She nodded and tried to get to her feet. Seeing that she was struggling, he stepped forwards to help her.

'I am fine,' she insisted.

He immediately let go of her but stayed close until he was sure she was steady. 'You're not fine. You're in desperate need of a bath.' He thought she might blush, but she just looked up at him, then away.

Leksi took the reins of his horse from Charis and

mounted. When he reached out for her, she took a few hurried steps back. Straightening, he rested his hands on the pommel of his saddle. 'You planning on walking to the manor?'

She hesitated before stepping closer to the horse. Again, he leaned down and offered his hand, and she stared at it for a moment.

'You never told me *your* name.'

Charis cleared his throat. 'That is Sir Leksi. Syrasan's most skilled knight.'

The mentor did not appear the least bit impressed by the revelation. 'Of course, Prince Tyron's right-hand man.'

'I see you've heard of me also.' He gestured for her to come closer. She hesitated before taking his hand, and he pulled her onto the horse as though she weighed nothing. She held his shirt and stared nervously down at the ground. 'You all right?'

'Yes… it is just… I have not been on a horse in some time.'

He pushed his mare into a walk and her grip tightened. 'How long is "some time"?'

'Nine years.'

'All you have to do is hold on.'

CHAPTER 4

*A*s the horse walked between the rows of tents, Petra felt the curious stares of every man in the camp on her. What would they make of the filthy woman wrapped in a Syrasan tunic, riding behind the knight? Not just any knight, but Sir Leksi, famous for more than his fighting skills. "Notorious womaniser" was the most common term used to describe him whenever his name came up in conversation. But something in her gut told her she could trust this man, despite the fact that she had decided a long time ago to never trust anyone.

'Here we are,' he said, pulling up his horse.

Charis rushed over to help her dismount, but her hands were like tiny vices attached to the knight's shirt.

Leksi turned to look at her. 'You going to get off, or shall we do another lap of the camp?'

She saw the amusement in his eyes and let go of him. He offered her his hand while she awkwardly slid off the back of the horse. Charis caught her, but it was Leksi who held most of her weight on descent.

She stepped back from the squire and looked around, her fingers coming together beneath the tunic.

Press, press, press.

Leksi joined her on the ground and stepped over to the large tent, pulling the flap back to let her through. She remained where she was. Tilting his head, he regarded her for a moment.

'You're welcome to stay out here if you would prefer.'

She glanced at the other men, then, holding the tunic tightly, stepped past him into the tent. Coming to a stop in the middle of the space, she looked around at the simple arrangement. 'Is this where you sleep?'

'This is where I do everything right now.' He remained at the door. 'I'll organise a bath, a bite to eat and some clean clothes. Then we'll talk.' He gestured to the water flask on the small table. 'Drink.'

She glanced at the flask, then back at him. 'Thank you.'

He lingered a moment. 'We don't have any women here to assist you.'

'I do not need anyone to assist me.'

'Don't leave this tent,' he said before disappearing, the flap swinging back into place.

A few minutes later, Charis arrived with food and more drinking water. She tried to eat like a lady, but she found herself shovelling the warm soup into her mouth with surprising speed. When her bowl was empty, she slowly ate the bread and the small piece of salted meat, washing it down with more water. When she had finished, she looked down at herself and was almost brought to tears by the sight.

Charis reappeared with two men carrying a wooden tub, big enough for her to stand in. 'I'll bring some hot water.'

'Thank you,' she said, gripping the tunic with both hands. Afraid to sit or touch anything for fear she would soil it, she remained next to the tub.

Charis returned with a pail of steaming water, some soap and a towel. Then she was alone. She waited a few minutes, just in case anyone else came in, then reluctantly stripped off her filthy clothes and stepped into the tub, scrubbing her skin until it was pink and raw before lathering her hair, rinsing it with the remaining hot water. As she dried herself, she looked around and realised that no clothing had been left for her. There was no chance of her putting her dirty dress back on.

As she was wrapping the towel around her, she spotted one of Leksi's shirts crumpled at the end of his bed. Glancing down at her bare legs, she was aware that the knight could return at any moment, so she snatched the shirt and slipped it over her head before wrapping the towel around her waist to cover the rest of her. The shirt was huge, the neckline gaping. She adjusted it as best she could before bringing the neck of the shirt to her nose to check if it was clean. It smelled like him—a far more pleasant scent than one would expect from a man who had spent months in a camp.

The sound of a throat clearing made her turn. Sir Leksi stood watching her.

Leksi took in the sight before him. She was wearing his shirt, and her wet hair had soaked through it, making it far more see-through than she probably realised. A gentleman would have looked away.

'It's not clean, if that's what you're wondering,' he laughed. She seemed momentarily flustered but recovered quickly.

'It was this or my dress.'

'Or just a towel.'

Again, she did not blush. Too well-trained. 'I could not see a clean dress anywhere.'

While she was far too prudish to be his type, there was no denying her beauty. But he would expect nothing less from the king's former Companion. Or current Companion. The lines were blurred in this instance. 'I have organised some clothes, though it might take a while for them to get here. Not too many women about the place.'

He had been forced to approach Lord Belen with the request and explain the rather suspicious circumstances of a woman in his tent in need of clothes. He could not tell if the man disliked him in general, or if perhaps some of the rumours had finally reached him.

'I suppose I owe you an explanation,' she said.

He noticed her hands fidgeting, though she showed no other signs of nerves. He almost felt bad for glancing down at her breasts a second time. 'I'm going to need something, because as you can imagine, harbouring King Nilos's runaway Companion will likely disrupt the peace.'

'I am not his Companion,' she said.

Her fingers continued to fidget. What on earth was she doing with them?

He shrugged. 'Former Companion, then. Either way, I'm guessing he didn't let you leave.'

Her fingers stilled, and he looked up at her broken expression. *So she's human after all.*

Stepping into the tent, he went to sit on the cot, patting the space next to him. 'All right. Let's hear it. And definitely don't skip the part where you rolled about in manure before coming here.'

Not even a hint of a smile. She watched him, as though considering how much to share.

'When will I be able to speak with Aldara?' she asked.

He rested his elbows on his knees. 'Probably never. They left for Syrasan this morning. I've sent a message to them. For now, it seems you are my problem.'

She swallowed. 'And I suppose you want to send me back?'

'You haven't told me anything yet, so how am I to decide?'

A nod, appearing to understand his position. 'If I knew where my son was, then I would have somewhere else to go.'

Leksi tried not to let her soften him up too much. 'It seems King Nilos wants him to remain hidden.'

She walked over to the bed and sat at the far end of it. 'Ask me whatever you like, and I will answer.'

He studied her, confident he would know if she were lying. She sat with the trademark good posture and composed face of a mentor, waiting. 'Whose blood is on your dress?'

She glanced down at the garment. 'Her name was Orla. She was Prince Felipe's Companion.'

'Was?'

'She took her own life yesterday.' The words were delivered in an even tone, but she looked down at her lap for a moment.

He kept his gaze trained on her. 'I've heard Prince Felipe has that effect on people.'

'He has a temper,' she said, looking up.

'But that doesn't explain why you're on the run. Did they try to pin the girl's death on you?'

Her hands gripped her knees. 'I… I realised I could not stay.'

'Why not?'

Her fingers were turning white. 'It was such a terrible shock, I suppose.'

'But no one else ran away, did they?'

She shook her head. 'No.'

'What were you afraid of?'

She stared at him, as though she was digging for the right answer. 'I think I realised that if I did not get out of that place, there was every chance I would make the same choice.'

They stared at one another for a moment. Before Leksi could reply, the tent flap went back and the woman he had booted from his bed earlier that morning stepped inside. She froze at the sight of Petra, then turned to glare at him.

'I realise how this looks,' Leksi began.

She threw the pile of clothes she had been carrying at him with surprising force for a lady of leisure, then stormed from the tent. Leksi gathered the garments and set them on the bed between them.

'An acquaintance of yours?' Petra asked.

He glanced at her, preferring not to have to explain. 'Probably safe to say *former acquaintance*.' He continued to look at her, then exhaled, adding, 'What am I going to do with you, runaway?'

Her expression gave nothing away. His gaze fell to the bruises around her wrists, and he realised he did not have it in him to send her back to King Nilos. He attributed the decision to the fact that he had a weakness for damsels in distress. As well as damsels not in distress, and those in between the two extremes.

'You can stay here for now,' he said, standing.

She stood also. 'And where will you stay?'

He suppressed a smile. 'Don't worry, I'll bunk with one of the other men.'

She looked visibly relieved.

'I'm not going to put a target on my back by sharing a tent with you.' He noted the dark circles around her amber eyes.

'Thank you, Sir Leksi.'

'You can just call me Leksi.'

She blinked. 'Where I come from, if a person has a title, you use it.'

'Then shall I address you as *my lady*?'

'Only the Companions address me that way.'

He should have known better than to waste humour on a mentor. 'Get some sleep. I'll be back to check on you later.'

CHAPTER 5

A small lantern burned in the corner of the tent, casting a soft glow of light. Petra should have been asleep. She was exhausted. Instead, she watched the shadows, her body tense as though she were bracing for something. She knew there were no safe havens as long as King Nilos was searching for her.

The flap of the tent swept back and she sat up in surprise, staring at her visitor, trying to connect the woman standing in front of her with the one she had mentored eighteen months earlier.

'Aldara.' She pushed her blankets back and got to her feet.

Looking as though she had seen a ghost, the princess released a breath, then rushed forwards. Petra stiffened as arms enclosed her. The only affection she had known in the previous nine years had come from King Nilos—and it had never been welcomed. This was very different. She felt a tightening in her throat but swallowed it down in order to remain composed.

Aldara stepped back to look at her, keeping hold of her arms.

'Are you all right?'

'Fine.' One word. A lie.

Aldara did not appear to believe her anyway. They had once existed in the same world, after all. 'How on earth did you get away?'

She really did not want to retell the story. 'It was not pretty' was all she said. 'I am sorry to come here, to put you in this position.' She paused. There was that tightening in her throat again. 'I... I did not know where else to go. I could hardly go to my family's home. The king will be looking for me by now.'

'Of course he will. He will send men to every corner of the kingdom.'

Hearing those words from someone else's mouth made her feel slightly less crazy. Only a handful of people knew how it really was between them. 'I need to find my son, before the king finds me.'

Aldara's expression softened. 'I have not stopped searching since I left Masville. Did you get my last letter?'

She nodded, the disappointment still raw. 'No new leads, then?'

Aldara shook her head. 'I am so sorry. I know how much you want to find him.'

Petra brought her hands together in front of her. 'At the very least, I need to know he is safe, that he is loved.'

'I understand. Not knowing anything must be the worst form of torture.'

'I need to see it with my own eyes.'

'Of course you do.'

They fell silent for a moment.

'Will Prince Tyron send me back?' Petra asked.

Aldara hesitated before answering. '*He* won't, but if King Nilos learns of your whereabouts, I am afraid the decision will be out of his hands.' She paused. 'Relations are fragile, and King Pandarus will—'

'It is all right. I understand how these things work. Your king does not owe me anything.'

The tent flap shifted, and the women turned to see a young boy watching them through the gap. Petra's heart pinched.

'Mako, what are you doing?' Aldara asked him. 'I told you to stay with your father.'

Petra's hands went limp at her sides. 'Your son?'

Aldara waved him in. 'When he is misbehaving, he is Tyron's son.' Mako came to stand in front of his mother, and she placed her hands on his shoulders. 'Mako, this is an old friend of mine, Petra.' The boy gazed curiously up at her. 'Without her help, we would never have made it home, and you would not have a sister.'

Petra looked up. 'You have a daughter?'

Aldara nodded, almost apologetically. 'I will not give up the search for your son. I hope you know that.'

'I know. That information is the only power King Nilos holds over me now. That is why he keeps it from me.'

Aldara thought for a moment. 'A smarter man would hand the information over freely. Not a very clever tactic for winning a woman's affection.'

Petra's hands went to her stomach. 'The time for that has long passed. He is so beyond the possibility of redemption now.'

'Do you worry your disappearance might jeopardise Xander's safety?'

Petra shook her head. She had already thought of that. 'Even Nilos is not foolish enough to sever the only tie between us.'

The tent opened and Prince Tyron appeared. When Petra looked up, she saw Leksi standing outside the entrance.

Their gazes met briefly before the canvas swung back into place. She turned her attention to the prince, a stark contrast from the wasting, bearded man who had emerged from Masville's dungeon all those months back.

'Petra,' he said with a nod.

She curtsied. 'My lord. I apologise if I disrupted your travel plans.'

'No need,' Aldara said. 'I have been trying to come up with an excuse not to go for months.'

Tyron went to stand by his wife, his hand coming to rest on her back. 'We have a problem.'

Something in his tone made Petra's insides turn cold.

The prince's gaze shifted to her. 'There are Corneon guards riding the boundary. They may already be suspicious of you crossing.'

'We could fight them,' Mako said, thrusting his hand forwards as though he were holding a sword.

Aldara's grip tightened, and Tyron patted the boy's head. 'Easy, soldier,' he said, then to Petra, 'Anyone else know you are here?'

'No one.' That did not mean King Nilos would not figure it out. She had passed enough others on her walk to the manor, and what a memorable sight she would have been. 'I have brought trouble to your door. I apologise.'

Aldara frowned. 'You had no choice. Where else would you go?'

Tyron was quiet for a moment. 'You cannot stay here.'

Aldara's eyes widened. 'Tyron—'

'I am not saying I will not help, but have you thought this through properly?'

Of course not—she had panicked. 'I really do not wish to cause you trouble. Your men have already been very kind. I have some jewels I can trade for some supplies. I can leave tonight, if you would prefer.'

'No,' Aldara said, staring at her husband.

One look at his wife softened his expression. 'The guards have dogs. They will find you straightaway.'

Dogs. She did not like dogs.

Tyron cleared his throat. 'If you returned now of your own accord, you could explain the situation to your king. He might even be sympathetic, show leniency.'

'The man is obsessed,' Aldara said. 'If she returns to him, he will never let her out of his sight again.'

'Any further delays in your return will only exacerbate the situation,' the prince continued. 'If you choose to run, we cannot predict the lengths King Nilos will go to in order to find you.'

She could. How many times had he told her that she belonged to him—mind and body?

She took a moment to think it all through, pushing past the fear and trying to think like a mentor. She thought about marching across the border of her own free will, approaching the guards on foot and asking them to escort her back to Masville so she might fall at the king's feet and beg his forgiveness. 'It was a lapse of judgement,' she would say. If she were clever, she would tell him she missed him, that she could not be apart from him. He would love that. She even thought about how she might make it up to him. Small things, like watching him move on top of her instead of averting her eyes. She could put her hands on his back instead of recoiling beneath him. It would be like hugging a bull to her. Then she would arch her back, murmur words he had waited years to hear. By the end of it all, he would give her anything within his power—except her son.

Mako, growing bored, wriggled free of his mother's grip and ran for the exit. Leksi was still waiting on the other side. 'Up, up,' Mako shouted, charging at the knight.

Petra listened to the squeals of delight through the canvas

as the boy was lifted into the air. 'I will not go back there until I see my son,' she whispered.

Aldara looked relieved, and Tyron just nodded before stepping away.

'You will have to trust us to continue the search for your son,' he said after a long silence. 'In the meantime, you need to go far away from here, somewhere you will not be recognised, somewhere safe. We will need time to figure this out.' He looked at Aldara. 'Which we will do from Archdale Castle. Cancelling the trip will only raise suspicion.'

It was the only plan available, so she could hardly say no when they were prepared to help her. 'Where will I go?'

'My family has some land near Veanor, south of the village. It has a house on it, which is currently unoccupied.'

Her heart seemed to stop beating. 'Veanor? That is the other side of Syrasan, is it not?'

Aldara placed a reassuring hand on her arm. 'The farther you are from King Nilos, the better.'

Petra looked down at the warm hand on her arm. Aldara had referred to her as an *old friend*. Mentors did not have friends, they had responsibilities.

'Leksi will go with you,' Tyron said. 'He can keep you safe for now.'

Petra looked up at the mention of the knight. The laughter outside died.

'Again,' Mako cried, but it seemed the fun was over.

'Is he not needed here? For more important things?'

'The mentor makes a good point,' came Leksi's voice.

'He is very trustworthy,' Aldara assured her. 'Even if he does eavesdrop on the prince's conversations.' Outside, Leksi coughed. 'He is very good at his job. There is not a man alive who could keep you safer.'

Tyron looked across at his wife. 'You do know I am still standing here?'

Aldara suppressed a smile.

'All right,' Petra said. 'There is a lot of personal risk for you in doing this. I am certain I will be more grateful once I have had time to process everything.'

Mako burst back into the tent, and Petra's gaze met Leksi's through the gap once more. He did not look overly pleased by his new assignment.

'The day you let my wife and I walk free from Masville was a great personal risk to you,' Tyron said, catching hold of his son. 'Aldara will pack some supplies for you.'

Petra swallowed. She had just agreed to travel across a foreign kingdom with a man she had only known a few hours. 'When do we leave?'

Tyron glanced at Aldara before answering. 'It's best you leave now.'

CHAPTER 6

*A*s if being sent to an isolated location for God knew how long was not bad enough, Tyron had rubbed salt into the wound by pulling him aside to lecture him on propriety. She was still on the run from the last man she shared a bed with, and he was quite capable of spending time alone with a pretty woman without it leading anywhere. Besides, no sensible man looked at a mentor in that way. They were the ones who prepared the *other* women, the ones it was perfectly acceptable to look at in that way.

A realisation dawned on him as they headed for the horses. He was not going to be able to escape into the village for his usual entertainment. There would be no evenings off, no long drinking sessions ending in drunken songs and easy women. It was going to be a sort of test. Perhaps that was why Tyron was sending him. Well, he was not one to shy away from a challenge.

'Are you all right?' Leksi asked, glancing sideways at Petra. They were headed for the horses, and she was out of breath trying to keep up with him.

'Fine,' she panted.

He could tell by her fatigued expression that she had still not slept. Charis walked in front, torch in hand to prevent them from stumbling in the dark.

'Are the woods safe at night?' Petra asked.

Ah, so she was afraid. 'You slept out in the open last night and nothing ate you.'

'Not by choice.'

A smile tugged at his mouth. Mentors had an answer for everything. 'You are quite safe when you are with me.'

'I too have a sword,' Charis said, swinging around and almost burning them with the torch.

Balancing their supplies in one arm, Leksi caught the boy's hand with the other. 'I'm sure the lady feels much safer now.' He shoved the squire forwards and stole a glance at Petra, who looked as though she might fall down from anxiety at any moment. Soon she would be too tired for worry. They would be riding overnight, and he would have to keep an eye on her in case she fell asleep in the saddle.

'Here we are,' Charis said. 'A gelding for the lady.'

Petra came to a stop beside Leksi, her feet frozen in place as she stared up at the tall horse.

'What's wrong?' Leksi asked. 'I assure you he's a calm mount.'

She looked between the horses. 'Am I to ride alone?'

Leksi studied her in the dark. She was visibly terrified by the prospect. He supposed nine years locked in a castle did that to a person. 'I could have someone else ride him, but that would defeat the purpose of this whole exercise, as you would still be here.' She did not laugh—not even a hint of a smile. The wrong time for jokes, perhaps. 'Why don't you ride with me, and the gelding can carry our supplies.'

He watched her exhale. 'Only if you do not mind.'

It was not ideal, but he suspected she would be fairly easy company if she could manage to stay on the horse.

Charis helped him secure all the supplies on the gelding, and then Leksi mounted his horse and pulled her up behind him for the second time that day. She smelled of soap and bread, a vast improvement from earlier. She grabbed handfuls of his cloak.

'Best you hold on properly,' he said. 'If you hold my clothes, you'll choke me when you fall.'

'Oh.' She moved her hands to his waist.

Once Charis was in the saddle, Leksi kicked his horse into a trot and they headed east towards the trees. Charis rode in front, lighting the way for them.

'What happens if the torch goes out?' Petra asked.

Leksi smiled to himself. 'Moments later, wolves descend, and we all die.'

There was a short silence before she replied. 'You do know I cannot see your face from back here to know if you are joking.'

He turned his head to look at her. 'Mentors. Such a serious bunch, aren't you?' When she did not answer, he faced forwards. 'You are allowed to laugh out here beneath the trees. Your propriety is wasted on me.'

'I shall keep that in mind if at some point you say something humorous.'

He shook his head. 'To answer your earlier question, I can find my way to Syrasan with or without light. All you have to do is hold on.'

They fell silent then, each returning to their private thoughts as they cantered beneath tall oaks towards the border. Above them, bats flew and owls hunted for food. Twigs snapped and branches rustled around them. Whenever a bird took flight or a hare ran for cover, Leksi felt Petra jump behind him. He said nothing, saving her the embarrassment and him the headache of constantly asking if she was all right. She would need to toughen up, or at least learn to trust him.

A few hours later, they crossed the border into Syrasan and the horses slowed to a walk. They emerged onto a wide road that would lead them west.

'Let me know if you need to relieve yourself,' Leksi said over his shoulder. 'Otherwise, we'll keep moving.'

Charis rode up next to them. 'I might need to go, my lord.'

Leksi turned to him, a tired expression on his face. '*You* should be able to last longer than a few hours.' Even in the dark, he could see Charis's cheeks colour.

The squire shifted uncomfortably in the saddle. 'I was busy getting everything ready and forgot.'

'You didn't go before we left?' He knew eight-year-olds who required less mothering. He pulled up his horse. 'All right, go on.'

The boy leapt from his mare and ran for the large tree at the edge of the road.

'Hopeless,' Leksi said. 'Would you believe me if I told you he was fifteen?'

Silence behind him.

'In three years, I'm supposed to send him into battle. I would bet my horse he forgets his sword on the day.'

'Perhaps you have forgotten what it is to be fifteen,' Petra said, sounding sleepy.

Leksi felt the weight of her head on his back. At fifteen, he had thought himself invincible and ready for war. He had taken risks that the older him did not want to think about. 'I had control of my bladder if that's what you're asking.' Her head remained pressed against him. 'What were you like at fifteen?'

For a moment, he thought she had fallen asleep because she took so long to reply.

'At fifteen, I attended the flag tournament and was

presented to King Nilos.' She yawned. 'At fifteen, I was sold. At fifteen, I was the king's Companion.'

He frowned as he processed the information. 'Fifteen? But coming of age in Corneo is sixteen, is it not?'

'Yes.'

The idea of a child sharing a bed with a king did not sit well with him. There were laws for a reason. 'Why didn't your father say no?'

'We could not afford to say no. The king never asked my age, and the answer probably would not have deterred him.'

'I'm trying to remember what the king looked like all those years ago.'

'Does it matter?'

'To a fifteen-year-old girl, it does.' Silence. 'Nine years is quite a sentence.'

Charis came running back, scaring his own horse in the process. It leapt sideways, narrowly missing them. Leksi shook his head and resisted the urge to lean over and clip the boy. Thankfully, his own mount was not so easily spooked.

They continued on their way until Leksi felt the weight on his back grow heavier. She was falling asleep. He thought about where they might stop for a rest. He had an uncle a few hours north of Arelasa, but was not keen on going south and adding more time to their journey. There was another option, but he had to consider whether it was worth the hassle. Perhaps pushing through was a smarter alternative.

His question was answered a few minutes later when he felt Petra's hands fall away and her head slide along his back. He reached back with one hand and caught her, and she woke with a start.

'Sorry,' she said, voice groggy as she straightened behind him.

Leksi stopped the horse, and when he was sure she was

fully awake, he dismounted. 'Climb up onto the saddle,' he instructed.

She frowned down at him.

'Trust me,' he said.

She hesitated before moving into the seat of the saddle. He slipped his foot into the stirrup and pulled himself up behind her. Threading his arms around her, he took hold of the reins.

'What are you doing?' she asked.

'Making sure you don't fall off.'

She went rigid in the saddle.

'I'm quite the gentleman unless a woman invites me to be something else. Since no such invitation has been extended, you can sit comfortably.'

She softened in the saddle, and he kicked the horse forwards. 'Charis, we're going to stop at the house for the night.'

The squire turned to him, visibly surprised '*The* house, my lord?'

'That's the one.'

Petra looked between them. 'Which house might that be?'

'It's around two hours north-west of here,' Leksi replied. He wished there was somewhere else he could take her, but it was late, and people would ask questions.

Petra turned in his arms. 'Who lives there?'

'My father,' he replied, staring ahead.

She faced forwards again. 'Oh. Your family's estate?'

'It's my father's estate' was all he said. Thankfully, for the first time in his life, Charis remained silent on the subject.

They rode at a steady pace for the first hour, and when Petra could no longer sit stiff and proper in the saddle, he slowed his horse to a walk.

The house was about an hour's ride from Archdale Castle.

Leksi had done that ride so many times as a child he was confident he could do it blindfolded.

When they arrived at the front gate, he saw its hinges had rusted through and it was no longer in use. Weeds had claimed it. Every visit was more depressing than the last. The staff had slowly been reduced over the years until the only person who remained in the house was his father. The money had eventually dried up, or was more likely spent on drink.

'Not what you were expecting?' Leksi asked, reading Petra's face.

She closed her mouth. 'It must have been rather grand in its day.'

Mentors.

They followed the muddy path all the way to the modest house. There was no light, no smoke from the chimney. Inside, a dog barked, and of course, Petra jumped at the noise.

'This is where you grew up?' she asked.

Leksi stopped his horse, his eyes going to the front door, which was slightly ajar. He felt a pang of something resembling guilt as he tried to calculate the months since his last visit. 'I spent most of my youth at Archdale.'

Leksi dismounted and turned back to Petra to help her down. The dog burst from the house, running towards them. Petra stepped behind Leksi, pressing against him. He crouched down, and the dog stopped barking and began wagging its tail. He spent a few moments patting it before standing once more.

Charis stepped up to take his horse. 'Shall I put them in the stable, my lord?'

'If it's still standing.'

The dog ran back inside.

'There does not appear to be anyone home,' Petra said.

Leksi drew a breath. 'Oh, he's home.' What he did not say was he would be passed out from drink by now. He would deal with his father in the morning. He gestured towards the door. 'After you.'

~

Inside, the house smelled of dust, lard, and fried eggs, and the floor was sticky underfoot. Leksi led Petra up a creaking stairwell that she was certain would not hold the weight of them at the same time. She exhaled when they stepped onto the landing at the top.

'Wait here,' Leksi said before disappearing into one of the rooms.

Moments later, light filled the space and he returned holding a lantern. Petra could make out two bedrooms, and one of them appeared to be occupied. She looked up at Leksi, waiting for an explanation.

'Don't worry, nothing will wake him now. He surfaces in the morning.'

Petra followed Leksi into the second bedroom without asking any questions. Inside, a veil of dust covered every surface, and the mattress was bare. She shivered. It was no warmer indoors than out.

'You can sleep in here.' Leksi walked to the end of the bed and opened the trunk, pulling out some linen and a folded blanket. 'They are clean. I washed them myself last time I was here.'

'When was that?' She spoke quietly.

He paused to think. 'Going on a year.' Placing the lantern on the table, he moved to make the bed.

'I can do that,' Petra said, stepping up and taking the linen from his hands.

Leksi nodded and looked around the room. 'I'll leave the

lantern here for you. Charis will bring you some water shortly.'

She was about to object, to tell him he could take the lantern to find his way downstairs, when she realised she did not want to sleep in the dark.

'Goodnight,' Leksi said, stepping away and walking over to the door. He pulled it closed as he stepped through it.

'Goodnight, Sir Leksi,' she called, just before it clicked shut.

After she had finished making the bed, she sat with the bag Aldara had packed for her and rummaged through it. It contained a nightdress, some undergarments, a few cotton dresses and a hairbrush. There was also a rolled-up towel, a sage and salt paste for her teeth and a small piece of soap inside. The princess had thought of everything.

A knock came at the door and she went to open it. Charis stood holding a basin and a jug of water. He blinked against the light, visibly tired. 'Can I get you anything else?' he asked after setting the items on the small table by the window.

She shook her head. 'No, thank you. You go get some sleep. You look exhausted.'

Alone again, she had a long drink, a quick wash, and then changed into the nightdress. She had just slipped beneath the blanket when she realised she needed to use the chamber pot.

Sitting up, teeth practically chattering in the cold room, she looked around. She crawled to the end of the bed and opened the trunk. No sane person would store a chamber pot with their linen, but she was desperate to avoid going outside. No pot, just a pile of what appeared to be clothes for a baby. She picked them up, studying the beautiful stitching on the simple shifts. They looked new. She folded them carefully before placing them back in the trunk and closing it as she resigned herself to the fact that she would have to go downstairs.

Wrapping her cloak around her shoulders, she picked up the lantern and walked barefoot over to the door, opening it as quietly as she could. As she crept across the landing, she saw the fire was now lit downstairs. Leksi sat in front of it, knees up, watching the wood burn. She walked as quietly as she could down the stairs, mindful not to wake Charis, who slept curled beneath a blanket against the wall.

When she reached the bottom of the stairs, her gaze went to Leksi, who appeared to be either asleep sitting up or very much lost in his thoughts. For a moment she considered sneaking past and relieving herself on the grass so as to not to bother him. He deserved a few hours' break after carrying her on his horse for most of the night.

Shaking her head, she realised she was not brave enough to venture outside alone. She took a few steps towards him and was about to whisper his name when a low growl sounded. She froze as the large dog leapt to its feet and came for her, its bark deafening. A small scream escaped her just as Leksi reached out and grabbed the animal by the scruff of the neck.

'Easy, girl,' he said. 'She's with me.' He looked up at her then, frowning. 'What is it?' His gaze flicked to his sword before moving past her.

'Nothing,' she replied, taking a step back from the dog, who continued to bare its teeth. 'That is… I do not seem to have a… chamber pot.'

Leksi relaxed. 'Sit,' he said to the dog, and it immediately sank to the floor.

Petra hid her trembling hands behind her back, eyes remaining on the dog.

'Don't tell me you're afraid of horses *and* dogs,' Leksi said.

She cleared her throat. 'Most people are afraid of growling animals.'

The knight gave the dog a quick pat before releasing his

grip and standing. 'She was just giving you a solid warning because you were sneaking up on me.'

She wanted to look him in the eye, but her gaze kept returning to the animal at his feet. She did not trust it. 'Warning heeded. And I was not sneaking up on you, I was being considerate to those fortunate enough to be sleeping.'

They both glanced at Charis, who had not stirred throughout the noisy ordeal.

'He will sleep through anything,' Leksi said, crossing his arms. He watched her for a moment. 'Are there any animals you are not afraid of, then?'

She thought for a moment. 'The stuffed kind mounted on walls.' She shook her head. 'Actually, I take that back. I always avoid those rooms when possible.'

He grinned. 'Come pet her,' he said, crouching again.

Horrified by the suggestion, she took another step back. 'Absolutely not. A moment ago that animal was about to maul me.'

'And now she is calm and has accepted you, despite your hostile body language.'

She looked down at herself and then at the dog. 'He can read body language?'

'She. And yes, she can. Come.' He gestured, and when she did not move, he added, 'Would you like a chamber pot? Or would you prefer to take your chances outdoors?'

His tone was serious enough for her to step forwards.

'Best to crouch down to her height so she doesn't feel threatened.'

'So *she* does not feel threatened?' Gathering the bottom of her cloak and nightdress, she did as she was told.

'Hold out your hand,' he said. 'Let her smell you.'

She cast a worried look at the knight. 'Why?'

Leksi rubbed the dog's back. 'Just do it.'

Petra slowly extended her hand, and the dog stretched its

neck to sniff her. 'Well, she is no longer growling, so I suppose that is progress.'

'Now pet her.'

She stiffened. 'I think we have done enough bonding for one night.'

Leksi tilted his head. '*Pet her.*'

She reluctantly reached out and ran her hand along the dog's back. The fur was surprisingly soft. She continued stroking, eventually relaxing enough to look up at Leksi. 'Why are you not asleep? You must be tired.'

He shifted so he was seated more comfortably on the ground. 'I have trouble sleeping in this house.' He paused. 'Too many memories.'

She studied him. 'Not good ones, judging by your expression. I gather your father has a drinking problem?'

He nodded.

'How old were you when it started?'

'He's been a drunk for as long as I can remember. I was eight when it became a problem.'

She sat down also, her legs tucked beneath her. The warmth from the fire helped relax her. 'What changed when you were eight?'

He stopped petting the dog and leaned back on his hands. 'My mother died during childbirth, the baby with her.'

The dog rolled onto its back and stared up at her with large, pleading eyes. She hesitated before rubbing its belly. 'I am sorry. That would have been hard on you being so young.'

'I'm a firm believer that the events of our childhood decide the type of person we'll be later in life. Mine made me tougher, and a much better fighter than I might've been otherwise.'

She watched the dog for a while. 'Maybe that is where I went wrong. I had a dull, uneventful upbringing. I was not prepared for my life.' She looked up, suddenly feeling as though she had said too much. 'About that chamber pot…'

Leksi grinned. 'It's under the bed, behind the trunk.'

'Oh.' She had only taken a brief look under there, fearing she might spot a rat peering back at her. When she stood, the dog jumped up also. 'What is she doing?'

'She follows the attention.'

Petra took a few steps back and the dog walked with her. 'Where do you think you are going?'

Leksi got to his feet and rocked on his heels. 'You've made a friend for life now.'

Petra was about to object and send the animal back to Leksi when she realised the company might be nice. 'What if she turns on me suddenly?'

'She won't. Trust me.'

She looked up at that. She had learned to read people, to sum them up within a few minutes, especially men. How else could she help the women in her charge survive? It might have been foolish, but she believed him. 'Goodnight, Sir Leksi.'

He bowed his head. 'Goodnight.'

As she walked away, she kept a wary eye on the dog trotting alongside her.

CHAPTER 7

She woke to the sound of someone chopping wood. Something shifted against her legs, and she glanced down to where the dog was curled in a ball, its eyes on the door. Looking in that direction, she was surprised to find a man leaning in the doorway, staring at her with a confused expression. She sat up with a gasp, causing the dog to jump down and trot away.

'Who are you?' he asked.

Even from that distance, she could smell the stale drink on his breath. She saw the similarities then, the strong jaw and broad shoulders. Though this version of Leksi had a red face and thinning hair. 'I am an acquaintance of Sir Leksi's.'

He studied her for a moment. Outside, an axe came down. 'He's here?'

She nodded, the blanket pulled up to her chin.

Leksi's father sniffed. 'He get you pregnant?'

She hid her horror at the suggestion well. This was his house, and she needed to be respectful of the fact. 'No.'

He nodded before turning away, and she listened to the

stairs creaking as he made his way downstairs, no doubt in search of his son.

Pushing back the covers, she crept over to the window and peered out. Leksi stood next to an enormous pile of wood, axe in hand. He was sweating from his efforts, despite the cool morning. Wiping his forehead with the back of his hand, he set another piece of wood on the chopping block and split it in two. His firm body was visible beneath his wet shirt, and even she could see the appeal. What a difference to the men of Masville, whose flaccid bodies did not match the power handed to them.

As though sensing he were being watched, he turned and looked up. She stepped back from the window just in time, feeling ridiculous.

After she had dressed, she headed downstairs, where the smell of eggs frying drifted from the kitchen. When she stepped inside the room, she found Charis busy cooking at the stove, and Leksi's father slumped in a chair. His food sat untouched in front of him. He did not appear to have much of an appetite.

'Good morning,' she said, walking over to Charis.

'Morning,' the squire replied, looking far more energetic than the previous night. 'Food's limited. How does an egg sound?'

She forced a smile. 'Lovely, thank you.'

'Didn't know to expect company,' Leksi's father grumbled from his chair.

Petra cleared her throat and decided to start again with him. 'My name is Petra. Sorry about earlier. I was just a little surprised by your… visit.'

He looked up at her, grey-faced and red-eyed. '*You* were surprised? That boy only shows up when he needs something.'

So it was not going to be an easy breakfast, then. 'Sorry, I did not catch your name.'

'I didn't give it.'

Leksi stepped through the door at that moment, and she could tell by the expression on his face that he had heard at least some of the exchange.

'This is Thom,' he said, glaring at his father's back.

Thom looked between them. 'You know, this one has a different woman every week,' he said, nodding towards his son.

'All right,' Leksi said, shaking his head. 'We'll be out of your way soon.'

'Still haven't managed to get rid of this one, I see,' Thom said, waving a finger in Charis's direction.

The squire just carried on cooking as though he had not spoken. Clearly he knew what to expect from the man. Petra glanced at Leksi, embarrassed on his behalf and a little sorry for him. He did not meet her eyes, instead stepping up to the table and sliding the plate closer to his father.

'You should try to eat something.'

Thom shoved the plate away, and it would have flown off the table had Leksi not caught it. 'I'm going back to bed,' he said, standing unsteadily, his chair scraping on the floor. 'Don't bother chopping any more wood.' He narrowed his eyes at his son. 'It won't last a year.'

Petra stepped back as he shuffled past her and returned upstairs. Only then did Leksi finally look at her, appearing uncomfortable for the first time since they had met.

'Would you like me to wash the linen and hang it out to dry before we leave?' she asked, trying to save him from an embarrassing explanation. His expression softened.

'Don't bother. It'll still be hanging there next time I come.'

Charis walked over and handed her a plate. The smell made her mouth water.

'Thank you,' she said.

Leksi pulled a chair out for her and sat opposite, dragging his father's cold plate in front of him and snatching up a fork. She picked up her own cutlery, inspecting it for a moment. There were smudges on the blade of the knife.

Leksi stopped eating, his loaded fork poised. 'Something the matter?'

She immediately lowered the cutlery to her plate, shaking her head. He already thought her a snob, and she was in no position to complain when they were kind enough to house and feed her.

The moment Leksi finished eating, he stood. 'I'm going to prepare the horses. I'll meet you both out front shortly.'

Petra stared up at him. 'Would you like me to let your father know we are leaving?'

He glanced at her. 'No need.' With that, he fled the kitchen.

Charis came to collect the plates from the table. 'This is how it's always been. He'll be fine once we leave.'

Leksi seemed eager to put as much distance between them and the Corneon border as possible. Or perhaps it was his father. They moved almost at a gallop for the first hour, farmland and the odd house flashing past them, before finally slowing to a more sensible pace. She noticed he checked their surroundings constantly, always on the lookout for something. As much as she knew he resented the role of bodyguard, he took it seriously.

'What village is this?' she asked when they finally slowed to a walk. Children had come out of their houses to wave at them, all eyes on Leksi. He looked every bit the heroic knight in his red tunic.

'Pelaweth,' he replied. 'This is where the flag tournament is held each year.'

She watched as a woman ushered her young sons off the road. 'Everyone is so friendly,' she said, waving.

'It probably just seems that way after spending the night in my father's home.'

She surprised herself by smiling. She looked the other way to hide the fact, but he must have seen it.

'Was that a smile?'

'No.'

He looked rather pleased with himself. 'I made you smile. You think I'm funny.'

'No, I do not.'

A satisfied grin settled on his face. At least she had managed to bring him out of his mood.

'I'm finely tuned to the ways in which women respond to me, and *you* think I'm funny.'

She shook her head. 'I thought *one* comment you made was funny. That is not the same thing.'

'When was the last time you laughed?'

What a ridiculous question. So why did it make her uncomfortable? Probably because she could not remember. 'Out loud?'

He turned and looked at her as though she were crazy. 'Yes, out loud. How else does one laugh?'

Inwardly, like every other emotion she had felt over the past nine years. 'Masville was a little lacking in humour.'

He chuckled softly at her response. 'Last stretch of the journey now,' he said, kicking his horse into a canter.

She took hold of him again, and Charis followed behind with the spare horse.

An hour and a half later, they reached the outskirts of Veanor. Instead of continuing along the main road that led to the port, they veered left and rode south through a patch of forest, emerging on the other side to sandy grassland. She could smell it then. She had never visited the coast, never smelled the ocean, but somehow she knew it was close.

They climbed a gentle hill, and when they reached the top, Leksi stopped his horse and loosened the reins.

'The Arossi Sea,' he announced.

Petra looked past him. For just a moment, the raw beauty of it silenced every thought. She watched as waves built and crashed against the rocks, the water moving as though it had a pulse.

'I love the ocean,' Leksi said, breathing in deeply. 'It can wash away anything, you know.'

She continued to stare. 'It is beautiful.'

He turned in the saddle, a curious expression on his face. 'Have you ever seen the ocean before?'

She shook her head. 'No.'

'It's not warm enough to swim yet,' Charis said, stopping next to them. 'You'll likely freeze to death if you go in.'

'I can't swim,' she replied, eyes on the water.

Leksi walked the horse on. 'Let's get to the estate first. Then I'll show you to the ocean.'

They continued south for another twenty minutes before a small wattle and daub house came into view, a good distance back from the water's edge. Behind it was a fenced garden and a small yard with shelter for the horses. In front was a grassy slope leading down to a stretch of pristine sand, enclosed by rocks at either end.

'This is the... estate?' Petra asked.

'This is it,' Leksi replied. 'Been in the family for years, though no one makes use of it.'

'I can see why.' It was tiny, and underwhelming as far as royal houses went.

'It's perfect for our needs.'

'Discreet,' she said. 'Is it leaning?'

He smiled. 'It's not much to look at, but it does hold up well in the cold season when those coastal winds hit.'

Thankfully, the cold season had just come to an end, and the grey clouds would disappear soon. Petra was looking forward to some warmth.

Leksi stopped in front of the house and helped her down from the horse. Her legs were shaky and sore from the long hours in the saddle, and she had to hold on to him for a few moments until she was steady.

'I could carry you over the threshold if you like,' Leksi offered, teasing.

She immediately let go of him.

Charis dumped all of their bags at the door and then led the horses away in the direction of the yard. Petra followed Leksi into the house, recoiling at the musky smell that greeted her. It was dark and dreary inside. Walking to the closest window, she pulled the curtain back and let light pour in.

'It's been closed up for some time,' Leksi said before disappearing into one of the rooms.

She wandered around the space. Aside from a few pieces of furniture, it was otherwise bare. She paused at the log bench, running her fingers over its rough surface. It was a far cry from the polished appearance of Masville, and yet it was charming in its own way.

'We're going to need to buy some supplies,' Leksi said, stepping back into the room. 'They don't tend to keep anything at the house.'

'It will only get stolen if there is no one here to watch it.'

He looked around. 'At least it's been kept clean.'

She was tempted to disagree. Her hands were itching for some warm water and a scrubbing brush.

'But I'm guessing you'll clean every inch of it again,' Leksi said.

So he had picked up on the fact that she was a little particular in that regard. 'Well, I have some jewels you are welcome to trade for supplies.'

He watched her for a moment. 'Coin is not an issue. Keep your jewellery.'

Petra was beginning to feel bad that he was stuck at the edge of the world in a tiny seaside house—with her. She wanted to help. 'Shall I cook us some food?' Except they did not have any food, or pots for that matter. 'Are there fish in the sea?'

He cocked his head. 'In this sea?' He nodded in the direction of the water.

'Yes.'

He suppressed a smile. 'Last time I checked, yes, there were fish in the sea.'

She scowled, not enjoying being laughed at. 'At Masville, we used to eat fish that was wrapped in leaves with lemon and herbs, and cooked in coals. No utensils required.'

He blinked. 'And how do you plan on catching the fish?'

She crossed her arms also. 'There are many ways to catch a fish.' She had never caught a fish in her life, but she had read books on the subject.

'I can catch us some fish,' Charis said, stepping inside and saving her. He placed a stack of saddles in the corner of the room, away from the fire. 'All you need is a long sturdy stick, a dagger and a bit of rope. Crab you can get by hand.'

'There you go,' Petra said. 'Charis will catch us some fish, and I will find us some large leaves.'

Leksi had the most amused expression, and it infuriated her.

'There are only pine trees in this part of the world,' Charis said, almost apologetically.

'Charis grew up in these parts,' Leksi explained.

She cleared her throat and glanced around the room. 'All

69

right, then I shall stay here and start cleaning up while the two of you go get supplies.' When Leksi frowned, she asked, 'What is the matter now?'

He closed the distance between them, and she made a point of not stepping back. 'I cannot leave you. Where I go, you go. That's how it works from now on.' He turned away. 'And it's safer if you stay away from the village. Charis will go into Veanor and bring back all we need.' He faced the boy. 'I can't write you a list, so I'm counting on your sharp mind to remember everything.'

Charis tapped his head with one finger. 'No need for a written list, my lord.'

Petra suspected he was the type of boy who most definitely needed a list, but off he went, confident in his abilities. She began rolling up her sleeves, preparing to get to work. Leksi stepped closer, and she looked up at him.

'First things first,' he said, taking her by the hand and leading her out of the house.

The action should have made her nervous, but as always with this man, for some unknown reason, she followed. 'Where are we going?'

He grinned over his shoulder at her. 'I told you I would show you the ocean.'

Now she was nervous. 'And you do remember I cannot swim?' He did not slow down. 'We are not going *in* the water, are we?' Her spare hand pressed against her stomach.

'Next best thing.'

They stepped down onto the soft sand, and she turned her head to look at the trail of footprints behind them. Her tongue moved in her mouth, tasting salt.

'Just up here,' Leksi said, keeping hold of her.

She was forced to run in order to keep pace with his giant strides. Finally they reached the rocks at the end of the beach and she stopped next to him, looking up.

'Start climbing,' he said. 'I'll help you.'

She turned to him, wide-eyed. 'What do you mean, "start climbing"?'

'That's how we get to the top.'

She stepped forwards and placed her palm on the cool rock. 'It does not look safe to climb.'

He stepped up behind her and grabbed her waist. 'What have I told you? You're safe with me.' With that, he hoisted her into the air so her hands and feet scrambled on the surface of the rock until she found her footing. 'Just keep climbing,' he called to her. 'I'm right behind you.'

With her heart pounding in her chest and hands trembling, she gripped the jagged edges of the rock and pulled herself up until she reached the top. She glanced back over the edge, both scared and a little thrilled by the height.

'Now what?' she asked as Leksi joined her.

He took her hand again. 'Follow me.'

She held tightly as he stepped onto the neighbouring rock. A step for him meant a jump for her, but she kept up. They continued that way for a number of minutes. At one point she lost her footing, but he righted her before any part of her touched the surface.

They came to a stop at the edge of the final rock, and Petra held her breath as she peered over the edge, where the water swirled and crashed below. She looked in both directions. They were standing on the most western point of the shoreline. Wind whipped at her hair, pulling pieces from her braid, but she made no effort to tame it, breathing in greedy lungfuls of crisp air instead.

'Wait for it,' Leksi urged, tightening his grip on her.

She turned to him, confused. 'Wait for what?'

Before he could reply, a giant wave smashed against the rock, sending a spray of seawater high into the air. She gasped as it rained down on them. Looking at her wet dress, she licked her lips, tasting the water. It was revolting and delicious all at once.

'Like I told you,' Leksi said, 'the ocean can wash away anything.'

She turned to him, frowning. 'Hopefully it does not wash us off this rock.'

'I've got you,' he replied, sounding confident in his ability to keep her safe.

She looked down at the water building up once more, splashing higher up the rocks with each wave. Her skin burned where the water sat on it, and she started to think he might be telling the truth about its powers.

Up went the water, and then down it came. But she was ready that time, eyes closed, bracing for the cold. Her skin tingled at the feel of it.

'Believe me yet?' he asked.

She opened her eyes. 'I suspect I am going to need more than a few waves.'

'Well, you have an entire ocean at your feet.'

She nodded absently, knowing it still would not be enough.

CHAPTER 8

They transformed the house into something more closely resembling a home. Leksi helped her clean it once, and then Petra went over every inch of it again. Leksi did not comment, not even when she rewashed the windows he had scrubbed spotless. He had no idea how long they would be stuck there, and he wanted her to feel comfortable.

Not one to sit idle, Leksi had Charis help him build a pell so they could train together. They would spend hours sparring and practicing their archery before washing off in the frigid ocean. In the afternoons, he would collect Petra from the garden behind the house, where she spent most of her time tending seedlings as though they were babies. They would take a long walk, either in the nearby forest or along the rocks. She never said no to him, never complained, but she never appeared to enjoy herself either.

He kept waiting to witness some miraculous change in her. There was a part of him that wanted to figure her out, get inside that head of hers and see what demons were lurking, but the only time she gave anything away was when he received letters. She would linger as he read them, holding her breath.

'Did they find him?' she would ask the moment he had finished reading.

He did not need to ask who she was referring to. It was all there in that hopeful expression, right before he disappointed her.

In the evenings, Petra would sit in her chair close to the hearth and stare out the window. He could not tell if she was waiting for her son to miraculously appear, or for King Nilos's men to show up and drag her back to Masville.

Of course, he felt sorry for himself also. He too was forced to sit idle, waiting for news. Evenings were the hardest. Nights were for drinking, socialising and women. Instead, he sat across the room from Petra's blank face, his sanity hanging by a thread—sober. It was not as though he were not allowed to drink, but rather that he would feel uncomfortable doing so under Petra's scrutinising gaze. The awkward situation made for a lot of early nights.

Three weeks into their sentence, he sent Charis to the market and then wandered over to the edge of the garden, watching Petra sow vegetables. It seemed she had retained some useful skills from her youth after all. She had asked Charis to bring her manure and sand from the beach, and every day she worked it through the soil.

'In Pamid, the soil is full of clay. Nothing grows,' she said, not looking up at him. 'You have to put in the work if you expect anything to survive.'

'Food scraps help also.'

She was kneeling in the dirt, wearing the same empty expression she always wore. 'There was no such thing as food scraps where I grew up.'

He looked down and cleared his throat. 'Your rows are crooked.'

She sat back on her heels and studied the perfect lines. 'No, they are straight. I marked every point before I began planting.' She turned to look at him, taking in his playful expression. 'Oh. I suppose you meant that as a joke.'

The garden was immaculate to the point of terrifying. God help any weed that tried to make a home in her space. She was that way with most things. Whenever he cooked, she would wash all the pots, then line them up on top of the hearth with the handles pointing in the same direction. Naturally, during times of extreme boredom, he would go and turn them all in different directions, then sit across the room and wait for that moment when she noticed. He would smile to himself as her body went rigid, watch her fingers working over her nails while she fought the urge to straighten them.

As he watched her dig into the earth with gloved hands, an idea came to him. 'Time for a break,' he called. 'Come with me.'

She looked up at him, tiredly. 'Come with you where?'

He tutted. 'Always so suspicious. To the behourd.' He thought the term might make her smile, something he was yet to witness properly. Instead, she frowned at him.

'You mean to the grain sack you stuffed with straw, mounted on a stick, and stuck in the ground over there?'

'That is our pell, located within the behourd.' He could have sworn her eyes showed some life for a moment.

She stood and brushed dirt off the skirt of her dress. 'You want me to watch you train? Put on a big manly display? Is that it?'

'Actually, I thought I would let you have a turn.'

'A turn at what?' she asked, folding her arms delicately in front of her.

He stepped on the bottom rail of the fence he had built for her; it was supposed to keep the hares out, but it was a work in progress. Reaching down, he pulled a dagger from the sheath strapped to his ankle. 'We'll start small.'

She glanced down at the weapon in his hand and shifted her weight. 'You want me to stab the sack?'

'So many questions,' he said, waving her over. 'Come, let's see if we can release some of that tension you're holding in.'

She hesitated before exiting the small gate he held open for her, stepping past him without so much as a glance. They walked over to the cleared area and she stopped next to the pell, crossing her arms in front of her, waiting.

'Right,' he began, throwing the dagger in the air and catching it by the blade. He offered it to her, and she stared down at it. 'Go on,' he encouraged. 'I'll show you what to do.'

She exhaled before reaching out and taking it from him, holding it out from her as though it might turn on her at any moment.

'Take a firm hold,' he said. He watched as she adjusted her grip. 'Now distribute your weight evenly between your feet, like this.' He showed her with his own feet, and she copied him. 'That's it, that foot behind. Good. Now I want you to step forwards, and at the same time, thrust the blade like this.'

'Into the straw bag?'

'Not just yet. Show me the action first.'

She looked entirely uncomfortable as she took a small step forwards and extended her arm.

His eyebrows shot up in surprise. 'Really? That's it? Where's all that anger you're holding on to?'

She looked at him. 'I am not angry, Sir Leksi.'

'I disagree.' He walked over, moving behind her. 'May I?'

'May you what?'

'Engage the enemy,' he joked.

She turned her head to him. 'Probably not a great idea when I am armed.'

He put his hands up and stepped away. 'Good point. I shall talk you through it.' He moved so he was in her line of sight. 'Step up to the pell.'

She stared at him blankly.

'The straw sack,' he said, pointing.

She stepped forward.

'This time you're going to stab it. Give it all you have,' he instructed.

Drawing a breath, she narrowed her eyes and widened her stance before thrusting the dagger into the sack. She stepped back to admire the one-inch hole with a satisfied expression, as though she had excelled at the task.

'That's all you have? Really?' She looked a little taken aback. 'Hold on a moment.' He dashed off and returned a minute later with some flexible twigs and long pieces of grass.

'What is that for?' she asked.

He held a finger up, telling her to wait, and got to work bending and binding the sticks together to form a circle. When he was done, he set it on top of the pell, like a crown. 'You remember this guy, don't you? I present King Nilos of Corneo.'

Her hand went limp around the dagger as she stared at the pell.

'More straw stuffing required?' Leksi asked, trying to read her expression.

She blinked and looked down at the ground.

He stepped up beside her, lifting her dagger hand again.

'Don't lower your weapon,' he said gently. 'This man stands between you and your son.'

She flinched and looked up at him. 'I do not want to do this anymore.'

He studied her face. She was shutting down, right in front of him. What on earth had the king done to her to initiate

77

such a response at the mere mention of his name? 'I think you should. Let it out, or it will eat you up.'

She raised her eyes to the pell.

'I want you to reflect on the past nine years,' he continued. 'Every painful moment. I want you to feel it. Don't push it down. Just let it out—every ugly part of it.'

'I can't,' she said, dropping the dagger. 'My mind does not work like that. I am a mentor, not a soldier.'

Again he stepped forwards, picked up the dagger, and placed it in her hand. 'I've seen the bruises. I'm guessing you're more like a soldier than you realise.'

She glanced at him as though deciding if she should trust him.

'Tell me about your son. How old was he when the king took him?'

Her hand went to her stomach. 'Four days old.'

'But you remember him.'

A nod.

'Say it. Say, "I remember him".'

'I remember him.'

'And did the king share his plans with you?'

'No.'

'What did he do?'

'He stole my baby.'

Leksi watched the change in her face when she said the words. 'While you slept?'

She nodded.

'I want you to say it.'

'He stole my baby, from my arms, while I slept.'

'And you hate him for it.'

She closed her eyes, shaking her head.

'You don't hate him?'

No response.

'Why don't you know where he is?'

Her eyes opened. 'He will not tell me.'

'Why not? You're his mother.' She was trembling, but he continued. 'What *has* he told you?'

'He told me once that he was living with a distant relative.'

Leksi watched the threads holding her together come loose. 'That's all he's said in five years?' No reply. She was struggling now. 'Do you believe him?'

She shook her head.

'A thief *and* a liar. Do you think he should pay?'

No reply.

'I said, do you think he should pay?'

'Yes.'

'So make him pay.' He took another step back. 'He's standing right in front of you.'

Narrowing her eyes on the pell, she lunged forwards with surprising speed, driving the dagger through the material. She stilled, staring down at the giant tear where a few strands of straw now poked out. Then pulling the dagger out, she thrust it in again. Leksi remained where he was, watching the raw emotion play out on her face. She held it with both hands this time, driving it into King Nilos's straw heart. A noise escaped her—a sob and a roar forming a single sound.

Leksi realised at that moment that years of suppressed anger and pain might be too much for her all at once. He could only guess at what had taken place behind those walls. Perhaps the reality was much worse than he had imagined.

By this stage, she was slashing the pell, all composure gone, her hair coming loose with each swing of her arm. He had a choice: stop her or let her finish the job. He went with the latter.

'Talk to him,' Leksi called to her. 'Tell him why you're doing this.'

'Because I hate you!' She reached for the sack with her spare hand and began pulling at one of the holes until it tore open. 'You took him from me!' Straw began to fly everywhere, floating down around her. 'You drugged me, and you stole my baby, right from my arms.'

Leksi looked down at the ground. He had heard the story from Tyron, but this was something else.

'Then you called me to your bed, night after night, knowing I hate you!' Another tear, another puff of straw. 'Why didn't you leave me alone?' She shoved the pell, and when it did not budge, she began kicking at it. 'Where is my son?' she screamed.

It was no longer safe for her to continue, so Leksi went to her, keeping an eye on the dagger in her hand, worried she might accidentally hurt herself. When he took her arm, she turned on him, blade swinging. He leapt backwards, angling his body so the weapon passed him without making contact. She froze and her gaze went to the dagger, staring at it like she had forgotten she was holding it. It fell from her hand, right before her knees gave out.

Leksi stepped up, caught her, and lowered her gently to the ground. He did not keep hold of her, instead sitting in the dirt next to her while she cried into her hands. After a few minutes, the crying stopped.

'I am so sorry,' she said, barely able to look at him. 'Are you all right?'

He laughed through his nose. 'It would be fairly embarrassing if I wasn't. I've learned how to avoid a blade over the years.'

'I did not mean to—'

'I know.' He was surprised by how much he hated seeing her cry. After a long silence, he asked, 'He really drugged you?'

She sniffed and pulled her knees up, hugging them to her.

'He knew it was the only way. I would never have handed him over.'

For once, Leksi was at a loss for words, slightly out of his depth on this one. He had most definitely underestimated the extent of her anger. 'I thought it better out than in.'

She studied him. 'Probably safer for both of us if my feelings remain buried in the future.' Looking down at herself, she said, 'I am a mess. Is this how you train your men?'

'Sometimes. Depends on the man. They don't tend to cry as much though.' He usually ran in the other direction when women cried in front of him. He was a bastard like that, especially given he was usually the cause of the tears—he had broken a few hearts over the years. Something about their puffy red faces and desperate expressions made him want to flee, so he was very surprised to find that instinct had not kicked in. It helped that she was one of those rare people who looked beautiful when she cried. Stunning, actually. 'It doesn't bother me if you make a mess of yourself. You do the laundry.'

She glanced across at him. 'This is probably one of the most mortifying moments of my adult life.'

He shrugged. 'I've seen men twice your size in far worse states.'

'I never cry in front of people.'

'I would be more concerned by the fact that you just tried to stab me.'

Almost a smile. 'There is that.'

He leaned back on his hands. 'They'll find your son.'

'How can you be sure?'

'You've met Aldara. She isn't one to give up.' He reached out and plucked a piece of straw from her hair. 'How old is your son now?'

She rested her chin on her knees. 'Five. I have missed so much of his life.'

'They'll be watching him especially close at the moment, just in case.'

'If I knew where he was, I would go to him anyway.'

'That's why I'm here, to protect you and to stop you from doing anything foolish.' He watched as she pushed some hair off her face. 'If it makes you feel any better, I don't remember the first five years with my mother.'

'What about the last three?'

He thought for a moment. 'I remember some things. Not events, but moments and feelings. I think I remember her face, but I'm not entirely sure I trust my memories.'

Charis had arrived back from the village, and they watched as he approached the house on horseback.

'I was with my mother for fifteen years, but the memories are fading.'

'What was your mother like?' he asked, conscious that their time alone would soon be over.

She straightened her legs and leaned back on her hands, a mirrored reflection of Leksi. 'Hard-working, a good wife, and a good mother given our circumstances. She was always too tired to be much fun, but we were always fed and clothed.' She attempted to tidy her hair. 'What was your mother like?'

He had not thought about her in some time. It was easier not to. 'She loved to laugh, and she had a wild imagination. She used to make up funny stories, to make me laugh. I don't think my father appreciated our sense of humour. I don't remember him ever laughing, but I know he loved her.'

'Why do you say that?'

He thought for a moment. 'Because of how he grieved.'

They fell silent, watching Charis unsaddle his horse in the yard.

'I hope I laughed often enough in those eight years. I wish I could see myself through her eyes.' Leksi looked around, not really believing he had spoken those words aloud. His gaze met Petra's.

'I have no doubt the two of you spent most of those eight years in absolute hysterics.'

He cleared his throat. 'Is that your way of admitting I'm funny?'

Her eyes shone at him. 'Obviously I am not going to appreciate your humour as much as your mother.'

'That is a rather long-winded way of saying no.'

She held his gaze. 'I will admit to finding you amusing.'

'Very generous of you.'

Charis had spotted them and was now heading in their direction. Standing, Leksi offered his hand and pulled her to her feet, holding her hand for a moment. 'How do you feel?'

'Embarrassed, and in need of a wash.'

He released her hand, stepping back from her. 'Then my work here is done. I should go note down all the things Charis forgot to buy so we don't forget them next time.'

'Sir Leksi,' she called to him.

He turned, waiting.

'Your only job is to keep me safe. I feel as though you have gone above and beyond what is expected.' She appeared to be struggling with her words. 'I suppose I just wanted to say thank you.'

He suspected he would not go above and beyond for any other woman. Something was broken in her, and he had an irrational need to fix it. He watched as her fingers worked over her fingernails.

Press, press, press.

'Best stay alert,' he said. 'I have a bad reputation when it comes to women.'

She studied him for the longest moment, then shook her head. 'No, I think Aldara was right. You are a good man, Sir Leksi.' She gathered the skirt of her dress and stepped past him. 'Your mother would be very proud,' she added.

The comment landed with a thud. He had received compliments from women before, but not like this. This was different to the post-climactic murmurs of a woman quivering beneath him. This one left something warm humming inside him.

CHAPTER 9

There was no news of her son. What had she expected? There were no shortcuts simply because she was desperate. And she *was* desperate. At some point, Prince Tyron's generosity would run out, or his hand would be forced, and then she would be on her own.

Six weeks after fleeing Masville, another letter arrived from the prince. She could tell by Leksi's face that it was not good news. She had watched him over the weeks and had learned to read him.

'Bad news?' she asked, reminding herself to breathe. They were sending her back. She was sure of it.

Leksi lowered the letter, his expression serious. 'King Nilos has been in communication with King Pandarus. He's demanding your return.' He handed the parchment to her so she could read it.

'He knows I am here.' She handed it back to him. 'He will come for me if you do not hand me over.'

Leksi shook his head. 'He's bluffing, chasing confirmation of your whereabouts.' Folding the letter, he shoved it into his pocket. 'That's not to say there's no danger. King Pandarus is likely aware of the fact that you're in Syrasan. Prince Tyron will have to manage that.'

Her hand went to her forehead. 'I have brought him so much trouble. Perhaps it is time for me to return to Corneo, search for Xander on my own.'

'You'll be caught before you even get a chance to make enquiries.'

They stared at one another. As much as she did not want to admit it, she felt much safer with him around. 'If the order arrives to hand me over, you will have no choice but to obey your king.'

'I'm quite aware of the workings of a monarch, thank you.'

She turned away. 'I need a walk.'

'I'll come with you.'

Her lips pressed together. 'There is really no need. I am just going down to the water. You must be tired of my company by now.'

'I thought I would be, but I'm not.'

She swallowed and was about to reply when she heard a wagon approaching. Leksi turned just as Charis came running from the house.

'Wagon, my lord!'

Leksi rolled his eyes. 'Well spotted.' His hand went to the hilt of his sword, and he began walking in the direction of the carriage. 'Take her inside,' he called to his squire, then glanced back at her. 'Don't come out of the house.'

She nodded, and with her heart hammering in her chest, she followed Charis into the house and waited nervously by the door. She listened as the horses came to a stop and the wagon door groaned. The exchange sounded friendly, and she frowned at Charis.

A moment later, footsteps approached, delicate ones that

could only belong to a woman. Charis stepped forwards to open the door and a pretty brunette stepped inside, looking around before her gaze settled on Petra.

'There you are,' the woman beamed. She closed the gap between them and took both of Petra's hands in hers. 'In the flesh, exactly as I imagined you.' Her eyes moved down Petra's dress. 'Though clearly styled by Aldara. You poor thing. Never mind, I come bearing gifts.'

Petra looked to Charis for help, an introduction, or at least a clue that he knew who she was.

'Lady Hali,' the squire said.

The woman's eyes widened as she realised her mistake. 'Oh, how rude of me. Please, just call me Hali.' Seeing Petra's blank expression, she added, 'I'm a good friend of Aldara's. She sent word that you were cooped up in this sad little house with Leksi, so I thought it best that we stop by and ensure our notorious knight is behaving himself. Now that I've seen you, I believe it was a wise decision.' She leaned forwards in a conspiratorial manner. 'Leksi has a bit of a reputation with the ladies.'

'So everyone keeps telling me.'

Leksi chose that moment to enter the house, though she could not tell by his face whether he had heard. His eyes met hers briefly as he held the door open for someone else. An older gentleman stepped through and smiled at her. He had a kind face.

'Lord Yuri,' Leksi announced. 'And I see you have already met his lovely wife.'

Petra curtsied. 'My lord.'

Yuri inclined his head. 'Forgive the intrusion. My wife was rather keen to meet you. I suggested we send a messenger first, give you some warning, perhaps come by tomorrow—'

'I was never going to wait until tomorrow,' Hali said.

'Quite.' Yuri's eyes smiled.

'We are staying for dinner.'

Petra's eyebrows shot up, and she looked to Leksi, who gave a small shrug.

'Don't worry about a thing,' Hali went on. 'Our cook is on her way with plenty of food. We shall make a feast of it.'

'If that is all right with the lady of the house,' Lord Yuri added, eyes on Petra.

She looked between the expectant faces. Leksi seemed comfortable in their presence, which was good enough for her. He had been starved of company for weeks; their visit would probably do him some good. 'That sounds wonderful, thank you.'

Hali clapped her hands together. 'Excellent, but first things first. Let's get you out of your peasant clothes and into something befitting guests.'

'I am afraid I do not have a very extensive wardrobe,' Petra replied.

'Don't worry, I brought some things with me. I too was a mentor once.'

Petra glanced at Leksi for confirmation. He nodded once, his lips turning up.

'And married to a lord?' Petra said. 'That must be quite a story.'

'And a long one. Best reserved for dinner, perhaps,' Yuri replied. He turned to Leksi. 'Perhaps you could give me a tour while the ladies ready themselves for dinner.'

More horses arrived outside, and Leksi excused himself before stepping out. A minute later, he returned with two women laden with baskets of food. Leksi pointed them in the direction of the hearth, and after exchanging a surprised glance, they rolled their sleeves up and got to work.

'It'll be a short tour,' Leksi said.

'Be sure to show Lord Yuri the behourd,' Petra said with the straightest of faces.

Leksi's eyes met hers, and the most brilliant smile spread across his face. Such a small thing, but she was rather pleased with herself.

The men walked the grounds, and the women shut themselves in Petra's bedroom. Hali was surprisingly easy company given they had never met before. She fussed and chatted, often jumping topics before Petra had even commented on the last one. How the woman had ever become a mentor, Petra had no idea. Hali clearly wanted to feel useful, or was perhaps lonely. Either way, Petra just let her do whatever she wanted, happy to sit back and let someone else do the talking.

With the weather finally warming up, she accepted the offer of a green silk dress to wear, enjoying the feel of the luxurious fabric after weeks wearing nothing but plain cotton. Aldara had, of course, been thinking practically, and it was not as if Petra had anyone to impress while she was in hiding.

Hali sat beside her on the bed with a collection of paints and brushes, lifting Petra's face to her. 'You must be going out of your mind stuck out here,' she said, studying Petra's complexion before deciding on colours.

She was going out of her mind waiting to hear about her son. The rest was not so bad. 'It is a welcome change from life at Masville.'

Hali nodded in agreement. 'Oh, I can imagine. I hear King Nilos is a piece of work.'

Petra said nothing.

'The audacity to give you the role of mentor and then to continue to invite you to his bed, right under the noses of his Companions,' Hali went on. 'Bet those women stared daggers at you across the table at every meal.' She stopped painting.

89

'And what sort of man separates a baby from his mother? It's no wonder you fled.'

So she knew everything. 'Yes' was all Petra said. 'Do you have any children?' she asked, attempting to move the conversation away from her.

Hali resumed painting. 'I entered this marriage with realistic expectations as far as children go. Yuri is older than me. His sons are all grown up. Such a big house, so many empty rooms.'

Despite her smile, there was something in her tone that made Petra think she was not so relaxed inside. 'Perhaps it will just take a little longer for the two of you.'

Hali found a smile. 'Yuri says the same thing about forming new friendships, but the reality is much harsher. All of his friends are of noble blood, and they're devastated that he's married so far below him.'

'You do not seem like you would have trouble making friends.'

'Oh, the servants love me, but any woman of standing flees in the opposite direction the moment I enter a room.'

'I take it they are aware of your previous… adventures.'

Hali laughed, a pretty, warm sound. 'They think I'm a big whore, if that's what you mean.'

Petra opened her eyes and watched as Hali mixed a colour for her lips.

'I too was the king's Companion once,' Hali said. 'Though he wasn't king at the time.'

'Companion to a prince is still an honour.' She had no idea why she said that. Years of internalising the lies fed to her, most likely.

'Pfft, hardly. He sold me to King Jayr of Zoelin first chance he got.' She shook her head. 'Now there's a fun man.'

Petra observed her. 'I have met him a number of times. A very intelligent man.'

90

'Oh, he's smart enough. Charming, even. Behind closed doors is another matter. Have you seen his wife?'

'Queen Cora? A few times. I hear she is not a fan of Companions.'

Hali leaned in. 'You know, she was Sir Leksi's biggest admirer for a number of years.'

Petra was not one for gossip, but this comment held her attention. 'Oh?'

'If she wasn't such a horrid person, I might feel sorry for her. In love with a knight for most of her life, then forced to marry a monster.'

'The queens of Zoelin are treated better than queens of their neighbouring kingdoms.'

Hali appeared sceptical. 'Do you actually believe that?'

'I suppose there are more ways to hurt a person than just physically.'

'Exactly.'

They were silent for a moment, Hali's eyebrows drawn together in concentration as she applied a few final touches. A question burned inside Petra, and she could no longer contain it.

'Queen Cora's feelings for Sir Leksi… were they mutual?'

Hali seemed surprised by the question. 'Are you asking if Leksi was in love with her?'

Petra's cheeks burned beneath the paint. 'You do not have to answer.'

Hali shook her head. 'I doubt it. They flirted endlessly, of course, but it's a well-known fact that Leksi loves all women far too much to settle for just one.'

Petra swallowed. 'Queen Cora is famous for her beauty.'

'And her vile temper.' Hali was silent a moment. 'What was King Nilos like as a lover? I'm picturing him as rather lazy.'

Petra's gaze fell to her lap.

. . .

'Look at me.'

'No.'

He gripped her face, forcing her to meet his gaze. 'See what you do to me. Look at my face. I love you.'

She closed her eyes. 'You do not love me.'

'Look at me!'

'No.'

He grabbed a handful of her hair and yanked, jolting her neck at an unnatural angle. 'Tell me you love me.'

'I love you.' Her tone was flat, empty.

'You do not mean it.'

She opened her eyes. 'I do not mean it.'

Letting go of her hair, he cupped her face with both hands. 'What do you want? Anything you want, it is yours. Tell me.'

She looked down. 'My son.'

'I am trying to forget,' Petra replied. It was the truth. She had spent nine years trying to shut him out.

Hali's face filled with pity. 'Sorry, it's none of my business. I'm simply starved for company, as you have probably figured out.'

Yes, she had figured that out. 'I too appreciate the company,' Petra lied. She had always preferred to be alone—though she had tolerated Leksi's company rather well of late. 'And the dress, and the hair.'

Hali stepped back to admire her work. 'You look absolutely beautiful. No wonder King Nilos is completely besotted with you.' She must have noticed the change in Petra's face, because she added, 'Of course, he'll never get past your bodyguard.'

'I am very fortunate he agreed to help me.'

Hali chewed her lip. 'Has it been all right here?'

Petra glanced at the window. 'Yes, actually. Sir Leksi has been very kind.'

'I hope he isn't forcing you to address him in such a formal way,' Hali scoffed. 'I wouldn't put it past him, of course.'

'Not at all. Old habits and all that.'

Hali gestured for her to stand and fiddled with the neckline of the dress so it showed just the right amount of cleavage. 'You need jewels.' She stepped over to her bag and began sifting through it. 'Leksi basically grew up at Archdale, you know?'

Petra stared at her back. 'After his mother passed away?'

Hali was only half listening. 'Queen Eldoris practically raised him like one of her own.' She returned with some gemstones. 'His father all but threw him out.'

Petra watched as Hali fitted a gold cuff around her wrist. 'That must have hurt him tremendously.'

'He's no wilting flower.' She stepped back for a final look. 'Stunning. I must say, I'm surprised Leksi has not tried anything untoward.'

Petra looked out the window to where the men were returning from their walk. Leksi had shown no interest in her beyond the occasional flirt, which she suspected he did with all women. They had become friends of sorts. Probably out of necessity. 'I am not his type, which makes this situation easier for everyone.'

Hali picked up the small mirror from the bed and held it up. 'Are you ready to forget your troubles for one evening?'

Petra barely recognised her reflection. It was not just the paint and the jewels, it was the absence of dark circles around her eyes, fuller cheeks and sun-kissed skin. Six weeks and she was already changing. What would a year away from King Nilos look like? A lifetime?

TANYA BIRD

She squashed down the hope, far too practical for dreams.

'I think you're wrong, by the way,' Hali said. 'I think you are exactly Leksi's type.'

Petra's gaze returned to the mirror. She would know soon enough.

CHAPTER 10

$\mathcal{T}$he wine went straight to Leksi's head, or perhaps it was the speed at which he drank it. When Petra had stepped out of that room, he knew he was in trouble by the way his body reacted at the sight of her. All that soft flesh on display, those gentle curves, those lips painted in just the right shade of red to make his mouth turn dry. He had always thought her beautiful, but this was something else.

He immediately sent Charis to one of the bedrooms for the remainder of the evening, unable to watch the boy stare, open-mouthed. He remembered what it was to be fifteen, and he did not want to see his own private thoughts play out on the face of his squire.

'What do you think, gentlemen? Isn't she lovely?' Hali had asked, clearly proud of her efforts.

Lord Yuri had agreed wholeheartedly, eyes on her face like the true gentleman he was. Then everyone had waited for Leksi's reply, and he had stood there like a gaping fool, with no idea where to look. Breasts, hips, legs, breasts again. *Dear God*. He had finally settled on her shoes, though one creamy ankle was visible through the small split of the dress. It was still too much for him.

'Very nice,' he had managed. He considered himself quite the wordsmith when it came to women, and never in his life had he uttered the words *'Very nice.'* Clearing his throat, he had encouraged everyone to take a seat. He needed to cover her with a table before he embarrassed himself.

Now he sat across from Hali, and every now and then he caught her gaze. She had a mischievous glint in her eye.

She knew.

He tried to focus on the food, as it was one of the best meals he had eaten in weeks. Petra had tried to cook a few times, and the three of them had sat around the table making appreciative noises while chewing the mutton for twice the amount of time than usually required. Leksi offered to cook most days to spare them the performance and Petra the embarrassment. He could manage the basics: bread, soup, and stew, but nothing like the mouth-watering fare spreading the length of the table in front of them: fish, eggs, an assortment of vegetables, and fresh bread.

'We might have to keep hold of your cook,' Leksi said, reaching for another helping of fish. He was seated next to Petra, plenty of distance between their chairs.

'I am afraid I have not been much help in that regard,' Petra said. 'It has been years since I have needed to cook anything.'

'I wish I could tell you she is being modest,' Leksi said. Everyone laughed, and when he glanced at Petra, he found her half smiling into her food. Just once he would like to see a full smile.

'Leksi tells me you are not very confident with animals,' Yuri said.

Petra looked up. 'Did he now? A rather kind way of

saying that I embarrass myself every time I am confronted with one.'

'Not entirely true,' Leksi said, swallowing his mouthful of food. 'She met my father's dog and they ended up spending the night together.'

'How very scandalous,' Hali said, winking at her.

'I thought we agreed to never speak of it,' Petra said, turning to Leksi.

He looked into her smiling eyes. Normally he would have replied with something funny that would bring the whole table to laughter, but the moment passed, and he reached for his wine. His eyes met with Hali's once more. He really wished she would stop assessing him.

'One of our dogs had a litter of pups recently,' Yuri said, placing his knife and fork on the plate and pushing it away. 'I mean to sell them, but Hali has become somewhat attached.'

Hali took a large sip of wine before speaking. 'They're just babies! We'll sell them when they're older.'

'They were weaned from their mother weeks ago.'

Leksi watched as Petra filled her cup and took a long drink. She seemed suddenly uncomfortable.

'So that's it?' Hali said. 'I'm supposed to look into those adorable brown eyes and say, "You've had your few weeks with your mother. Time to be given away to a stranger"?'

Petra froze next to him. Leksi stood, causing everyone to look at him, except Petra whose gaze was fixed on her plate.

'It's stifling in here with the food, the hearth, and the wine. I'm going to get some air.' He turned to Petra and offered his hand. 'Would you care to join me?'

Without looking up, she slipped her hand into his and stood. 'Excuse me.'

Lord Yuri also stood, only returning to his seat once they had exited the house.

It was one of those clear evenings when the air burned

your lungs, but the blazing stars above made the cold worth it. Leksi released Petra's hand and watched as she stepped away. She was slightly turned away from him, hands on her stomach.

'Are you all right?' he asked.

She nodded.

'I've known Hali for some time. She probably doesn't even realise—'

'It is all right,' Petra said, turning to him, eyes shiny. 'She has been nothing but kind. This evening has been wonderful.'

Leksi's weight was on one foot, his arms at his sides. They stared at one another, neither really knowing what to say next.

'Perhaps the wine was not such a good idea,' she said, attempting a smile.

'I can send them home if you would prefer,' he said. 'They'll understand.'

She shook her head. 'Do not do that. You deserve some pleasant company for just one evening. You should go back inside. I will be along in a moment.'

He watched her, bathed in light from the window, and swallowed. 'I like your company. That's what I was trying to say before they arrived.'

She tilted her head in a manner that suggested she did not believe him. 'There is really no need for you to be careful of my feelings. I might be afraid of horses, but away from animals I am rather resilient.'

His eyes travelled over her. Every hair was in place, with just the right amount of skin on display to make his pulse quicken every time he looked at her properly. In that moment, she was the perfect Companion, the most upstanding mentor, and yet he had seen another side of her. He had lifted her off the forest floor, her lips blue. He had seen her cry and kill a man made of straw.

'You look absolutely beautiful, by the way.' The words came out with ease that time. He was not trying to be charming; it was just an honest observation.

Her eyes widened a little, but that was her only reaction. She was too well trained to be embarrassed. 'That is a very kind thing to say.'

He gave a small shrug. 'I'm not trying to be kind. It's the truth.' The wine helped him—a lot. Though having her within reach was probably not a good idea. He reminded himself that the last thing she needed was some man leering at her, grabbing her, kissing the paint from her lips. And then there was the promise he had made to Tyron. She was off limits. But she continued to hold his gaze, as though waiting to see what he would do next.

'Can you smell that?' he asked, glancing at the house.

She sniffed the air. 'Honey and ginger.'

'Stewed pears,' they said in unison.

He offered her his arm. 'Would you care to join me for dessert before it all disappears?'

She slipped her bare arm through his. There were still two layers of clothing between them, and yet he could feel the warmth of her through the fabric. He kept his eyes ahead and his thoughts on the food.

By the time the wagon pulled away from the small house, Petra had drunk more wine in a few hours than she had in her nine years at Masville. She stood outside in the dark, warmed by drink, conversation and laughter. Others' laughter, but it was enough. She had enjoyed watching everyone around her, telling their stories, completely unafraid of being judged. No shame, no propriety, just raw human spirit so contagious that Petra felt the walls shift inside of her—just a little.

'You must be freezing,' Leksi said, looking down at her bare arms.

She drew a long, cleansing breath. 'I am certain it is cold, but I honestly cannot feel it.'

'That doesn't surprise me. I saw how much you drank. I'm impressed at how well you hold your liquor.'

She peered up at him in the dark. He was a full head taller than her. 'Were you counting my drinks?'

'It's my job to watch out for you.'

'Hmm.' Her head was cocked to one side. Dear God, she was flirting. Fuelled by the wine, she took a step towards him. 'And is it your job to sneak glances at the neckline of my dress?'

'Ah, you noticed that?'

Her lips curled into a smile. 'It is my job to notice the reactions of men, Sir Leksi. The more you drank, the less discreet you were.'

He continued to watch her. 'You know you can just call me Leksi, right?'

Her heart was pounding so hard in her chest that she was worried he would see it through the sheer fabric. For years she had taught women the art of seduction, introducing them to the workings of a man's mind. It was an act, a performance, a lie.

This was different. This was not a sequence of planned gestures. There was an energy moving through her, and for the first time since they had met, she was forced to admit to herself that she was drawn to him. She had been convinced that part of her was missing or broken, but there it was, attraction in its most primal form.

And it felt good.

'What are you doing?' he asked when she took another step towards him.

'I am not entirely sure.' She held his gaze. 'Should I stop?'

Conflict played out in his face. 'Not yet.'

She took one more step, their bodies almost touching. 'It seems you find me attractive in this dress.'

His eyes travelled down her body and back up again. 'Honestly? I find you attractive in any dress.'

She swallowed, waiting for her sensible side to shut down whatever was happening. 'Did you think about kissing me earlier?' She could not believe she had just asked that.

He was so still. 'I've thought about it before this evening, but before you get cross, I never planned on acting on those thoughts.'

She lifted her face a little, and she could have sworn he was about to lean in but stopped himself. 'Because I am not your type?'

He frowned and pulled away slightly. 'Why would you say that?'

'I take no offence.'

That time he did lean in. 'Trust me, in that dress and with those lips, you are every man's type.' He reached up and ran one finger down her bare arm. Tiny bumps prickled her skin. 'If there's something you want, all you have to do is ask.'

She felt slightly dizzy and slightly something else. More than anything, she felt confused by her actions. What *did* she want? He was going to make her say it.

'I think I want you to kiss me.'

'You think?'

Her mind was fuzzy. 'I suppose I will not know for sure until it happens.'

He moved so slowly that she had time to examine every part of his handsome face. 'I need you to be sure before it happens.' He waited.

'I am sure.' Yes, she was ready. Why else would she remain in front of him, face turned up and mouth slightly parted?

She closed her eyes as he leaned in, brushing his lips over hers so gently she felt a bit cheated. Her eyes opened as a pleasant sensation lingered. His breath smelled of pears and sugar. He was watching her, taking in her reaction, assessing her. Whenever the king was that close, she would turn her head, but she did not want to turn away from Leksi.

'More, please,' she whispered.

Apparently that was his undoing, because he gripped her arms and his lips came down on hers, firmer that time. Something must have shifted in her mind, because suddenly she could not feel him anymore. She could not feel anything. Her body stopped responding to his. It just stopped period.

He pulled back and stared down at her, his expression confused—worried, maybe.

'What's the matter?' he asked.

'Nothing,' she lied.

He let go of her arms but did not move away. 'I felt it.'

Tears threatened to spill over. 'Felt what?' It was definitely worry she recognised on his face now.

'The moment I lost you.'

She understood then what had happened. Her body had done what she had trained it to do—it had shut him out.

She took a step back from him. 'Sorry.' The wine no longer warmed her, but rather made her feel sick.

'Don't be sorry,' he said. 'I shouldn't have taken advantage of you in your current state.'

My current state? Oh. He thought her drunk, or worse, damaged. Maybe she was.

She shook her head, embarrassed. 'You did not take advantage. I asked you to—'

'And I moved too fast.'

No, the speed had been perfect. 'I should go to bed.' She

forced herself to look at him. 'I… I am very sorry about… all that.'

'Don't apologise.' He went to move towards her and then stopped. 'Go get some sleep. In the morning, we can pretend this never happened.'

She all but flinched at his words. Of course he wanted to forget it. What a mess she was. 'Goodnight, Sir Leksi,' she said, turning away and trying very hard to keep a slow, composed pace.

'Goodnight,' he called to her back.

CHAPTER 11

The following morning, Leksi stepped out into the early grey light while the rest of the house slept as a messenger pulled up in front of him, his horse heaving and lathered with sweat. Taking the proffered letter, Leksi stepped away before tearing it open. He recognised the handwriting of his father's neighbour, and a feeling of dread enveloped him. He had received similar letters his entire life, every time his father made trouble in one of his drunken stupors, like when he had slaughtered one of their neighbour's sheep, believing it was a boar.

Now what?

'I regret to inform you of your father's passing...'

He stilled, his chest turning to lead. So many feelings, all crashing inside him at once. The house had burned down, his father inside it, likely asleep or too drunk to get out. By the time his neighbour had dragged him from the house, he was already dead.

Leksi's throat ached and his eyes blurred, all while the messenger waited for a reply behind him. He worried he might not be able to give one. Looking to the house, he saw

Petra standing in the doorway, a blanket pulled around her, watching him. They stared at one another for the longest moment; then, as though sensing he needed her, she walked over and gently pried the letter from his hand. He hoped she did not notice the slight tremble.

After scanning its contents, her hand went to his arm, and his throat threatened to close.

'You should go to him,' she whispered.

He gave a small cough, just to test his voice. 'Why? So I can bury him in that shithole?' He stared at the house because he did not want her to see what was in his eyes.

Her hand fell away and she walked over to the messenger, giving him instructions and sending him on his way. Returning, she said, 'We will bury him here.'

He looked at her then, his lips pressed into a thin line.

She gave him the smallest of smiles. 'The ocean can wash away anything, remember?'

To stop from embarrassing himself, he walked down to the water and stripped off his trousers, wading into the sea before diving beneath its surface.

He did not know how long he stayed in the water. Hours maybe. Petra watched him from the top of the slope, giving him the space he needed while letting him know she was there. In his experience, women were not good at reading signals, but her skills were exceptional—though what else did he expect from a highly trained mentor.

When he finally exited the water, he stepped into his trousers and shoved his feet into his boots, then walked straight past her to the garden at the back of the house. Snatching up the shovel, he marched all the way to the back of the property and got to work digging a grave.

By mid-morning, the pile of dirt beside the hole was nearly as tall as him, but he could not stop digging. Sweat poured off his brow and ran down his back and chest, but he paused only when a surge of emotion threatened to tip him over. What that emotion was, he did not know.

The sun was high in the sky when he became aware of the blisters forming around his calluses. He stopped, examining the hole he stood in. It did not seem big enough or deep enough to bury all that needed to be buried.

Charis wandered out to see if he needed help, but one glance from Leksi made him turn and walk in the other direction.

'It is big enough,' Petra reassured him, coming to stand by the grave.

He said nothing in reply, just stepped past her again and disappeared inside. He did not speak one word to anyone for the rest of the day.

The next morning, his father's body arrived in the back of a cart. Leksi pulled the blanket back and stared down at the corpse. The red face he had come to recognise over the years was now an unsettling shade of grey. He had seen more dead bodies than he cared to think about, but there was something different about gazing down at his dead father. Misplaced grief twisted inside of him: not grief for the man he had lost, but for the father he was robbed of. How different things might have been if his mother had lived, if his sister had lived.

He wanted desperately to be the man everyone expected him to be in that moment, strong and unshakable, but he was neither of those things. He was supposed to carry the body, but his feet refused to move.

Once again, Petra acted when he could not. She covered the corpse with the blanket once more and instructed Charis and the driver to carry it inside. There, she washed the body, changed his clothes, and wrapped him in a white linen shroud which she sewed closed. Leksi waited outside, unable to enter the house. Instead, he watched the waves crash against the shore.

An hour or so later, a priest arrived from the village. She had thought of everything. The body was placed inside the grave, and prayers were spoken aloud, though not by Leksi, whose throat seemed to have closed over again. Then it was time to fill the hole. That, he could do.

Picking up the shovel, he began pushing the mountain of dirt into the grave. Only once the white sheet was no longer visible did the air return to his lungs. Petra walked the priest to his horse while he and Charis continued working. They did not stop until the job was done.

Leksi leaned on his shovel, panting as he stared down at the mound of dirt. He would have liked to saddle his horse and ride to the closest tavern to drink himself into a stupor— with enough liquor, he could forget about the entire thing— but he could not leave Petra. And if he was honest, he did not want to. There was comfort in having her close by.

Charis took the shovel from his hand and walked off towards the house. Leksi remained at the grave, staring at the unnatural patch of dirt. Grass would cover it eventually.

The priest rode away and Petra returned, coming to stand next to him.

'I am so sorry,' she said, staring down at the grave.

He nodded. 'Not much of a loss, really.'

'He was still your father, even if he was not a very good one.'

Leksi was silent for a moment. 'Ironic that he probably died in a fire started by the wood I cut during my last visit— if you can call it that. The only thing I ever did to help him killed him in the end.'

She looked at him. 'His death is not your fault.'

Another nod. She was right, of course, but it did not stop the guilt.

'If you need to leave for a while, clear your head, I understand. Do not stay here on my account.'

He shook his head. 'I'm not abandoning you too.'

She narrowed her eyes on him. 'What do you mean?' Silence. 'You did not abandon him. He pushed you away.'

Another lump formed in his throat. He felt vulnerable and could not stand it. 'I'll stay. I suspect I can't outrun this feeling anyway.'

She slipped her hand into his, and his fingers closed around it. Neither of them spoke for the longest time.

'When they took my son, I thought I might die from the pain of it,' she said.

He squeezed her hand. 'But here you are.'

'But here I am.'

More silence.

'Thank you for today,' he said. 'For some reason I just couldn't...'

'He is your father, and his mistakes do not change that fact.' She let go of his hand and stepped back from the grave. 'You should go for another swim. I will cook dinner.'

'Is you cooking supposed to make me feel better or worse?'

A smile formed and faded. 'All right, Charis will cook dinner.'

He cleared his throat and glanced past her to the house. 'Don't wander off while I'm in the water.'

'Would not dream of it, Sir Leksi.'

CHAPTER 12

A week after his father's passing, the fog began to lift from Leksi's mind, but the heaviness in his chest remained. He was surprised by the way he felt. He had always expected to feel a strange kind of relief at hearing of his father's passing, but he had been wrong.

He thought about writing to Tyron to tell him the news, then decided against it. The prince would send someone to take his place, insist he have some time off to grieve and get his affairs in order, and he wanted to remain at the house.

Petra came looking for him when he was tending the horses. He stopped what he was doing to watch her approach. He did that a lot lately. She seemed to grow more beautiful with every passing day, now that there was colour in her cheeks and light in her eyes.

His gaze swept down her simple dress and bare arms, and for a moment, he forgot about the grave near the trees behind him. He placed the pail he was holding on the ground and turned to her.

'You look rather pleased with yourself,' he said.

Her eyes shone at him. 'Charis and I found something I think you are going to love.'

'You *found* something?' He leaned against the fence post, fighting the strange urge to reach out and touch her pink cheek. 'What is it?'

'You have to come with me.'

Her hands were linked behind her back, like an excited child. It was infectious. With a grin, he snatched up the pail of water and poured it into the trough for the horses. 'All right. Where are we going?'

'This way,' she said, turning and heading for the water.

'Should I be worried?' he asked, falling into step with her.

'Almost there.'

They descended the slope, but instead of heading for the water, Petra turned right and wandered towards the rocks.

'Close your eyes,' she said, facing him. 'And do not open them until I say so.'

He closed his eyes and crossed his arms over his chest. He heard the sound of something being dragged along the sand, mixed with Petra's heaving breaths as she struggled with the weight of whatever she was moving.

'All right,' she said, panting. 'Open your eyes.'

He did as he was told and looked down to see a small boat sitting on the sand between them. 'Where did you find that?' he laughed.

She pointed to a large rock. 'In there, hidden in the gap. Whoever put it there was smart enough to cover the opening with branches and seaweed.' She looked up at him. 'Charis showed me how to row. I thought I might take you out on the water.'

He watched her, so very amused. 'You think *you* can row us?'

She nodded, looking sure of herself. 'You always have to

take me on your horse, so I thought I might return the favour by taking you on my boat.'

'*Your* boat?'

She shrugged, a rare gesture. It was possible she was beginning to relax more in his presence. 'I found it.'

He laughed through his nose. The truth was, he liked taking her on his horse. He could not really explain why, but he had quickly gotten used to her being behind him. 'It's not as easy as you might think. You have to make it over the waves without overturning the boat.'

She all but rolled her eyes. 'Yes, yes. Charis told me to row straight towards them. The boat will only overturn if we are sideways.'

'Sound easy, does it?'

She stared up at him, her expression defiant. 'I am quite capable of using oars.'

He shook his head and bent to remove his boots, then dragged the boat towards the sea. 'This should be entertaining.' Once it was in the water, he looked at her while holding onto it. 'Where shall I sit?'

She waved a knowing finger at him. 'I see what you are doing. You are testing my knowledge. You will be seated on the stern thwart, because *I* need to sit on the centre thwart with my back to the bow in order to row, and you will be too heavy for the front end.'

He nodded, impressed.

'Are you surprised by my boat knowledge?'

'I'm never surprised by a mentor's knowledge. I will most definitely be surprised if you can actually row the thing though.'

She tutted and gestured for him to get in.

'You should climb in first,' he said. 'I'll hold the boat steady.'

'You weigh more, so you should probably get in first.'

That made no sense whatsoever, but since she seemed determined to prove herself, he did as she instructed while she struggled to keep hold of the boat as it rocked. When a small wave tried to drag the boat out to sea, she stumbled in the water but remained upright. Then a wave splashed up the side of the boat and sprayed the front of her. She gasped, eyes wide.

Smiling, he asked, 'How's it going so far?'

'Fine, thank you.' She wiped water from her face and pushed herself up on the side of the boat. It tilted, and she would have fallen in face first had Leksi not caught her and lifted her in.

'Thank you,' she said, not looking at him. She settled herself on the seat and picked up the oars. As she tried to secure them in the rowlocks, the boat was thrashed about in the water, throwing them from side to side, the oars getting wedged in the sand each time. She cleared her throat and let go of one oar while she tried to reposition the other one. The abandoned oar slid towards the water, and Leksi caught it. Petra gave him a sheepish glance and took hold of it once more. She sat a little straighter, keeping a firm grip on each oar that time. Then she began to row, awkwardly, trying to turn the boat without success.

'There was no book on this at Masville?' he asked, tone light.

She glared at him. 'I just need to get the bow—' she puffed, '—to face the other way.'

'A solid plan.'

She moved the oars in opposite directions and then stopped when she realised they were turning the wrong way. Before she had a chance to correct the error, a small wave pushed them towards the shore and the bottom of the boat became lodged in the sand.

'Are we stuck?' she asked, chewing her bottom lip as she peered over the side.

'It would appear that way.'

She turned to look at him. 'All right, I admit, this is not going to plan. I meant to cheer you up, let the ocean work its magic, not put you to work.'

Funny, but it never felt like work with her around. He noted the sincerity in her expression. 'This rather comedic ordeal has definitely lifted my spirits.'

'Not in the way I had hoped.' She narrowed her eyes on him. 'Are you... are you laughing at me?'

'Not out loud.'

'Oh, what a gentleman.' She shoved the oars towards him. 'All right, clever man. Show me how it is done.'

He glanced down at the oars. 'I don't want to tread on your toes.'

She pressed her lips together at the threat of a smile. 'I believe you have made your point, Sir Leksi.'

He rolled his trousers up to his knees, then jumped into the water, placed the oars inside the boat and held onto the side. With a gentle push, the boat came unstuck, and he ran a few paces before leaping back into the boat and taking up the oars. 'Hold on tight.'

She immediately gripped the seat. He watched her face change as they climbed the first wave and came crashing back down. A small squeal escaped her, and a smile broke out on her face. It was such a beautiful sight with the sun behind her and water spraying around them.

He continued to row, never looking away from her. Up and down went the boat, until finally they were behind the waves, drifting on calm water. After a few more minutes of rowing, Leksi pulled the oars in and rested his arms on his knees. He turned his head towards land, and she followed his gaze.

'The house looks so small from out here,' she said.

'I prefer the term quaint.'

'Quaint,' she repeated. 'I grew up in a house even more quaint, if you can imagine it.'

His eyes went to her. 'Siblings?'

She nodded. 'Three brothers.'

'That must've been fun. What did your father do?'

She met his gaze. 'What most people in the south of Corneo do—try to survive.'

'He didn't work? Surely your brothers did.'

She kneaded the fabric of her dress between her fingers. 'They all worked when it was available.'

'Farmers?'

Another nod. 'Farmers need crops and animals. Not sure if you have heard, but neither seem to survive that far south.' She gave a tight smile.

'Is that what all those pesky wars are about? Good to know.' They were quiet for a moment before he asked, 'Can you imagine yourself living in such a house now?'

'You mean after the luxury of Masville Castle?'

'Yes.'

She squinted against the sun. 'I would happily live in a hole in the ground if my son lived there also. The house does not matter to me, but rather who I share it with.' She studied him. 'Will you take over your father's estate now that he has… passed?'

He shook his head. 'Everyone in my family died in that house. I think it burned to the ground for a reason.'

'I suppose you are too busy to keep an estate. You go where the prince sends you.'

'I prefer to be busy, to have a purpose. I designed my life that way.' He had never admitted that out loud before.

'I get it,' she replied, holding on to her knees. 'You stay busy so you do not have to think about all the other things.'

He frowned. 'What other things?'

'The painful things, the serious parts of life, like the loss of your family.'

'I just refuse to let those things dictate my happiness. I've seen what it does to people.'

She studied him for a moment. 'I suspect if I were not here, your grief would take a different form.'

'How do you mean?'

'You would bury it beneath wine and women, would you not?'

He shrugged. 'Nice to know you hold such a high opinion of me.'

She held her hands up. 'I am not judging you. Who knows what kind of person I would have become had I been given the choice.'

'A low-life like me, perhaps?'

'Those are your words.'

His eyes smiled at her. 'How would you describe me, then?'

She pretended to think on the matter. 'Casually inclined?'

'That's the politest version of *womaniser* I've ever heard. You mentors really are lyrical geniuses.'

She suppressed a smile and looked out at the water. 'I only know this version of you, so it is very difficult to imagine the man others describe.'

He only wanted her to know this version of him. 'Do you want me to teach you how to row the boat?' he asked, changing the subject.

She frowned. 'Is my theoretical knowledge not adequate?'

'No,' he laughed. 'It really isn't.' He shuffled back on the seat, opening his legs wider and patting the seat in front of him. 'Sit here.'

She looked down at the spot between his thighs. 'Someone might get the wrong idea.'

He looked around. 'Lucky for us there's no one here to judge.' He patted the seat again. 'Come on.'

She hesitated, then moved and sat in front of him, her back brushing his chest. The scent of soap lingered on her despite the saltwater. Her loose hair shifted in the breeze, brushing his face.

'All right,' he said, placing his hands below hers on the oars. His chin hovered above her left shoulder, his lips close to her ear. 'I'll get you started, and then I'll move out of your way.'

She glanced over her shoulder at him. 'Your confidence is very reassuring.'

'I have complete faith in you while we're in calm waters.'

He saw the shape of her cheeks change. She was smiling, but he could not see it. He rowed slowly, allowing her to get the feel of it. After a minute, he let go of the oars, and she continued on her own.

'There you go,' he said. It was time for him to move. Much safer if he did, because having her that close did things to him. He moved awkwardly around her before finally landing on the seat opposite.

'Very smooth,' she said.

'Thank you.' He bowed his head, then watched in silence for a moment. 'How are the hands holding up? They'll blister in no time.'

'My hands are fine, though I suspect my arms are going to be sore tomorrow.'

The sun shone down on her, highlighting golden tones in her brown hair. She had tucked the loose pieces behind her ears, but it still blew around her face. In some ways, she had really let herself go. Wild hair, unpainted face and plain clothes, and yet he had never found a woman more attractive. His gaze travelled along her salt-crusted arms, watching her hands work and finding the motion strangely erotic. It really had been too long between women.

'You are staring, Sir Leksi.'

He blinked and looked away, clearing his throat as he did so. 'Do you think you can get us back to shore?'

She stopped rowing and glanced in that direction. 'With your help, perhaps.' Making room for him, she shuffled forwards on the seat again.

He swallowed, wondering if perhaps it was not a good idea to sit behind her a second time.

'It is all right. I trust you,' she said.

He could not have said no to her even if he wanted to. There was light in her eyes, and he tried to read her expression, but she averted her gaze before he had a chance to assess her properly. Stepping carefully over the oar, he settled himself behind her, his hands covering hers. 'You're freezing.'

Petra said nothing, but he noticed she watched their hands as he turned the boat and began rowing them towards the shore.

Whatever space he was trying to put between their bodies did not last. As the sea grew rough, Petra leaned her head against his shoulder; her scent and the feel of her windswept hair against his neck were too much. He stopped rowing and pulled the oars in just as the first wave lifted them high into the air. She closed her eyes and clutched her stomach as the boat dropped once more, and his arms went around her, holding her in place.

'I feel like I am falling,' she said, bracing for the next drop.

Leksi's cheek brushed the top of her head. He felt it too.

CHAPTER 13

'Y̌ou know, I'm not sure this is a good idea. I'm supposed to be keeping you away from the village,' Leksi said.

They were standing outside a tavern near the port in Veanor, voices and music drifting out onto the street. Leksi could see Petra was putting on a brave face before they entered, even though the entire thing had been her idea, another attempt at cheering him up.

She glanced at Charis, who was waiting with the horses, before speaking. 'If anyone asks about me, just use a pretend name.' The door swung open and she winced as drunken laughter spilled out before it shut again. 'A few cups of wine and—'

'Ale,' the squire corrected.

She frowned before continuing. 'Ale,' she repeated, already sounding less sure of her plan, 'a dance with a pretty woman or two, or whatever your usual number is, and then we will return to the house.'

Leksi could not believe how far she was prepared to step out of her comfort zone for him. Little did she know he was coping just fine without drink and women. 'So, you're going to enter a noisy tavern, full of sweating, shouting men, and drink ale from a dirty mug?'

She swallowed. 'The mugs are dirty?' Realising her mistake, she shook her head. 'Of course they are. It is fine. The whole thing is completely fine.'

He glanced down at her cloak. 'You're not wearing the green dress under that, are you? I can't be wrestling men off you all night.'

She shook her head. 'That would not help me blend in with the locals, now would it?'

'No, it wouldn't.' He glanced at the horses. 'All right. One drink, and then I'm taking you home.'

Once again, looking very pleased with herself, Petra turned towards the tavern. Before she had taken her first step, two men burst through the door, one drunk and stumbling, the other guiding him out to the street. Leksi recognised the sober man as Hamon, the owner of the establishment.

'Home with you,' Hamon said, facing the drunk west and giving him a gentle push. 'Before your wife comes looking for you.' As he was turning back, he locked eyes with Leksi and stopped. 'Sir Leksi?'

Unbeknownst to Petra, Leksi was well-known in taverns all around Syrasan, so her plan of a discreet, quiet drink and easy departure was not going to be quite so straightforward. 'Evening, Hamon.'

The man grinned. 'I'd heard rumours you were in Veanor, but no one seemed to know where exactly.' Pushing open the door, he called, 'Guess who's here?' The room fell quiet. 'Sir Leksi.'

Cheers erupted and Petra turned to him, one eyebrow raised. He cleared his throat.

'After you,' he said, gesturing to the door, then looked at

Charis. 'Stay alert, and don't move.'

Hamon held the door open and waited for them to step inside. Leksi wanted to see Petra's initial reaction when the smell hit her and her shoes stuck to the floor, but he was behind her and missed it. Once inside, her gaze swept the room, and she looked completely lost amid the rowdy men and women, mugs in hand, all raising their drinks to him. Some walked up to shake his hand and pat his back. Women smiled and laughed amongst themselves, adjusting the necklines of their dresses as they did so.

Why did I think this would end well?

'Drink?' he said, stepping into Petra's view. She was surprisingly composed.

'Ale, please.' Delivered with a straight face.

'Clear a table for them,' Hamon said to one of the barmaids, then turned to Leksi. 'Sit, enjoy yourself.'

A table was vacated, wiped down, and Leksi pulled one of the chairs out for Petra, checking it was clean before sitting her in it. Another barmaid returned just as he took a seat, a half-smile on her face.

'There you are,' she said, looking only at Leksi.

He looked up, trying to remember her name, and more importantly, if there was a reason he ought to remember it. 'Here I am,' he replied.

'The usual?'

He glanced at Petra, who was pretending not to watch the exchange. 'And also for the lady.'

The barmaid turned, as though noticing Petra for the first time. Her eyes moved up and down, assessing her competition. 'Oh.' She looked between them. 'You don't normally *arrive* with a lady friend, Sir Leksi.'

Oh God. 'Tonight I do.'

The barmaid nodded. 'Very well. I'll fetch your drinks.'

'Thank you,' Petra said, watching the woman's swaying hips as she walked away.

Finally they were alone, glancing at one another and then away. A few tables down, a man was playing the lute. He was not very good, but it did not stop people from dancing. Petra watched him for a moment, her nose scrunching up in disapproval.

'You're not at Masville anymore,' Leksi said, his eyes laughing.

'Clearly.'

The barmaid returned with a jug of ale and two mugs, winking at Leksi as she set them on the table. Petra continued watching the lute player while he poured their drinks.

'Should I have let you inspect the cup first?' he asked.

'Absolutely not,' she replied, turning back to him. Picking up her drink, she sniffed the frothy liquid. 'Oh,' she said, leaning away from it.

Leksi smiled. 'Have you ever drunk ale before?'

She shook her head. 'Does it taste better than it smells?'

'Only one way to find out.' He clinked his cup against hers. 'Ready?'

She drew a breath and nodded. They drank at the same time, Leksi taking a large gulp and Petra taking a tentative sip. Her hand went over her mouth as though to stop herself from spitting it out.

'An acquired taste, perhaps,' she said.

He laughed, feeling warm and easy in her company—as he always did.

Her gaze returned to the lute player.

'You never asked me what my talent was,' she said, turning back to him.

He frowned. 'Your talent? You mean, when you were a Companion?'

She took another sip of ale, screwing up her face. 'Yes, when I was a Companion.'

He leaned in to better hear her. 'Oh no. Did you play the lute?'

Up went her cup, a longer drink that time. She nodded. 'I played the lute.'

He was genuinely surprised. 'Really? The *lute*?'

She studied him over the rim of her drink. 'Why do you say it like that?'

'It just doesn't seem very...'

She tilted her head. 'Very what?'

'I don't know. Noble? Feminine? What word am I searching for?'

Her eyes widened. 'Feminine? What is that supposed to mean?'

He reached for the jug and topped up their drinks. 'I would've guessed the harp, or singing perhaps.'

'Not dancing?'

He shook his head. 'You're far too prudish for dancing.'

'Far too...' She leaned back in her chair, unable to finish her sentence. 'Is this the sort of establishment where it is acceptable to throw one's drink at a man?'

Keeping a straight face, he replied, 'This crowd will burn you alive if you waste perfectly good ale.'

She tapped a finger on her mug. 'All right, you leave me no choice.' Bringing her drink to her mouth, she drank until there was only a small amount left in her cup, then stood, blinking away the bad taste.

His eyebrows rose. 'What are you doing?'

Removing her cloak, she draped it over the back of her chair. 'Showing you and your friends what this extraordinary instrument can do.'

His eyes went to the lute player, then returned to her.

'You start playing some pretty ballad and people *will* throw their drinks at you.'

She stared down at him. 'What a snob you paint me as. Have you forgotten where I grew up?'

He leaned back in his chair, linking his hands over his stomach. 'All right, but don't come crying to me when they shout at you to hand the instrument back.'

Smoothing down her blue peasant dress, she strolled over to the lute player and the music stopped. Everyone who had been dancing complained and turned to see what had caused the disruption. Petra was bent down talking to the man, at one point gesturing to Leksi. The man eventually nodded, handed her his instrument, and vacated his seat. She remained standing, and the clientele watched her curiously, no doubt wondering if she could actually play.

Leksi found himself nervous on her behalf, not because he doubted her ability but whether her song choice would please this particular crowd.

She ran a few scales, warming up her fingers and getting a feel for the instrument. Then she plucked at the strings, a few pretty notes, adjusting the lute against her body as she readied herself. The crowd looked between one another, heads shaking, already growing bored. Leksi was perched on the edge of his chair, preparing to rush in and save her if need be.

With her gaze fixed on the instrument, Petra began tapping her heel on the wooden floor, loud enough to capture the attention of the room. All eyes were on her. Then, much to Leksi's surprise, she burst into a lively version of "The Lord and his Lady." He should not have been too surprised by the fact that she knew a Syrasan folk song; it was the job of a Companion to know songs and dances from all the kingdoms their kings had relations with, and many of their songs had originated from Corneo anyway.

'Aye!' called the men, bringing their hands together to clap in time with her foot.

Only then did she look up, watching the reaction of the room as more people stood to dance. They spun in circles, smiles on their faces. Halfway through the song, Petra's foot stopped. Her fingers played a single note, so softly that everyone looked over, trying to anticipate what would follow next. Her fingers stilled, and then down came her foot, the tempo shifting, faster that time. More cheers followed, and she smiled at their response, her teeth on display for all to see.

Leksi sat transfixed by the sight of her, his heart in his throat. She glanced at him, her smile only growing. He grinned back at her. It was not just her toe tapping now but her whole foot, thumping the floor. Only once the dancers were dizzy and the spectators giddy with laughter did the song come to a heart-pounding stop.

The entire room turned to her, applauding. She gave a small curtsy and handed the instrument back to its owner. He immediately began playing another song to which everyone knew the words and joined in singing. Petra was about to return to Leksi when one of the men pulled her into the group of dancers. Leksi shot up from his chair, searching for her among the crowd. He was about to start shoving people aside when he spotted her—*dancing*.

At first, she seemed a bit unsure, watching the feet of the others, no doubt trying to gauge if she could keep up. He stayed back, ready if she needed him, but in no hurry to steal the moment from her if she was happy. If anyone deserved to let down their hair, it was her.

Moments later, she was stomping, clapping and spinning with the rest of them. She was a little out of time in places, but no one seemed to notice, or care for that matter. Leksi crossed his arms, eyes never leaving her. Down the line she went, weaving between the men before joining hands with a partner at the end. The man spun her round and round, until the most magical thing happened.

Laughter.

Not the sweet, tinkling variety that Companions were prone to at social gatherings, but raw, unfiltered laughter. He swallowed, fixated.

When she finally stopped spinning, she turned, looking for him. He could tell the moment she spotted him, because her face relaxed into a smile. Breathless and sweating, she reached one hand out in his direction, gesturing for him to join her amid the barflies.

Leksi realised at that moment that he was going to have a lot of trouble letting her go when the time came—and it would come. At some point she would return to Corneo, and he would be forced to say goodbye. There was every chance she would be handed back to the very man who had crushed her spirit and stripped her of her self-worth.

Another wave of her hand, beckoning him, as a new song began. Then she was swept away by the other dancers.

Blinking, he took a step in her direction, finding her in a line of women on the other side of the room, clapping as men shuffled past them. He went and stood opposite her so he would partner her in the next section of the dance. Their eyes met again. Another smile.

Dancers moved between them, and they watched each other through the gaps, clapping along with the others. Men on one side and women on the other. A border between them.

Then it dawned on him. It was the first time in his life that he had stood in a roomful of available women, watching only one.

CHAPTER 14

The following morning, Petra woke to the sound of horses outside her window. She sat up, heart racing, trying to gauge the time as light filled the small room. She never slept in, but she also never danced in a tavern until closing time. Swinging her legs over the edge of the bed, she dressed quickly. Perhaps there was news of her son.

Men spoke in low tones, back and forth as they exchanged information. She knew the routine: wait in her room, still and quiet until Leksi came for her. Except the visitors had dismounted their horses and did not appear to be going anywhere. She watched as two strangers led their horses past the window, both wearing red tunics marked with an *S*. At least they were Syrasan soldiers.

A knock came at the door, and Petra stepped forwards to open it. Leksi was unshaven, his shirt rolled up to his elbows. It was an odd thought, but he did have the most beautiful hands.

'What is going on?' she asked, raising her eyes to him. Perhaps they were sending her back. She had been preparing herself for that possibility for some time, so why was she so afraid?

'They aren't taking you anywhere, if that's what you're thinking.'

She tried to hide her relief. 'All right.' Then why did he look worried?

'There are Corneon soldiers, here in Syrasan, looking for you.'

She let the words settle between them. 'Oh.'

'Prince Tyron has sent two additional guards while he... figures things out with King Pandarus.'

She drew a breath. 'He will have no choice but to hand me over now. King Nilos would never send his men across the border unless he was desperate.'

'He has clearly lost his mind. He is prepared to go to war in order to get you back.'

Her hands came together in front of her, fingers pressing. She looked down, surprised when the action did not hurt. The bruises had faded and her nails were strong. At some point she had stopped without even realising it.

Leksi took hold of one of her hands and lifted it, inspecting each nail.

'These men are here to keep you safe, not hand you over. Don't fall apart just yet.'

The warmth from him was so comforting, she was tempted to step closer and bury her face in his chest, but he let go of her hand and stepped back.

'I'll help the men get settled in,' he continued. 'Then I need to head into the village for a few hours.'

Her eyes searched his for a moment. 'Want me to go with you?'

'No. It's safer if you stay here.' He shook his head. 'Last night was reckless. I should've known better.'

She stared up at him. Last night had been one of the best

nights of her life. 'What happened to "where you go, I go"?' She cringed at her words, feeling like a child.

'Now you have two guards camped outside your bedroom window.'

She nodded and took a step back from him. 'Of course.'

He watched her for a moment. 'I would never leave you unprotected, especially now.'

'I know that.' And she did. But she also sensed a shift in him, as though he were withdrawing from her.

Leksi glanced at the cot against the wall where Charis was still fast asleep.

'He will sleep through anything,' Petra said.

Leksi shook his head. 'Let's see if he sleeps through the toe of my boot in his side.' He went to turn away, then stopped. 'You knew the lengths your king would go to in order to get you back.'

She nodded.

'But you ran anyway.'

'I ran anyway. It was foolish, I know, but I wanted to see my son, just once. I know how this ends.'

He seemed annoyed by her response. 'With you happily back at Masville?'

'Not happily.'

'But you will go?'

'You make it sound as though I have a choice.' He was not looking at her anymore. 'I know Nilos well enough to know he will not stop, and I cannot hide forever. You are already in danger because of me.'

He nodded at his feet. 'Nothing will change. It won't be any better than before.'

'No, it will be much worse.'

He ran a hand down his face. 'So you're just going to give up and give in?'

'As opposed to what? Do you expect me to go to war with

my king?' Tears prickled her eyes, but she held them in. 'I have nothing to fight with.'

'You have me,' he said, voice slightly raised.

Her expression fell. 'Sir Leksi,' she whispered. 'I have no doubt you are the greatest knight Syrasan has ever known.' She paused. 'But you will not win that fight.'

There was a scuffle behind them as Charis got to his feet, stumbling about as he pulled on his trousers. 'Horses, my lord! I hear horses outside,' he said, panic in his tone. He tripped over one of his boots, cursing as he fell.

Leksi watched him for a moment before turning back to Petra. 'When you're ready, come outside and I'll introduce you to the men.'

Then he was gone, pulling the door closed behind him.

CHAPTER 15

*T*here were eyes on Petra every waking hour. Even at night, someone stood guard.

The young soldier's name was Josse, and she learned he was in his nineteenth year. The older was Morris. He did not say much, but she guessed him to be around forty. They both went about their business, watching her, watching the house, watching the trees on the horizon. There was always someone watching.

Leksi seemed to sleep less and less. Whenever she retired to bed, he would saddle his horse and ride the boundary. She often heard him lecture the other men about what they needed to do better, as though they were incapable of performing their roles. Never mind the fact that Morris was at least ten years his senior.

With Leksi in what could only be described as battle mode, it was rather lonely at the house. He was away often, meeting with various people who had fresh information regarding the latest sightings of Corneon soldiers. He shared nothing with her, offering only a stern expression in place of his usual jokes.

'Where are you going?' she asked him one morning. He was in the yard, saddling his horse, not looking at her.

'Nothing for you to worry about.' His usual response. 'I'll be back in a few hours.'

For two weeks they had existed like that. Ever since the guards had arrived. She had spent most of her time in the garden, trying to keep hold of her sanity, and he had spent most of his time avoiding her questions, no doubt believing he was protecting her in some way.

'Leksi,' she said, waiting for him to look at her.

He checked the girth of his saddle again before turning. 'Yes?'

What could she say that did not sound like whining? 'Be careful.'

She received only a nod in response.

She watched him ride out while Josse stood behind, watching her. Leksi glanced over his shoulder before he disappeared from sight.

She felt a familiar pull in her chest whenever he left. As much as she hated to admit it, she had grown dependent on him. He was the only friend she had, except for Hali of course, who often 'found herself in the area' and called in for a quick visit that often stretched across the entire afternoon.

'I am going for a walk,' she said to Josse. She was already resigned to the fact that he would trail behind her, always lingering at the edge of her vision.

It was just past noon and the sun was high in the sky, the air sticky as the warm season headed to its peak. She removed her shoes and wandered down to the shore, standing at the water's edge and gazing out. She must have stood there for some time, because eventually, water ran over her feet. The tide coming in, but instead of stepping back, she let the sea wash over her, not even bothering to lift the skirt of her dress. It felt good, so she took a few steps forwards, the water splashing up her calves.

The ocean can wash away anything.

Soon her dress became heavy as it soaked up the water. If the young guard had not been standing behind her, she might have taken it off. She waded forwards, deeper, until she was thigh deep.

'Miss,' the guard called to her.

She stopped and held a hand up, indicating that she was fine. A large wave rose and broke, white water rushing around her. She squealed, completely wet now and not caring at all.

'Miss!' The guard was more urgent that time.

She turned to look at him as she moved deeper into the sea. He was standing at the water's edge, stepping back every time a wave raced towards his feet.

'I am fine,' she called to him, laughter in her tone.

He glanced back at the house, looking unsure.

Turning away from him, she took a few more steps so the water rose to her chest. She had a strange urge to dip below the surface and let the ocean work its magic. Drawing a deep breath, she sank down into the sea. A wave rumbled over-head, and she watched through murky water as small pieces of seaweed and debris swirled around her. Pushing off the sandy bottom, she emerged and drew a deep breath, surprised to discover a smile on her face as she wiped water from it.

'You better come in now,' Josse shouted.

She really wished he would shut up and leave her alone. 'In a minute,' she called absently. She moved out deeper, held her breath, and slipped beneath the surface once more. The water rocked her gently, making the skirt of her dress balloon around her. She surrendered to the sensation. Even with the roaring noise above her head, it was possibly the most peaceful moment of her life. It was a shame she needed to draw breath at all.

Her feet felt for the ocean floor so she could push herself up, but it took her a moment to get her bearings as the waves rolled her over. Finally her toes brushed the sandy bottom.

She was about to push herself up when two large hands took hold of her. Surprised, she inhaled, taking water into her lungs as she was dragged to the surface. The moment her head emerged, she coughed violently, trying to take in air and failing. Then she was face-to-face with Leksi, who was chest deep in the water, his hazel eyes burning at her.

'What are you doing?' Another cough. 'You almost drowned me!' She glanced at the shore, searching for Josse, who was now wading out of the water, clothes dripping.

'What am *I* doing?' Leksi replied, his grip on her tightening. 'Saving your *life*.'

He was awfully close to her face, and angry. 'What are you talking about? I was fine until you scared me half to death. I swallowed half the ocean.'

'You could've drowned,' he said, his tone filled with accusation.

She tried to pull herself from his grip. 'You are being ridiculous. My feet can touch the bottom.' Of course, at that moment they could not, because he was holding her up to better shout in her face.

She looked him straight in the eye. 'You are hurting me.'

He immediately let her go, throwing his hands up in the air. A large wave arrived, crashing over her head and knocking her underwater. Two hands grabbed her once more, that time dragging her towards the shore while she struggled to find her footing. More coughing.

'I was just putting my feet in the water,' she said as he

pulled her by the wrist. Then realising how ridiculous that explanation sounded, she added, 'It seems I got carried away.'

He made an exasperated noise, eyes straight ahead. 'Did you forget the part where you can't swim?'

He was moving too fast for her and she fell to her knees. He pulled her up without slowing down, hurting her wrist.

Now it was her turn to be angry. 'Slow down or let go of me,' she said, almost falling again.

'I'll let go when we're standing on the shore.'

'Sir Leksi—'

'Don't.'

She closed her eyes and staggered after him, the weight of her wet dress making the basic act of walking rather challenging. She had never seen him truly angry before, at least not at her. It was unsettling.

When they were finally standing on dry land, Leksi released her arm and approached the young guard so fast that he took a step back. 'You wait for me at the house,' he hissed.

Josse nodded nervously before scurrying off in the other direction. When Leksi turned back to her, she knew it was not over. She made herself as tall as possible as he stormed towards her.

'You are completely overreacting,' she said, getting in first.

He stopped a few feet from her, his hands going into his wet hair as he drew a long, shaky breath. 'I expected to find you dead,' he said. 'That's assuming I found you before the tide carried you out to sea.'

She glanced at the water. 'I told you—'

He held up a hand to silence her. 'There are undercurrents in that water, and you can't swim. If I hadn't reached you in time, you would likely have drowned.'

Petra realised at that moment that all of his anger was

really just fear. Lifting her chin, she said, 'I did not know that. I am sorry.'

He just shook his head, but at least he was looking at her now. 'I'm not really interested in your empty apology.'

'It is not empty. I really did not think I was in any danger.' She hugged herself, shivering in her wet clothes. 'I am sorry,' she said again, putting feeling into the words.

His eyes moved over her. 'You're freezing.'

'I am fine.'

He walked over to where his tunic lay in a crumpled pile next to his boots and snatched it up. Going to her, he said, 'Take your dress off and put this on.'

She glanced at the house, then back at him. 'What?'

'I assume you're wearing something beneath it,' he said.

'That is hardly the point—'

'I've seen you covered in blood and horse shit. Take off the dress.' He stood holding the tunic open for her, staring out at the water.

She hesitated before removing the garment, numb hands fumbling with the buttons. Stepping out of her dress, she turned so he could wrap the tunic around her shoulders. The fabric was warm from laying in the sun, and she shuddered beneath it.

'Thank you.' She secured it around her and looked up at him. Still, he could barely look at her. 'You are still angry at me. I told you I am sorry.' She felt vulnerable standing in front of him when he was holding so much anger towards her, but she did not step away.

'Let's get you inside,' he said.

She needed him to look at her, to know everything was all right between them. 'Leksi—'

'Oh, now it's *Leksi*?' He was walking away. 'What happened to *sir*?'

She caught up to him. 'Tell me what I have to say to fix this and I will say it.'

'Spoken like a true Companion. How about some sincerity for once?'

She stepped back as though he had slapped her, and he stopped walking, bringing a hand to his jaw, clearly regretting his words.

'I didn't mean that,' he said.

She looked down at the sand, then stepped past him and headed for the house. 'Yes, you did.'

He linked his hands on top of his head. 'I thought… I thought you meant to drown yourself.'

She stopped walking and turned to him. 'Why would you think that?' It was almost a whisper.

He threw his hands up again. 'Why *wouldn't* I think that? We can't find your son, you're faced with the prospect of being handed over to a man who hurts you, and…' He had to take a moment to regain his composure. 'And the first day I met you, you told me you left because you knew if you stayed at Masville, you would make the same choice.'

She stopped shivering, all of her energy going into recalling her words. Yes, she had said that, and at the time she had probably meant it. But that was before Veanor and the ocean. That was before she had rediscovered laughter, enjoyed food with friends and danced because she wanted to, not because she was instructed to. 'I did say that,' she admitted. 'But that was before all of this. That was before *you*.'

A pained expression crossed his face, and then he closed the distance between them, taking her head in both hands and kissing her. She grabbed hold of his wrists, and for a moment she was not sure whether she was going to push him off or pull him closer. It was a hungry kiss, but he held her so tenderly it melted away all of her hesitation. The warmth of him, the taste of him. Then she felt the same pull at the base of her belly that she had felt the first time, but she could not blame it on the wine any longer.

Her eyes sank shut.

'Keep your eyes open,' he murmured into her mouth. 'I don't want to lose you this time.'

She nodded, but the sensation of him was too much and her eyes closed once more.

'Look at me,' he whispered.

She did. Pushing up on her toes, she let go of his wrists and slid her hands up his neck and into his wet hair. Her body leaned into his, and she felt as though she were submerged in water once more. He placed a hand on her back, drawing her in closer, if that was possible. Her mouth opened in response, her own need matching his. Leksi pulled away and studied her face.

'Are you all right?'

She nodded.

His gaze fell to her mouth. 'You're so cold,' he whispered. 'Your lips are blue.'

She really did not want him to stop kissing her. 'So warm them,' she breathed, raising her face to him again.

'My lord!' came a voice.

Leksi kept hold of her, his forehead on hers for a moment while he composed himself. They were both breathing hard. After a few seconds, Petra turned her head and watched as Charis ran down the slope towards them.

'Your squire wants you.'

'I'm going to drown that boy with my bare hands,' he replied, releasing her.

She felt a pang of disappointment as her feet flattened on the sand.

'There better be an army riding this way,' Leksi called to Charis as he stepped back from her.

The squire held up a letter. 'From Lord Yuri.'

Exhaling, Leksi walked towards him, snatching the letter from his hand. He broke the seal with a quick slip of his finger and unfolded the parchment. Petra remained where she was, her heart hammering away, her entire body trembling from cold and something else. She gripped the tunic with both hands and pulled it tightly around her.

'What does it say?' she called to Leksi, unable to read his expression.

He frowned at the letter for a moment longer before folding it up and handing it back to Charis. 'Nothing for you to worry about.' Though he did not look at her when he said it.

Charis's eyes widened suddenly. 'My lord, you're wet!'

Leksi patted his squire's shoulder. 'I see those sharp observation skills aren't failing you. Go saddle my horse.'

'I just unsaddled her,' he said, looking confused.

Leksi pinched the bridge of his nose. 'All right, well, apologise to her for the mixed signals, and then pop the saddle on her back.'

'Where are you going?' Petra asked.

He offered her a reassuring smile. 'Lord Yuri has asked to speak with me.'

She walked towards him. 'Did he say what it is about?'

'I'll be back in a few hours' was his reply. 'You go inside and get yourself dry and warm.'

Petra looked at Charis. 'Could you give us a moment, please?'

The boy looked between them before turning and walking off in the direction of the house.

'What's the matter?' Leksi asked once they were alone.

'I might be speaking out of turn,' she began, 'but I feel very much in the dark about everything at the moment.'

'As I told you, it's nothing for you to worry about.' He

bent and kissed her forehead, like one does a child. 'I'll be back as soon as I can.'

She studied his face, an uneasy feeling growing inside her.

'Come,' he said, taking her hand. 'I need to have some stern words with the guards before I go.'

CHAPTER 16

*P*etra sat on her bed, drying her hair with a towel. Every now and then she brought her fingers to her lips, remembering the feel of Leksi's mouth on hers. She had never really known desire, and now the knight had woken something long dormant inside her.

The sound of a distant horse made her still to listen. Leksi had not long left, but perhaps he had returned for something. She looked down at her still-wet clothes and leapt off the bed, peeling off the wet undergarments and slipping into the dry clothes she had laid out. The bath would have to wait.

Exiting the room, she walked to the window closest to the hearth and peered out. Charis was out front, cleaning tack, but the sound had caught his attention also. Before long, Josse and Morris passed the window, their eyes on the road. She leaned closer to the glass, trying to get a better look. It was not one horse she had heard, but many.

Five mounted soldiers appeared on the horizon—all in gold uniforms.

They had found her.

Charis turned to the house, eyes meeting hers through

the glass. She ran for the door, reaching it at the same time Charis burst through it.

'They are Corneon,' she said, pulling him inside.

'I know.' He looked around the room as though searching for something. 'Go to your room and don't come out until I come get you,' he said, doing his best impersonation of Leksi. Then, spotting his bow, he went to get it.

She shook her head and grabbed his arm as he went to run past her. 'You cannot fight. You are not even of age.'

He scowled. 'I cannot hide in the bedroom either.'

She dragged him towards the room. 'You are not going to hide. You are going for help.'

'I can't leave you,' he protested. 'Leksi will have my head.'

They stepped inside and she gripped his arms. 'Let the guards do their job. The best thing you can do for me right now is get word to Leksi.'

The sound of swords clashing made them both glance at the door. She let go of him and shoved her feet into a pair of shoes before walking over to the window.

'Stand back,' she said.

Charis stepped away, looking confused. Raising her foot, she put it straight through the glass. It sprayed the grass on the other side. She continued to kick at the remaining shards until the frame was mostly clear.

'Go,' she said, stepping up to him and shoving him towards the window.

'You should come with me.'

'They will not chase down a frightened child, but they will if I am with you.'

'I'm not a frightened child.'

'Of course not, but we do not want them to know that.' She gave him another push. 'Go. Quickly now.'

He jumped through the window and sprinted towards the

yard to fetch a horse. Thankfully, the bridles were still hanging on one of the fence posts.

Fear prickled her skin. She held her breath as he galloped towards the trees, expecting an arrow to reach him at any moment. Only once he had disappeared did she release the breath she had been holding.

She ran back out to the main room and peered through the front window. It was the worst possible timing, because at that moment a sword went through Josse's stomach, exiting his back. Her hands went over her mouth, pressing tightly to stop herself from screaming. Two Corneon soldiers lay dead on the ground, but there were still three very much alive, and only one Syrasan guard between her and them. A mounted soldier fixed his gaze on the house, then turned his horse, riding towards her.

Petra backed away from the window, her mind racing. There was nowhere for her to hide where they would not find her.

She turned and rushed back to her bedroom, opening the drawer beside her bed and snatching the cloth bag containing her jewels. Shoving them into the pocket of her dress, she crawled through the window, careful not to cut herself on any shards that remained in the frame. She practically fell through it, landing on the grass with her hands outstretched to break the fall.

She winced as glass pierced her hand, but without giving it another thought, she pushed herself to her feet and turned to the remaining horses in the yard. She immediately dismissed the idea, as she had no clue how to bridle a horse, or get on one without a saddle, or ride it for that matter. She had only her own feet and bad sense of direction. That would have to do.

She took off at a run towards the trees, confident they had not travelled across Syrasan only to shoot her in the back. When she reached them, she stopped and looked behind her. The soldier was probably searching the house; as soon as he saw the broken window, he would know where she was, and he would come for her.

Ignoring her bleeding hand, she took off at a run. She was disadvantaged on foot. Add to that the fact that she had no weapons or fighting skills of any kind, and the odds seemed very much stacked against her.

She moved in what she hoped was a straight line, north towards Veanor. The village was a twenty-minute ride, so she figured she could run that distance in around thirty minutes. Except that a few minutes into her frantic sprint to safety, her chest began to ache and her legs tired. She pushed through it. Was it really so much to ask to see her son just one more time?

The pounding of hooves behind her made her stumble. She stifled a sob, looking around for a place to hide. Where were the tall oaks with their wide trunks? Skinny pines were no good when she needed cover.

Legs trembling, she had no choice but to keep running. Faster she moved, and louder came the hooves behind her. She was certain they would have spotted her by now.

She looked above her, trying to gauge if she was still heading in the right direction. Blinding light flashed through branches, not helping at all. Nothing was familiar. There were no tracks, roads, paddocks, sheep or anything that might give her a clue as to where she was.

She turned right, hoping to lose the rider behind her, but then she heard a horse approaching from the right. She darted left without breaking speed while the horse approached at a gallop. All she could do was keep running, because Leksi would never forgive her if she just stopped and gave up. She would not forgive herself. So she ran, even when the sound of hooves pounded so close she was sure the animal would trample her. Tears streaked her cheeks, and she would have screamed, but all of her energy was going to her legs.

Hands grabbed her, snatching her off the ground.

No.

She struggled, legs kicking as she tried to break free from strong hands. Arms enclosed her and a scream rose in her throat, but before she could release it, a hand went over her mouth.

'Shh' came Leksi's familiar voice in her ear.

She went still, turning to check that it was actually him, that she was not losing her mind. His horse slowed to a canter, weaving between the trees. He took his hand away.

'Hold on,' he whispered.

She nodded, her legs to one side and arms wrapping his middle. One of Leksi's arms went around her, crushing her to his chest. Her eyes closed and she listened for horses. She forced herself to breathe as the image of a sword protruding from Josse's back replayed in her mind. The pounding of hooves whispered through the trees, eventually growing softer as Leksi steered them this way and that, until they faded altogether. She remained pressed against his chest, too scared to move or speak.

'You're bleeding,' Leksi said, slowing his horse to a walk and inspecting her hand.

She opened her eyes, disappointed to see they were still among the trees. 'It is nothing.'

'Did they hurt you?'

'No.' She looked up at him, eyes welling again. 'They killed Josse, and probably Morris.'

He nodded, then closed her hand, pressing her fingers tightly. 'Keep a fist to stop the bleeding. We need to get to the manor.'

He pushed his horse into a canter once more, hoisting her

higher so she would not slip off. His eyes searched the trees around them, then suddenly he pulled up his horse, its front legs leaving the ground momentarily.

Petra held on and turned her head to see one of the Corneon soldiers. Another emerged from the trees on their left, an arrow pointed at them.

'Get behind me,' Leksi said calmly, his gaze shifting between the two riders. He drew his sword. Once she was safely behind him, he reached down and retrieved the dagger that sat above his boot.

'Hand her over and we might let you live,' said one of the guards, advancing.

'A generous offer, but I've never negotiated with a man wearing gold before, and I don't intend to start now.'

'There is an arrow pointed at your neck,' the soldier said. 'Don't be a fool.'

'My neck?' He whistled. 'Your arrow will go straight through me at that proximity. Shoot me, and you'll kill the lady. And we know how your mad king would feel about that.'

The man with the bow glanced at the other rider, but the soldier ignored him, addressing Leksi once more. 'Don't try to be a hero. You can't fight both of us.'

Leksi shrugged. 'Sure I can.'

Petra closed her eyes. If she went with the men, they might let him live.

She pressed her forehead against Leksi's back. 'Just hand me over. It is not worth your life.'

He kept his gaze trained on the men. 'Have a little more faith,' he said. 'Here's *my* offer. I'll let you both ride away, but only if you leave now.'

The men chuckled as they closed in. 'Hand her over,' said the man with the bow.

Petra heard the bow creak in his hands. She had just

made the decision to slip down from the horse and surrender herself when Leksi's body jolted. Her head snapped up, expecting to find an arrow protruding from him. Instead, the soldier with the bow tilted sideways in the saddle and fell to the ground, Leksi's dagger in his neck. Her hand went over her mouth, holding in whatever was rising in her throat.

'I respectfully retract my offer,' Leksi said, turning to the second rider. The man stared down at his friend, who continued to choke on the ground. 'Care to see what I can do with a sword?'

The soldier narrowed his eyes. 'You Syrasan bastards are all the same. Think you're the centre of the world. Come on, then,' he said, drawing his sword.

Without turning, Leksi reached back and took hold of Petra's arm. 'You're going to stand right here.' He lowered her to the ground. 'Don't move, no matter what.' When she did not reply, he said, 'Understand?'

'Yes.' She anchored her feet, hands shaking.

Leksi's horse lurched forwards, and her eyes snapped shut as steel screeched a few feet in front of her. She decided to keep them closed so she would not have to watch or be tempted to move. If Leksi wanted her to remain in that spot, she would remain in that spot. Only when someone cried out did she open them. Leksi thrust his sword up and twisted before pulling it from the soldier's side. There was no choking that time; the man was dead before he hit the ground.

Leksi swung his horse around and reached for her, pulling her up behind him once more. 'How many Corneon soldiers died at the house?'

She gripped his waist, her mind not working properly. 'What?'

'Charis said there were five soldiers.'

She shook her head, trying to think while corpses bled out on either side of her. She blinked.

'Petra, how many?'

'Two,' she said, jumping at the sound of her own voice. 'I don't know about the other. I left before…'

Leksi's eyes went to the trees.

'You should have just handed me over,' she said, bringing her hand to her face. 'All these people are dead because of me. *You* could have died.'

He returned his sword to its sheath, not bothering to wipe the blood from the blade. 'Those fools were never going to kill me.'

The comment infuriated her. 'You cannot just assume you are a better fighter than every other man.'

He looked over his shoulder at her. 'I *am* a better fighter than every other man.'

She turned away. 'Those poor guards at the house—'

'Were clearly not up to the job.' He faced forwards and dug his heels into the sides of his horse. 'We'll talk at the manor.'

She grabbed hold of him and glanced back at the dead men. 'What a mess I have made. And for what? The king has made it impossible for me to reach my son.' She buried her face in his back, and Leksi slowed the horse to a walk.

'Look at me,' he said, turning to her.

She raised her eyes to him, feeling broken.

'I went to the manor to organise additional men for your transportation,' he said.

She stared at him for a moment. 'Transportation to where?'

'Archdale Castle.'

Searching his face, and a little afraid of the answer, she asked, 'Why?'

'They found your son.'

CHAPTER 17

*H*ali sat Petra down on a large bed in one of the many upstairs rooms while maids rushed in and out with pails of hot water. Petra barely noticed the elaborate furnishings and expensive rugs; her eyes were fixed on the door, waiting for Leksi to return. He was with Lord Yuri, securing the manor. Once she was safe, he would head to the house to take care of his men.

'*Then I will tell you everything,*' he had promised.

'This is one of my favourite rooms,' Hali said, collapsing on the bed beside her.

Petra forced herself not to be rude, taking a quick glance around the room. 'It is lovely.'

'A result of too much time on my hands. You know, you're the first to see it outside of Yuri's sons who occasionally stay. I once thought it would make a lovely nursery with its large windows.'

Petra immediately thought of Xander. Four days she had spent with her son before they had drugged her and taken him. One day for every pregnancy terminated before him. She was going to Hell, but the worst part was that

148

Nilos would be there also. Even then she would not be rid of him.

'Occasionally, Yuri's sons bring their own children to visit, but their mothers prefer to keep them away.' She looked down at her hands for a moment. 'It sounds bad, but they simply wish to minimise scandal in their own lives. Can't say I blame them,' she added.

The door opened and Petra shot off the bed, hopeful. A maid entered and poured another pail of water into the tub before leaving, pulling the door closed behind her. Petra and Hali looked at one another.

'You are welcome to stay here as long as you need,' Hali said, smiling reassuringly.

Petra's fingers moved over her nails. 'Thank you, but I need to leave as soon as possible. Did you hear? They found Xander.'

'That's wonderful news,' Hali said, her face creased with concern.

'What is the matter?' Petra asked. 'I thought you would be happy for me.'

Hali reached for her hand and studied the cut. 'I don't want to worry you, but the situation is complicated. You can't just ride into Corneo and visit him. Once King Pandarus hears of what happened at the house, he'll have his own agenda.'

Petra stared at her. 'I… need to see him. Whatever must happen after that, so be it. Leksi promised to help me.'

Hali tilted her head, as though Petra should know better. 'Leksi's hands are tied. He'll follow the orders of his king.' She paused. 'Actually, he serves Prince Tyron first, his king second. Though Prince Tyron's hands will be tied also, because he's forced to deal directly with Pandarus.'

Petra pulled her hands away. 'A piece of me left with him the day he was taken. I need to know that he is loved, that he is safe, that he forgives me for all my failings as his mother. And I need him to know that I came looking for him, even if I could not stay.' A tear escaped and she wiped it away. 'Honestly, I am growing tired of people standing in my way.'

Hali swallowed. She was about to say something when a knock came at the door. 'Come in.'

Leksi stepped into the room, looking surprisingly fresh-faced given the events of the day. The man never seemed to tire.

His eyes went to Petra. 'Let's talk.'

The conversation went nothing like Leksi had imagined it. Somewhere between the house and the manor, Petra had lost all ability to have a rational conversation.

'I am not even asking you to come with me,' she said, throwing her hands about as she paced the length of the entranceway. 'I am simply asking that you let *me* go.'

Hali had abandoned him, leaving them to their quarrel. Lord Yuri was also suspiciously absent. Even the maids and servants had disappeared into the secret burrows of the house. Leksi leaned against the front door, a physical barrier, his arms crossed in front of him. 'As I've already told you, probably fifty times now, it isn't safe for you to go anywhere alone. King Nilos has men combing the kingdom. You'll never make it.' He let out a long breath. 'My orders are to bring you to Archdale.'

She stopped walking and turned to him. 'That is not what we agreed on. It is all well and good to locate him, but not much help if you keep me from him.'

'I'm not keeping you from him. I'm protecting you so you might actually get the chance to see him.'

She shook her head. 'No, you are following orders. I get it, you cannot go to Corneo, but you can let me go.'

His hands curled into fists, which he brought to his eyes. 'You're not listening. It's not safe.'

'I do not care.'

He pushed off the door. 'Well I do.'

Her hands went over her face and then fell to her sides. 'What is it with you men and your need to control? If you do not wish to help, fine, but get out of my way.'

Up went his hands. 'Not helping? We found him, didn't we?'

Her eyes pleaded with him. 'What is the point in knowing where he is if I cannot go to him?'

Leksi stared at her, visibly torn. 'You know I can't just let you go. My orders are to bring you to Archdale.'

She stepped closer to him. 'Please. If you take me to Archdale, there is every chance King Pandarus will hand me over and I will never see my son again.'

'You don't know that.'

She took another step towards him. 'I cannot tell if you are lying to me or yourself. What does your gut tell you? Do you think your king is going to risk men by sending them into Corneo on my behalf?'

He stared at her, silent.

'You promised to help me,' she whispered, turning away.

He reached out and caught her arm.

'What do you want? Name it.'

'You know what I want.'

'Do you want to be queen?'

'Corneo already has a queen.'

He bit into the flesh above her breast, groaning into her skin.

'You will always be my queen. I cannot live without you. Tell me you feel the same.'

'I feel the same,' she said absently.

He pulled back and brought his hand down across her face. She turned away, eyes dry. 'You know I hate it when you lie to me.'

That was true. But he did not like the truth either.

'Forgive me,' he whispered, pressing against her once again. Pinning both her wrists above her head with one hand, he pushed her knees apart with the other. 'Open for me, my queen.'

She stared down at the hand gripping her arm.

Taking in her blank expression, Leksi let go of her. He placed a finger under her chin, raising her face to him. 'Where did you go?'

She blinked and stepped back from him, his hand falling away. 'You have a job to do. I see that now.'

He narrowed his eyes on her. 'I want you to see your son, but we need to be safe—'

'And you need to follow orders.'

There was something in her tone that got to him. 'What are you doing?' He shook his head. 'You need someone to blame? Is that it?'

Her lips flattened into a thin line. 'I came to Syrasan of my own accord, and you are treating me like a prisoner.'

He took a step towards her. 'You *trespassed* into Syrasan. I found you near death and felt sorry for you. If I had known you were going to be such a pain in my arse, I would've left you in the woods.'

Before he could snatch the words back, her face collapsed.

'I trusted you,' she said, breaths coming sharply and eyes brimming with tears. 'You can hand me over to your king, or hand me over to my king. It does not matter which.' She took an unsteady step back. 'You're all the same.'

Leksi felt sick to his stomach as she turned away from him. He went to follow her, then stopped himself, instead watching her disappear around the corner. Only then did he exhale, listening to her soft footsteps on the stairs. There was a process, and it was his job to ensure that process was followed. Perhaps she just needed some time to see sense. He could give her some time, and him some time. Then he would apologise for the things he said, and she would realise that he simply wanted her safe.

Leksi stayed in his room for the rest of the afternoon. He told Charis to keep an eye on Petra's door and tell him if she emerged. He had a wash, changed his clothes, and wrote to Tyron telling him they would be arriving at Archdale the following day. A servant arrived to invite him down to dinner, and he asked if Petra was downstairs.

'She would not open the door, sir. I thought it best not to disturb her.'

Leksi thanked him and went to fetch her himself. He was trying to be patient, understanding, because he knew how much she wanted to go to her son, but he was also prepared to knock her door down if she refused to open it to him.

He found Charis leaning against the wall, head slumped forwards, snoring. Shaking his head, he kicked the boy's foot, startling him awake.

'Sorry, sir,' the squire said, pushing himself up onto his feet.

Leksi knocked on the door and waited for what he thought was a reasonable amount of time. 'Petra,' he called. No reply. 'I'm coming in,' he said, pushing against the door and finding it was unlocked. He opened it and stepped inside, staring around the dark, empty room.

He turned to his squire. 'Where is she?'

Charis looked past him. 'Is she not in there?'

Leksi resisted the urge to kick him again. 'How long were you asleep?'

'Not long,' Charis replied, unconvincingly.

The knight stepped past him, head shaking. They made their way downstairs and entered the hall where Lord Yuri and Hali were seated at the large table, waiting for their guests to join them. Leksi stopped in the doorway, an uneasy feeling growing inside of him when he saw she was not there.

'Where's Petra?' he asked, his mind ticking over.

Hali frowned and glanced at her husband. 'In her room, I imagine. How about I go?'

'She's not upstairs.'

'Well, she cannot have gone far,' Yuri said, gesturing to the servant waiting nearby. The man stepped forwards. 'I want you to ask around and locate our missing guest. Check the entire manor.'

'Yes, my lord,' the servant replied before rushing from the room.

Leksi turned to Charis. 'Saddle my horse, just in case.'

'In case of what?'

He did not want to admit the possibility aloud. 'And ensure I have enough supplies to last a few days.'

Charis looked confused. 'Why?'

'Just do it.'

'Leksi,' Hali called, rushing after him.

He turned to her, jaw set.

'Does she know the location of her son?'

'Yes.' He had handed Petra the letter to read for herself. It contained every detail they had learned about the situation so far. She deserved that. Of course, in hindsight, if she was going to resent him anyway, he should have kept the details to himself until he got her to Archdale.

Hali's face was pinched with worry.

'She would not attempt such a journey alone, surely,' Yuri said, walking over and joining them. 'If she had requested a horse, I most certainly would have heard about it.'

Leksi closed his eyes. 'She will be on foot.'

'Well she won't have gone far,' Hali said. 'It's a two-day journey to the Corneon border on foot.'

'Perhaps she just took a walk of the grounds to clear her head,' Yuri offered.

Hali chewed her lip. 'No. She has gone to her son.'

Lord Yuri frowned. 'She is a smart woman who would surely understand the dangers and ramifications of such a decision.'

'She's already proven that she doesn't care about the dangers and ramifications,' Hali said plainly. 'She wants to see her son.'

'But to go on foot,' Yuri continued, 'with no coin or supplies...'

Leksi suddenly remembered the jewels she had in her possession. Shaking his head, he marched out of the hall and headed for the front door.

CHAPTER 18

It was tempting to run, but Petra knew the journey would be long. Only a steady pace and some clever thinking would get her to Corneo. After she had been walking for about an hour, she moved off the main road to study the map she had stolen from Lord Yuri's study, one she had every intention of returning—after she had seen her son. She would need to veer north, to Soarid, in order to get some supplies. The most direct route was to Lirald, but without water, food or shelter, she would never make it that far. All she had was the map and the jewels. She would need to find a merchant or nobleman willing to trade them for coin or supplies.

The moment Leksi had announced he was taking her to Archdale, she had been wary. Her son was in Corneo, and she knew he would have no control over the situation once she was inside the castle walls. Leksi must have known it too, but he had followed orders his entire life and was incapable of disobeying them. She understood—as long as *he* understood that her loyalty was to her son. He could not expect her to follow him blindly to Archdale so another king could decide the best course of action. No, she was done letting men make those decisions on her behalf—Leksi included.

The knight would have likely figured out that she was missing by now. He had left Charis to play watchdog, and she had waited for the sound of his familiar snoring before opening the door, stepping over his legs, and slipping from the house. The entire manor had been secured so no one could get in. They had not been expecting anyone to sneak *out*.

Knowing it would not take him long to catch up, she decided to stay off the road. Instead, she walked parallel to it, continuing that way until she arrived at a fenced paddock containing sheep. They watched her with suspicion, and while she knew they were not aggressive animals by any means, she still returned to the road, just as the sun disappeared.

From Soarid, she would make her way to Lirald, and from there, she would cross the border. It would be at least another day of hard walking to get from the border to Paton in Corneo's north. That was where Xander was waiting.

A priest named Father Gabot had taken her son in, ordered to raise him in the church and committed to cleansing him of his sins. The idea of a five-year-old boy having sins made her fingers curl, but she decided to reserve judgement of the man until she could see for herself. That was as far as she let her mind go. Maybe he was happy, loved, part of a family, a community, destined to help people in need. She would not take that from him. But if she discovered he was being mistreated in any way, she would do whatever was necessary to get him out of there before King Nilos came for her.

Gravel crunched underfoot, and she watched her shoes as she walked. Better than watching the dark trees around her. Occasionally a dog barked or a bird sang, making her jump.

Nothing slowed her though. The lure of her son gave her an energy she could never have imagined. A sheep bleated nearby and she glanced at the paddock, adjusting the hood of her cloak so it covered more of her face.

She swallowed, recognising thirst, though she had only been walking a few hours. The entire night stretched out in front of her; she would need to toughen up if she was to survive the journey.

As soon as there was light, she would search for water. Until then, one foot in front of the other, towards her son.

Leksi tried to get inside her mind. She would take the most direct route to Paton. Or would she? As far as he knew, she had no food or water. Soarid was not too far out of the way; perhaps she would go there first and try to sell the jewels. He was certain she would not venture far from the main roads. She would be expecting him, so he was not expecting to find her in plain sight. The mentor was resourceful enough when she needed to be.

Sheep bleated nearby, and he slowed his horse to a walk so he could watch the trees either side. His eyes were highly trained at spotting men among them, perhaps even better trained to spot her. If she was around, he would find her, then throw her over his horse and take her to Archdale. Those were his orders.

'Pandarus wants her brought to Archdale.'

That was what Tyron had said in his letter. That was all the information he had needed in the past, but now he found himself asking why. He had spent too much time alone with her, too many hours watching her from across the room, musing at her need for sterile living conditions and marvelling at the soft curves of her body.

He had witnessed a change in her. She no longer looked through him. Her blank expression had been replaced by something warmer, more reflective. And they had kissed—twice. Not the sort of kiss he was used to, but the type that was an event in itself.

He shifted in the saddle as he replayed the moments in his mind. The first time was on her. He had tried to do the right thing, be the man people wanted him to be instead of the one they expected him to be. The second time was on him. He had not been in control of himself, fuelled by the fear of almost losing her.

He prided himself on his ability to keep a cool head. There were only a handful of times in his life that he had not been in complete control of his emotions, but seeing her underwater, her long hair and dress swirling around her as the waves rolled her over in the sea… it had undone him.

The relief he had felt when he pulled her from the water had not lasted, quickly replaced by uncharacteristic rage. Why? Because he cared—too much. Now if he did not find her before King Nilos's men did, there was a good chance he might never see her again, and the possibility turned his stomach to stone.

Petra arrived in Soarid just as the sun kissed the horizon. She had stopped at a well outside the village and now lingered near the market as the merchants set up for the day. It took some time before she finally worked up enough courage to approach someone, walking up to a young woman selling flowers and trying not to appear as exhausted as she felt.

The girl looked her up and down for a moment before replying.

'You won't find a jeweller here. You need to go to Veanor.'

She had just come from there, but was not about to announce the fact. 'Perhaps you know of another merchant who might be interested?'

By the look on her face, she did, but she hesitated a moment. 'Try the goldsmith. He has a workshop next to his house.' She pointed in the direction. 'You'll see on your left.'

Relief and gratitude showed on Petra's face. 'Thank you so much.'

Exiting the market, she made her way along the road, continuously glancing over her shoulder. She kept expecting to see Leksi. Perhaps he had passed her, or gone straight to Lirald. That was what she hoped, and a part of her wanted to lay eyes on him, revel in the safe feeling she always had in his presence, but a bigger part of her wanted to get to Xander.

She found the goldsmith already in his workshop. He was seated at a bench, polishing a candleholder. He looked up as she stepped inside, eyes moving over her the same way the woman's had. In a small village, everyone took notice of an unfamiliar face.

'Good morning,' she called to him, opening her bag to retrieve the jewels.

'Can I help you?' he asked, standing and putting the candleholder and cloth on the bench.

She tried to smile as she gathered the gemstones in her hand, wanting to appear friendly. He did not smile back. 'I am looking for a buyer for some jewellery.' She stepped up to the table and laid the items in front of him: two large rings and a gem-inlaid bracelet.

His gaze went from the items to her, no doubt trying to figure out if they were stolen. 'They yours?' he asked plainly.

'Gifts.'

His eyebrows rose in surprise. 'Generous gifts.'

'A generous lover,' she replied, hoping that would answer all of his questions and allow them to move forwards.

'I see.' He picked them up, one at a time, studying them. 'Fine craftsmanship. Were they made in Syrasan?'

He must have known they were foreign pieces if he was asking. 'I'm not entirely sure.'

He placed them back on the table, closer to her that time —a bad sign. 'I can't pay you what they're worth. You'll get a better price in Veanor.'

She was about to say she had just come from there when she realised the less he knew, the better. 'I only need enough to fund my journey.'

'Where you headed?'

'South,' she lied. 'To Braul.'

'Thought I recognised an accent,' he said, nodding. 'I'm afraid I can't even offer you that.'

She drew a breath. 'What about some supplies instead of coin?' She held up her small bag. 'As you can see, I left in a hurry.'

He stared at the bag for a moment. 'I'm not going to regret this, am I? I want no trouble.'

She lowered her bag. 'I assure you the jewels belong to me. They are not stolen.' She hoped that was enough for him.

Crossing his arms, he asked, 'Why'd you leave in such a hurry?'

What answer to give? 'My family needs me. Let us just say my lover was not keen on me leaving.' It was partly true.

He shook his head as though he was about to say no. 'What do you need?'

She exhaled, swallowing back tears. 'What would you recommend for a solo journey?'

The goldsmith disappeared and returned with a flask filled with water, a sheet of waterproof canvas and some rope that could be used for shelter, a large loaf of bread, a few apples, some salted meat, a wool blanket, a towel, and a piece of soap. He packed all of the items into a saddlebag.

'Where's your horse?' he asked.

She bit down on her lip. That explained the saddlebag. 'I am travelling on foot.'

He looked past her, as if she were lying. 'You're *walking* all the way to Braul?'

'It appears that way.'

He glanced down at her shoes and shook his head. 'Wait here.'

She was worried he was going to report her insanity to someone, or worse, bring her an animal of some kind. Instead, he returned with a pair of old boots and a dagger. Crouching in front of her, he measured one of the shoes against her foot.

'You'll be able to walk for days in these without getting blisters. And they'll keep your feet drier than your fancy shoes.'

She looked up at the clear sky. 'Thankfully, no rain in sight.'

He gave a low chuckle as she removed her shoes and shoved her feet into the boots, hoping he would not notice the blisters already visible on her heels. When she was done, he handed her the dagger.

'What is this for?'

'Just in case.'

She nodded. 'Thank you.'

'Don't be taking rides with strange men. Plenty will offer.'

Another nod.

'And watch out for wild boars in the South. Better if you were on a horse, but I'm afraid I can't spare one of those.'

Boars. She shoved the dagger into her bag.

'The dagger won't help much with those. Thick hides.'

'Then I shall refrain from stabbing them.' She attempted a smile.

He ushered her to the door before heading back to his workbench, shaking his head the entire time.

She stepped outside and turned to face the rising sun, fear and excitement fighting for room inside her. Then, drawing a breath for courage, she headed east.

CHAPTER 19

*T*he forest between Soarid and Lirald was dense and alive with creatures Petra had only encountered in books. Birds crowed, lizards clicked and colourful fur flashed in the shrubbery. She clutched the saddlebag in one hand and the dagger in the other. The goldsmith had mentioned boars in the South, but she preferred to err on the side of caution in case they had wandered north.

Tall pines loomed overhead, stretching in all directions. She should have moved off the track, but her fear of getting lost kept her feet firmly on the path winding between the trees. The setting reminded her of the night she had slept on the forest floor, certain that if the cold did not kill her, the insects would. She had eventually surrendered to sleep only to be woken gently by a rather handsome Sir Leksi.

Another glance over her shoulder. He was not there.

The sky rumbled overhead, and she stopped walking and looked up. At some point, clouds had swallowed the sun, their colour suggesting it might actually rain. That explained the goldsmith's laughter. She had almost forgotten that Syrasan was capable of rain in the warm season. That was why they had food while their neighbours wilted. It would probably just be a shower, and the trees would provide enough cover for her to continue. She resumed walking. The sooner she got to the border, the better.

A drop of rain splashed on her forehead and she wiped at it. Another rumble of thunder made her look around, worried she would not hear approaching horses over the noise. A sudden wind hit her from the north, causing all the hairs on her arms to stand on end. She reached up and pulled the hood of her cloak over her head as more rain began to fall. Within minutes, she noticed the heaviness of her cloak as it collected the water. Not quite the shower she had predicted, but rather steady rain, which seemed to have settled in the skies above her.

Another glance behind. She wondered how far she was from Lirald, not that she was planning to stop there. Leksi would likely be waiting for her to make a mistake so he could drag her back to Archdale. He would be expecting her to seek shelter indoors, but she had everything she needed with her, and she could survive outdoors if it meant reaching her son.

Water began to pool on the forest floor, the earth too dry to absorb it. Her boots held up well at first, keeping her feet dry. Then every part of her was wet, her dress soaked through, and her feet slushing in her boots. She stopped walking, looking around for shelter, but water seemed to trickle from every nook of the forest. With no idea how long the downpour might last, she realised that she was actually going to have to attempt to build some.

She blinked, eyes heavy from lack of sleep. Perhaps she would allow herself an hour's rest until the rain stopped. She moved off the track for the first time since entering the forest and moved among the thick trees in search of higher ground where there was less water. Crouching, she pulled the canvas from her bag and unrolled it. There were holes sewn in the corners, no doubt reinforced for the rope. She thought she had tied enough rope in her youth to know what she was doing, but when she tried to recall the different types of knots, nothing came to her. One of the most educated women in Corneo, but no one had taught her how to tie a good knot.

Standing, she shook the canvas out, blinking against the rain. The wind had picked up, and the moment the canvas was flat, it took off like a sail, pulling free of her hands and wrapping the closest tree. She stared at it while rain splattered her face, fighting the urge to cry.

Leksi didn't mind rain to a point, but he suspected this was going to be more of a downpour judging by the darkening sky. Thunder clapped around him, and he imagined Petra's face in that moment. She stood no chance against the elements, and he could not help feeling slightly pleased by the fact. She had chosen to run off, after all. Perhaps she would finally realise her mistake.

The thought left as quickly as it came, however, because he knew she would be afraid, and that did not sit well with him.

He kept to the path, eyes searching the trees, because the forest was too big to try any other tactic. The goldsmith informed him that he had missed her by an hour, so he felt confident he would find her soon enough. The man had frowned at him, almost hesitant to answer his questions.

'She told me the jewels weren't stolen,' he had said.

'The jewels were hers,' Leksi had answered honestly.

He had clicked his tongue before asking, 'You the man who gave them to her?'

Whatever story she had fed him did not seem to paint Leksi in a good light. Eventually he had gotten all the information he could before heading off after her. He disregarded the part about her travelling south to Braul. There was only one direction she was going, and that was to her son.

Something caught Leksi's eye in the trees, about ten yards away. He stopped his horse and squinted into the rain, all the tension leaving his body in one relieved breath. He could not see her face, but the sight of a woman wrestling with a large canvas was all the confirmation he needed.

Dismounting, he led his horse through the trees towards her. She had her back to him, but he could hear her cursing as she tried to keep hold of the cover in the wind. To her credit, she had managed to attach the rope to all four corners of the canvas. He watched as one of them flew up, whipping her face. She swatted at it, an angry noise escaping her. He really should have stepped up to help; instead, he leaned against the tree and continued watching. When she finally got hold of the rogue rope, she looked around, searching for somewhere to attach it. She gasped and jumped a full foot in the air when she noticed him standing there.

'What are you—' She pressed a hand to her chest. 'You scared me!'

He had his arms crossed in front of him, an amused expression on his face. 'What are you doing over there?'

She straightened and licked water off her lips while the rain continued to soak her. 'What does it look like? I am making a shelter.'

His gaze fell to the canvas in her hands. 'That's not what it looks like.' He watched her lips press together, holding in her anger before returning to the task at hand. She even went as far as turning away from him. He would let her go for as long she needed to prove her point. He had no intention of helping her until she asked for it—and she would eventually.

She glanced over her shoulder at him, her face determined. His own expression gave nothing away. It seemed she was not ready to ask for help yet, and he was prepared to wait her out. She wound one of the ropes around a tree and tied it in a feeble knot that had him shaking his head. She noticed.

'What?' she snapped.

'That knot won't hold.'

She ignored him, her hands travelling down to the opposite corner of the canvas until she had the second rope in hand. She stepped up to another tree and tried to reach around the trunk. It was too wide for her arms to pass the rope between hands, so she walked around it—more of a stumble, really—then pulled it tight. Leksi watched as the rope at the other end shook, loosening with every passing second. Any moment, it would go flying at her.

He *really* should have stepped forwards at that point, but she chose that moment to cast him a filthy look, so he stayed where he was in order to enjoy the show. She tested her latest knot before turning to him with a cocky expression.

Then the other rope gave out. The canvas swirled through the air, wrapping her like a second skin. She took a few unsteady steps, trying to free herself, then lost her balance, landing on her side with the canvas still wrapped around her.

Confident his point had been made, Leksi wiped rain from his face and stepped forwards to stand over her. 'Let me know if you need help. I don't want to make assumptions.'

She tore wildly at the canvas until her head was finally free, then stared up at him. He expected to see blind rage on her face by that point, but she just lay there, panting.

'Ah,' he said. 'If the other Companions could see you now.'

Her breathing slowed, and for a moment, he thought she might cry. But then something spectacular happened. She began to *laugh*. At first her hand went over her mouth to cover it, but then it fell away and laughter tore from her throat in uncontrollable bursts. Her eyes closed and she lifted her face to the rain, completely surrendering to it.

Leksi stared down at her, completely thrown by her reaction. Her hands went to her stomach, clutching it the way a child did when they had passed the point of being able to stop and everything hurt. He had seen her smile, a few times now. He had even seen her laugh a total sum of once—but nothing like this. She was completely lost to the emotion, and dear God, she was beautiful in that moment: wet hair clinging to her face, leaves and mud stuck to her hands and clothes. She turned onto her side, gasping for air, mud covering one cheek. It was like witnessing her rebirth, and he was at a complete loss for words.

It took a long time for the laughter to die down, but the smile remained as she lay in the mud, eventually rolling onto her back to look up at him. She took a few calming breaths, laughed once more, and then let out an enormous sigh.

'Better?' he asked, barely recognising his own voice. He cleared his throat.

Her smile softened. 'Better.'

His eyes moved over her. 'Look at you. You're a disgrace —an embarrassment to your own kind.' He stepped forwards and held out his hand.

'What kind is that?'

He pulled her to her feet, keeping hold of her. 'The kind that demands cleanliness and order. The prudish kind.'

She studied his face. 'That would be highly offensive coming from any other man.'

It was by no means logical, but he desperately wanted to kiss her in that moment. The dirtier she was, the better. His gaze fell to her lips, but he stopped himself. 'Would you like me to build you a shelter? Then build you a fire so you can dry your clothes?'

She looked down at herself, then at the muddy canvas. 'I believe your assistance is required, Sir Leksi.'

He pulled a pine needle from her hair. 'You're lucky I found you.'

She shook her head and stepped out of his way. 'I was expecting you to throw me over your horse and carry me off.'

'Let's get you dry first,' he said, bending to pick up the canvas. 'All right, watch closely. You might learn something.'

She went and waited by his horse, arms crossed against the rain. Within minutes he had all four corners of the canvas secured to the trees.

'It is on a lean,' she pointed out, sounding rather pleased with herself.

'That's so the water doesn't pool on top,' he replied without looking at her.

'Oh.'

He smiled to himself before walking over to his horse to fetch some things. In under ten minutes, he created a cosy nest with enough room for them and their supplies, adding an additional canvas on one side to protect them from the wind.

'In you go,' he said. 'Take off your cloak and boots first though.'

She glanced at the shelter, then back at him. 'Are you coming in?'

He really should have wrestled her onto his horse the moment he spotted her and taken her straight to Archdale, but the temptation to huddle beneath a canvas with her for an hour or two, under the pretence of bad weather, was too great.

'In a minute,' he said.

He watched as she peeled off her wet cloak before sitting

down to remove her muddy boots. Once she was settled, he went to lay their cloaks over their bags, under no illusion that they would dry without heat. He removed his sword but left his boots on before dropping down next to her. She was shivering beside him. As soon as the rain stopped, he would build her a fire.

He reached for her bag and pulled out the blanket he knew she had. 'It's a bit damp,' he said, wrapping it around her shoulders.

She pulled it tightly and looked him up and down. 'How is it you never feel the cold?' she asked. 'You always emerge from the freezing ocean as though you have just taken a warm bath. And now you sit here in wet clothes, hands warm.'

He eyed her. 'How do you know my hands are warm?'

'They are always warm.'

He sat with arms resting on his knees. 'Years of practice. This is nothing after sleeping in the snow.'

She watched the rain. 'You really should not have come after me.'

'You're lucky I did.'

She shook her head. 'I am not going to Archdale with you. I am going to Paton.'

He regarded her for a moment. 'If I decide you're coming with me, then you are coming with me.' She did not reply, her silence feeling a lot like defiance. He noticed her lips had a blue tinge to them. She really was freezing. 'Want me to warm you up?'

She narrowed her eyes. 'Is this one of your tricks you use on women?'

'I don't need tricks.'

'Hmm.' Another shiver. 'Let me guess, I take my clothes off, you take your clothes off, and we implement the skin-to-skin warming technique.'

He suppressed a smile. 'I had planned to leave my clothes on, but if you feel the need to get naked, I won't stop you.' Her cheeks flooded with colour, and he frowned. 'I'm not sure I've ever seen you blush before.'

Wrapping an arm around her, he pulled her to him. She was rigid at first, then eventually relaxed against him, her head on his shoulder. There was enough familiarity between them, enough time spent in close proximity, whether it be in the saddle or standing on the shore with his hands tangled in her hair. They were both looking out, watching the rain as it finally slowed.

'Even the elements are against me,' she said, all laughter gone from her voice now.

'No one is against you. Well, maybe King Nilos.' He thought for a moment. 'I met him once. A few years back. He was probably less crazy then.'

She was quiet for a moment. 'I remember that visit. Peace negotiations. But I do not remember you.'

'I was just the muscle. The princes took the meetings.' He pulled her closer, covering her icy hands with his warm ones. 'I would've remembered you. I never forget a pretty face.' Not entirely true. He usually forgot them the very next day.

'It was probably around the time Xander was born. I was no good to anyone then. The king kept me hidden away for months.'

The rain had stopped falling, but water still ran from the trees. The thought of her locked up, grieving and isolated made him shift. 'Even if you make it to Paton, you'll struggle to get close to him. They'll be on high alert with you still missing.'

She sniffed. 'Perhaps you do not realise what it would mean to me to see him at all. My memories of him are five years old, and they are fading.' She paused. 'I remember his dark eyes though.'

His arm tightened around her, then relaxed again. He was no good at comfort. He usually distracted people from their pain with crude jokes, but he knew any humour at that moment would fall flat.

'I'm going to make you a fire,' he said, pulling away.

She straightened, watching him. 'Everything is wet.'

'Have a little faith, mentor.'

She hugged her knees, and he was aware of her gaze on him as he wandered around collecting sticks and pine cones from secret nooks. The wind had eased to a light breeze, ideal for fanning a flame. Taking out his knife, he stripped the wet bark from the sticks before shredding the dry parts. He stacked his collection of tinder in a precise order, then went to his bag to retrieve flint and a fire steel. A few minutes of coaxing, blowing and failed attempts finally resulted in a small flame. When he was certain it would not go out, he went in search of more tinder, conscious of not wandering too far from Petra.

'Just the sight of the flames is enough to warm you,' she said when he returned. She was holding her hands out to the heat.

He added to the fire, giving it his full attention until he was satisfied. Next, he went to tend to his horse and returned with another rope, which he tied between two trees close to the fire. After he had hung their cloaks over it, he walked over to Petra and said, 'Take off your dress and hose. We need to get you dry.'

She hesitated before undressing beneath the blanket, keeping her undergarments on, and handing everything else to him. He hung it, along with his tunic and shirt, leaving his trousers on.

When he was done, he looked back at the shelter and saw Petra's eyes on him, unreadable as always. She looked away as he walked over and collapsed beside her, watching the flames.

'I'm guessing you didn't sleep last night,' he said.

She shook her head.

'Get some sleep now. I'll wake you when your clothes are dry.'

She turned to look at him, her cheek pressed against her knees. 'I am guessing you did not get any sleep either.'

He shrugged. 'I can survive without it.'

She placed a hand on his arm, and he looked down at it. 'When I wake, I am going east to my son.'

'You really think I'm going to let you walk all the way to Paton, alone?'

They stared at one another for a moment. 'I am not asking permission.'

He turned back to the fire. 'Get some sleep.'

Her hand fell away and she lay down beside him, curling herself into a ball beneath the blanket. His eyes went to the wet clothes, viewing them like an hourglass. When they were dry, his time was up. He was going to have to decide if he was travelling south to Archdale or east to Corneo. The only thing he knew for certain was that, whichever direction he chose, they were going together.

South to his king, his friends, his home? Or east into enemy territory, to the son stolen from her arms while she slept?

He dropped his head between his knees, inhaling the smoke. Follow orders or follow his heart? He had to decide— and soon.

CHAPTER 20

When Petra woke, it was dark. It took her a moment to remember where she was. She turned her head, looking for him. He was in the same spot next to her, his face illuminated by the flames as he stared thoughtfully at the fire. So serious. She had done that to him, stripped him of his laughter by running. What had she expected him to do as she fled towards danger?

As though sensing she was awake, Leksi suddenly turned and looked at her.

She gave him a weak, sleepy smile. 'Sorry. You should have woken me.' She pushed herself up into a seated position, warm from the fire.

'I didn't have the heart to wake you.'

When he said things like that, it triggered her guilt. 'Did you sleep?' He shook his head, and she continued to study his face. 'I am sorry to put you in this position, but I hope you understand why I cannot return to Archdale with you.'

He did not reply for the longest time, then he exhaled and looked heavenward. 'I understand. That's why I'm going to take you to Paton.'

She stared at him, hoping she had heard correctly. 'What about your orders?'

Leksi turned to her. 'Tyron told me to keep you safe. So I'll keep you safe.'

Thinking her heart might explode with gratitude in that moment, she hugged his bare arm and pressed her lips to his skin. 'Thank you,' she breathed. She did not let go, feeling such pure affection for him that she was afraid to move in case he changed his mind and left her. She kissed his arm again, his skin so warm beneath her lips as she breathed in his familiar scent. A hand came to rest on the back of her head, fingers kneading her hair. She leaned into it, her eyes closing, though she was not shutting him out—she was savouring him.

Her mouth moved up his arm until she reached the top of his shoulder. Only then did she raise her eyes to him.

'What are you doing?' he asked, looking a bit unsure.

She ran one hand over his hard chest, pausing at a long silver scar. 'I am showing my appreciation,' she finally answered.

'A simple thank you will suffice.'

Her eyes went to his, and she saw her own lust mirrored back at her. 'Thank you,' she whispered, then slid her hand up his neck, pulling herself up to meet his lips.

Her need was so primal in that moment, she feared she would scare him away. It was as though every wall she had spent the last nine years constructing just crumbled to dust. Every thought was muted, replaced by the sensation of him. She gripped his face and kissed him deeper.

His hands were on her then, as though they had been waiting for confirmation. He pulled her onto his lap and her chest brushed his, her knees landing either side of him. It was the strangest feeling to have him so close and yet need him closer still. His fingers pressed into her back, his thumbs rubbing her sides as his mouth travelled along her jaw and down her neck. She leaned into the sensation, exhaling as her head tipped back.

'If you want me to stop,' he murmured against her skin. 'Or slow down.' His mouth moved lower. 'Just say the word.'

Her hands went into his hair, pulling him closer. 'Don't stop.'

His hand slid up her leg. 'Would you like me to show you how it can be with a *real* man?'

She opened her eyes and looked down, assessing his half-smirk. Her entire body pulsed with her need for him. 'You want to teach the mentor?'

He brought his lips to her collarbone, kissing softly. 'Do you trust me?'

She nodded. 'I trust you.' To prove the point, she began removing her undergarments. He leaned back on his hands to watch, his gaze moving over her body. The raw flames of the fire warmed her back.

'You are possibly the most beautiful creature God ever made,' he said, his smirk gone.

She studied his face for a moment. 'You can drop the charming act, Sir Leksi. You already have me naked.'

His expression softened and he reached up, running his thumb over her lips. 'I wish it were an act. It would all be so much easier if it were.'

She swallowed and placed a hand on his chest. 'I know.'

He lifted her then and laid her down on the blanket, one hand cradling her head while the other wandered where it pleased.

Oh God.

Her mouth found his, and the lesson began.

$\sim$

He should never have fallen asleep, but Petra's incessant mouth and body had finally rendered him completely useless. He had been with a lot of women, but with her, it had been something else entirely.

As she lay nestled in the crook of his arm, her sleepy breaths on his skin, he listened for whatever had woken him. Nothing but the crackle and hiss of the fire sounded, but he did not trust it. Gently, he pulled his arm free and dragged the blanket up to cover her. His eyes went to his sword as he tugged on his trousers, and then he heard the snap of something underfoot on the other side of the canvas wall.

He did not jump to conclusions. Hungry people often spotted campfires and went looking for food. There was no need for anyone to die just yet. But as he reached for his sword, an arrow hissed past his head.

That changed everything.

He swung around, sword ready, and was about to call for Petra to get behind him when he noticed her moving in his peripheral vision. Sliding, actually. Someone had hold of her foot and was dragging her from the shelter. Her eyes snapped open.

'Leksi,' she cried.

He caught her arm, and without hesitating, he drove his sword through the dark figure holding her. The man groaned, hands going to his stomach.

Leksi was a reasonable person, unless someone tried to drag a naked woman from his bed.

Wide-eyed, Petra crawled away from the dying man, wrapping herself around Leksi. He held her, but his eyes searched the trees, knowing there would be at least one more armed man.

'We need to move,' he said, wrapping her in a blanket and dragging her away from the fire. They came to a stop in the shadows.

'Stay behind me,' he whispered, just as a weapon swung towards him. Leksi blocked it with his sword, then drove his blade through the assailant's thigh. The man screamed, clutching his leg. Leksi assessed the gold uniform before stepping forwards and slicing his throat, pushing the man backwards with his heel so he would bleed out on the ground instead of all over his tunic.

Taking Petra's hand once more, he led her over to the horse so she would not have to watch the man die. He brought a finger to his lips, listening and waiting. Satisfied there were no more soldiers, he turned to her. 'Time to go.'

She was holding the blanket to her chest, her breathing shallow and body trembling. 'Who were they? Soldiers?'

He pulled a dagger from a saddlebag and handed it to her. 'That's my guess.'

She stared down at the weapon. 'Where are you going?' There was panic in her voice.

He kissed her rosy cheek. 'I'll be right back. Don't move.'

'Leksi—'

'Don't move,' he said again before rushing off. He checked the corpses for any letters before taking their weapons and the clean tunic off one of the bodies. Then he went to fetch their clothes before returning to Petra.

'Get dressed,' he said, taking the dagger from her and handing her her clothes. He threw his shirt on and slipped the gold tunic over the top. 'There may be more men close by. We need to leave.'

She stared at his gold tunic while fumbling with her clothes. When she was done, he handed the dagger back to her, gathering their things before finally kicking dirt over the fire. Everything went dark.

'How are you so calm?' she asked when he returned.

He loaded up the horse, fingers moving quickly over the straps and ropes. 'Again, years of practice.' He glanced back at her. Shock was frozen on her face, and her fingers had turned white around the dagger. 'What have I told you?'

She swallowed, looking up at him. 'When you are here, I am safe.' She paused. 'Though I would feel a lot safer if you were the one holding the dagger right now,' she added.

He took the weapon from her and mounted his horse.

'Are you sure about this?' she asked as he pulled her up behind him. 'If you come to Corneo with me, you will be directly disobeying Prince Tyron's orders. I am guessing you have never disobeyed him in your life.'

'He might disagree with you on that point,' Leksi said, gathering the reins.

She held on to his waist. 'But this is different.'

'This is different,' he echoed. He turned to look at her. 'I need you to do exactly as I say from now on. I can't be worrying about you running off again or doing something reckless.'

She nodded.

'You have to trust me.'

'I do trust you,' she replied without hesitation. 'I trust you with my life.'

She had a way of stirring emotions he did not even know he had.

'Let's go see your son.'

CHAPTER 21

The moment they crossed into Corneo, Petra felt it. The air was stifling, and the forest seemed void of life. She watched the trees flash past from the safety of the horse, untouchable in Leksi's presence. It was a dangerous mindset, because one knight did not stand a chance against a king with an entire army at his disposal.

They kept as far north as possible, avoiding the Syrasan-occupied part of Corneo. Leksi did not stop until they reached the edge of the forest, where a normally dry stream held some water after the rainfall. They filled their flasks, washed and let the horse drink. Petra took some food from her bag and they sat down to eat, watching the sun paint the sky in the east.

'We're not going to stop again,' he said. 'There are only open paddocks between here and Paton. Nowhere to hide. People are very good at spotting foreigners.'

She swallowed her mouthful of apple. 'Only you are a foreigner. This is my home.'

He tilted his head, a playful expression on his face. 'All right, Lady Local. Which way is Ituco?'

She looked around, thinking, before finally picking a direction and pointing with confidence. 'That way.'

'Incorrect,' he replied, pointing south. 'It's that way.'

She took another bite of her apple. 'Close enough.'

'Close enough?' He leaned back on his hands, his legs stretched out in front of him. 'How you got as far as you did without me, I have no idea.'

She squinted against the sun. 'What is the plan when we arrive in Paton?'

He took a long drink of water before replying. 'It's best I go in alone and observe for a while.'

'To see if there are guards watching?'

'There will be guards close by. King Nilos is no fool.'

Petra offered the apple core to Leksi's horse. A warm muzzle moved over her hand before returning to the grass. 'And then... and then you will take me to see him?'

'If it's safe.'

'Leksi—'

'You said you would do as you're told.' He stood and stuffed his flask in the saddlebag. 'We need to be smart. If he takes you now, he has all the power.'

Petra went to stand next to him, smoothing her hair that was out in a tangled mess down one shoulder. She went to speak, stopped, then tried again. 'I have to see my son. After that, it does not matter.'

He turned to her, head shaking. 'You mean it doesn't matter to *you*.'

She stared up at him. 'You know what I mean. The outcome is inevitable.'

'Doesn't have to be.'

She reached out and took hold of his arm. 'You have done so much for me. I am not going to continue to put you at risk.'

'A little late for that. What do you think will happen to me when I'm brought before your king?'

Her hand fell away. King Nilos would inflict the worst death possible. 'You are right. Perhaps I should go alone.'

'No. I'll take you to see your son, but then you're going to return with me to Archdale.' He glanced at her. 'King Nilos doesn't get you that easily.'

She placed a hand on the horse's rump, watching Leksi. So many emotions swam inside her. Words sat on the tip of her tongue, but she said nothing. What could she possibly say that would adequately express her feelings in that moment?

Before she could say anything at all, he mounted and reached down for her. She watched his face as he pulled her up before settling her on the back of the horse once more.

'I think you underestimate my need to keep you safe,' he said, a hand resting on her leg. 'It's also possible that you have completely ruined me for all future women.' He paused. 'Last night was…'

'I know.'

He looked at her. 'I really need you to be smart.'

'I just… I cannot think past Xander right now.'

He nodded, seeming to understand. Digging his heels in, they headed east.

They rode hard through barren paddocks, seemingly untouched by the rain, where matted sheep stood in huddles, watching them. Leksi stayed off the roads whenever possible. If they happened to pass someone, he would slow right down, smile, and wave. They made good time, reaching the outskirts of Paton before noon.

Petra knew Leksi had planned to leave her somewhere safe while he searched for Xander, but something about the village had clearly given him an uneasy feeling.

'Best you come with me,' he said, eyes on their surroundings. 'I think splitting up is a bad idea.' He nodded a greeting at an approaching woman walking along the road carrying a basket. She scowled back at him.

'Not the friendliest village I've visited,' he said.

Petra moved her hands to the back of the saddle. 'It is probably the tunic. Might be a clever tactic to blend in, but it will not win you many friends.'

They passed a man chopping wood in front of his house. He stopped work in order to better glare at them. Petra gave a small wave, which he did not return.

They gave up on courtesy at that point and just kept their eyes forwards.

A few minutes later, a steeple rose on the horizon in front of them. Petra gripped the saddle a little tighter, but it did nothing to still her trembling hands.

Leksi glanced over his shoulder at her.

'Are you all right?'

No, she was most definitely not all right. It had been five years since she had laid eyes on Xander. The prospect of seeing him now was making her palms sweat and her breath hitch. 'Fine.'

Leksi faced forwards again, but he placed one of his hands briefly on her leg before returning it to the hilt of his sword. She reminded herself to breathe, gaze fixed on the steeple.

When the entire church finally came into view, Leksi veered left down a narrow path that led between two houses. Petra rested her forehead on his back for a moment, fighting her urge to jump from the horse and run towards the church.

'He's not just going to be sitting on a pew waiting for you,' Leksi said, as though reading her mind.

'I know.'

'It's important we don't look lost or do anything that raises suspicions.'

She glanced back at one of the houses and saw a woman

peering out of a window at them. 'I think they are already suspicious.' She watched the church through the broken fences and leaning houses. The horse eventually veered left, climbing a small hill. They stopped at the top, where they had a clear view of the entrance.

'We're going to eat, without staring. Understand?' Leksi said.

Petra's eyes returned to him, and she nodded.

Leksi retrieved a blanket and laid it in the shade of an oak while she prepared some food, taking her time laying the items out. They sat with their backs against a wide trunk, facing the church. Petra chewed her food without tasting it, freezing every time a person wandered in or out of the building.

'There are a lot of men loitering about the church for this time of day.'

'They're guards.'

She frowned. 'Really? They are not in uniform.'

'No, but they're armed. Why would peasants be carrying swords in a village this small?'

Petra stared down at her food. 'Do you think they are guarding Xander?'

'I think the king is prepared in case you show up.' He took a drink of water. 'We can't go in that church.'

She turned a chunk of bread in her hands. 'How am I to see him if I cannot search for him?'

He looked at her, his face apologetic. 'It's not safe to hang around too long. There are already people watching us.'

She nodded. 'I know.' Another glance at the church before looking back at her bread. 'Perhaps I could go pray before we leave.'

'No.'

She took another bite, chewed, swallowed, and tried again. 'Both of us might raise suspicions, but if I were to go in alone, there would be nothing unusual or threatening about that.'

Leksi stared at his boots while he chewed, and his silence only encouraged her.

'I will be quite safe in God's house,' she continued. 'Safer than I would be waiting up here alone.'

He looked at her. 'Do you think those men give a shit if you're in God's house? King Nilos has the entire kingdom looking for you.'

She blinked, silence stretching between them. 'It is not as though I would run up and hug the child. I just want to see him.'

He shook his head. 'You can't predict how you'll react.'

She lifted her chin. 'Perhaps you are forgetting that I am a mentor. Remaining composed under difficult circumstances is a large part of my job.'

He crossed his feet. 'This is different, and you know it.'

She was about to argue when a small boy wandered out of the church holding a pail. Her gaze snapped to him, fixated as he wandered along the road towards the well in the centre of the village.

'I think that is him.' Her words were barely a whisper.

Leksi looked over and watched as an armed man appeared at the entrance of the church, leaning in the doorway, no doubt keeping an eye on the child. The tip of his weapon was visible beneath his tunic.

Petra's eyes never left the boy. The truth was, she had no idea what her son looked like, but as she studied the frail arms and mess of dark hair, she somehow knew he belonged to her.

With her heart drumming, she leaned forwards and snatched up the flasks. 'I need to see him up close.' She shot up and Leksi also stood, grabbing both of her wrists. She looked at him, sure he would tell her no. *It's too risky*, he would say. *There are guards everywhere*. She knew all that.

He leaned closer. 'If anyone asks, we're husband and wife. You walk slowly, body language relaxed, arms swinging and head stooped like every other common peasant. Keep the hood of your cloak down, like you have nothing to hide. Understand?'

She released the breath she had been holding and blinked back tears. 'Thank you.'

He nodded and let go of her. 'Be smart,' he whispered.

She sucked in a shaky breath and then turned casually, making her way down the slope towards the road. As she stepped out onto the gravel, her eyes locked on the boy walking ahead of her. She committed everything to memory, just in case. The way his feet turned out slightly, like her brothers' did. The uneven height of his shoulders because the pail was too large and heavy for his frame. The length of his hair, and the exact shade of brown.

When he arrived at the well, he got straight to work, lowering the rope. The pail would be far too heavy for him by the time it was filled with water; how on earth would he carry it all the way back to the church?

She stopped a short distance from the well, as though waiting her turn, but her eyes did not leave him. She studied his plain clothes and slightly drawn face, until he finally noticed her standing there. Their eyes met, and she knew it was him. It had been five years since she had looked into those dark eyes, but she had not forgotten them.

He stopped, straightened, and her heart seemed to stop beating for a moment.

'You're not from here,' he said.

The sweetest voice she had ever heard, though she had trouble reconciling it with the urgent cries of a newborn baby. She was worried her own voice would fail her. 'I am just passing through.'

He continued winding the handle as he studied her clothes. 'Where are you from?'

'Thovaria,' she lied.

'You going to the flag tournament?'

She knew nothing of the tournament. 'Yes.'

The pail hit the water and he peered over the edge, staring down into the well.

'Careful,' she called. When he looked at her, she smiled and added, 'It is a long way down.'

He waited for the pail to sink below the water's surface. 'I pulled a dead bird up once.'

She swallowed. 'Oh? I wonder why it did not fly up instead of drowning.'

He began turning the lever in the opposite direction. 'Father Gabot said it was a reminder from God.'

He was struggling with the weight, so she stepped up to help him, hoping he would not notice her shaking hands. When she was close, she inhaled, certain she would recognise him by scent. How many nights had she slept with his small body tucked into the nooks of her own? Not enough. He smelled of incense. 'What was God reminding you of?'

He shrugged and leaned down, taking over again. 'I have to do it myself. Work is part of God's plan for my redemption.'

She froze, eyes fixed on him. 'Redemption from what?'

'The sins of my mother,' he replied without blinking.

Such a big statement from such a tiny boy.

She sank down beside the well. A mother and her daughter walked past and cast a suspicious look in her direction. She did not have much time.

'Do you live with your mother?'

He shook his head.

'Where is she?'

'Don't know.'

'Your father?'

A shrug.

Petra wanted to reach out and touch his face, to feel his skin; instead, she dropped to her knees and reached for the handle once more. 'Please, let me do that.' He took a step back, breathing hard from his efforts. 'Do you live with Father Gabot?'

The boy crinkled his nose. 'And his wife.'

'Are they kind to you?'

'They help a lot of people in the village.'

That had not been what she had asked, but she moved on, aware their time together was coming to an end. The pail came back into sight. 'Have they taught you to read? To write?'

He shook his head. 'Father Gabot says the son of a whore has to work harder to get in God's good graces. He taught me to scrub floors.'

Petra's heart tore into tiny pieces. 'You... you clean the church?'

Another nod.

She glanced in the direction of the building, where a man had exited and stood with his hand to his forehead, squinting in their direction. Her time was up.

'Do you get enough to eat?' she asked, helping pour the water into his pail.

'I got to earn it.'

Her eyes closed for a moment. 'You mean work hard?'

'And pray.' He put a small hand on hers to stop her pouring. 'You can use the rest for your flasks if you want.'

She stared down at the callused hand covering her own. *Callused*.

'What is your name?' she whispered.

His hand fell away. 'Boy.'

She raised her eyes to him. 'Boy? Your name is *Boy*?'

He shrugged. 'That's what everyone calls me.'

She swallowed down the emotion choking her. She could hear the man's footsteps approaching. 'A handsome child like you deserves a real name.'

He tilted his head, studying her with the same eyes he had years earlier. 'What name would you give me?'

'Xander,' she breathed.

He practiced the word aloud a few times. 'Xander.'

'Boy!' came a voice.

They both jumped and turned to look at the man striding towards them. Xander picked up the pail with both hands and by some miracle lifted it. As he tried to rush off, the water slopped over the sides. The man reached him then, clipping him over the head, causing more water to spill. Petra felt a roar forming in her throat but swallowed it down.

'Slowly,' barked the man. He paused to look at Petra. 'Who are you?'

Not the friendliest priest she had ever encountered. *His mother*, she wanted to say. *Touch my son like that again and I will tear your hand from your arm with my teeth.*

'Daria,' she lied. 'My husband and I are on our way to the flag tournament.' She regarded his sour face and decided she did not like or trust him. 'That pail is quite heavy for one so young.'

He continued to study her. 'Only God knows his limits.'

Xander glanced over his shoulder at her, and she noted the change in his face. She knew it well. It was the same expression she had in King Nilos's company. Gone was the curiosity of a five-year-old boy. She gave him a small smile before he faced forwards again and continued down the road.

'You from up north?' Father Gabot asked.

'Thovaria.' She looked the priest straight in the eye as she lied to him.

Before he could ask any more questions, Leksi approached them, his horse trailing behind. The priest turned to look.

'How long does it take to get water?' Leksi said, casting a knowing look at the priest at her expense. 'My wife is blessed with the art of conversation. Or cursed. I haven't figured it out yet.' He took the flasks from her and kissed her. 'Ready?'

She managed a smile. 'Ready.'

The priest took in Leksi's uniform, the one stolen from a soldier he had killed just hours earlier.

'God bless you on your travels,' Father Gabot said before turning away.

'Thank you,' Leksi called to his back.

He mounted and pulled Petra up behind him. Without another word, they exited the village.

CHAPTER 22

They had moved off the road and were standing amid the trees so Petra could come undone away from prying eyes.

'I cannot leave him there,' she said again. She was pacing, holding her stomach like she might be sick at any moment.

Leksi was being patient with her because he could see she was in pain—and it was killing him.

'They have made him a slave. What sort of priest makes a child pay for the sins of his mother?' She stopped and turned to face him. 'And what of the sins of his father? Who pays for *his* sins?'

He would let her cry, scream, shout, throw punches at him if it helped. He would hold her while she cried, comfort her, soothe her. What he could not do was let her go back to her son.

'And what sort of man refuses to give an innocent baby a name when taking him in? No man of God. He is a monster. My son is being raised by a monster.' She resumed walking, head shaking. 'I am sorry, but I cannot return to Archdale with you. I am going back for him.'

'Father Gabot is not going to just hand the boy over to you. He has made his opinion of you quite clear.'

'He does not even know me.' There was a curve in her back now, like she was in physical pain. 'I will not ask, I will just take him. You saw it for yourself, the guards do not shadow him.'

'You'll never even make it out of the village, and the boy doesn't even know you. Why should he trust you?'

'His name is Xander,' she snapped.

He looked down. He had been naive to think she would leave him afterwards. She was a mother first, after all.

Tucking her hair behind her ears, she wiped at her face.

'No child would choose that life.'

'Xander doesn't know any different. He's five.'

She stopped walking and looked at him. 'I will show him there is a better life.'

He took a slow step towards her. 'We aren't even meant to be here, and now you're talking about kidnapping the king's son.'

'*My* son!' she said, pointing to her chest. More tears fell.

He shook his head. 'Neither of our kings will see it that way.'

Her hands went over her face, and it took all of his strength to remain where he was. After a moment, she looked up at him, arms falling to her sides.

'You go. Return to Archdale, tell everyone you tried to track me and failed. No one will blame you.'

'I already told you, I'm not returning without you. And we need to leave.'

She stepped up to him and pushed his chest with both hands. 'And I already told *you*, I am not leaving my son with that man.'

Leksi's feet did not move. He reached for her, but she shoved his hands away.

'I just want to know he is safe and loved. That is all I want for myself. After that, you can all do as you please. Use me as a pawn in your game of war or lock me up. At least I go away knowing he has a better future.' She staggered back from him. 'That man'—she pointed in the direction from which they had come—'will break his soul. I got fifteen years before they stripped me of my identity and self-worth. My son was just a few days old…' She could not finish.

Leksi turned away, walking to the closest tree and leaning his forehead against it. His throat was tight and his head ached. He should have left her, but he knew there was no way he could walk away from her now. She had nowhere to go. There were no safe havens in Corneo.

He slapped his palm against the tree while Petra continued crying behind him. The thing was, he could get the boy out if he wanted to. But then what? He was going to be in enough trouble when Tyron found out he had willingly escorted her to Paton. He was supposed to have brought her to Archdale. No one knew where he was. What would happen if he showed up with King Nilos's son? He could start a war.

Petra walked over to him and fell at his feet. 'Please. All you have to do is get on your horse and leave. Whatever happens now is on me. It is my choice, and if it all goes wrong, at least Xander will know he has a mother who loves him.'

Leksi could not bear the sight of her tear-stained face or the sound of her broken voice. Pulling her to her feet, he held her against him. He knew what it was to be a boy in need of a mother's love. He got eight years with his own, and he had no doubt those years contributed to the man he was today— or at least the man he could be. What would become of a boy who knew no love at all?

He kissed the top of Petra's head, still gripping her tightly.

'I will get him out.' The words spilled out as though he had planned to say them all along.

She looked up at him, eyes red from crying. 'I cannot ask you to do that. This is my mess.'

He wiped a tear with his thumb. 'It seems we're in this mess together. I can't leave you.'

'What of your orders?'

'I still have every intention of taking you to Archdale. After we get Xander.'

Her arms went around his middle, squeezing tightly. 'Thank you,' she breathed.

He exhaled. 'Don't thank me yet.' He needed to actually get the boy first. There were a number of ways he could do it, but time was not on their side, and the longer they remained in Corneo, the greater their risk of being discovered.

He decided on the most straightforward and quickest option. Holding her at arm's length, he said, 'You are going to stay here, and you are going to stay hidden until I return.'

She nodded. 'All right.'

'If I don't return before dusk, it means I've either been captured or I'm dead.'

She went to say something, but then closed her mouth.

'If that happens, it means they also have your son. Don't return to Paton under any circumstances. Make your way to Lord Belen's manor in the West, tell them who you are and what's happened. Prince Tyron will come to you as soon as he hears. Tell him everything, hold nothing back. You can trust him as you do me.'

She stared wide-eyed at him. 'You are speaking as though you might not come back.'

He kissed the top of her head. 'I'll be back, but we still need a contingency plan should anything go wrong.' He went to step away but she grabbed his arm.

'I do not want a contingency plan. I want you to promise me that you will return.'

'Stay hidden.'

Her eyes searched his. 'But you will come back?'

'That's the plan.'

'One of the plans. What of the contingency plan?'

He pulled her to him again, fearing he might crush her bones if he held her any tighter. 'I'm going to get your son, but I need to know you'll do as you're told, just once, if anything goes wrong.'

She nodded, sniffed. 'All right.'

He released her. 'At sunset, you leave here no matter what. You walk west until you reach the forest, then follow the treeline south all the way to Wripis.'

Another nod.

'Promise me.'

'I promise.'

He frowned, doubting her. 'This is a new promise, because you broke the last one.'

A smile flickered and faded. 'I swear to you, I will do as you have asked.' She paused, swallowing. 'But please come back to me.'

Leksi left Petra hidden in a cluster of trees about a forty-minute ride west of Paton. He rode at a steady canter back to the village, straight down the middle of the main road, all the way to the steps of the church. There were a few ways he could play it, but he had already decided on the most direct approach.

He first suspected something was amiss when the guards were nowhere to be seen. Tying up his horse, he climbed the steps and strode into the church. He was not overly surprised to discover Xander was not in there. There was every chance their encounter had raised enough suspicion to justify removing him.

Walking down the wide aisle, he stopped in front of the altar.

'Can I help you?' Father Gabot called to him, appearing in a doorway at the front of the church.

Leksi turned, trying to read his expression, looking for clues as to how the conversation might go. 'Yes. I'll get straight to the point. I've come for the orphan in your care.'

Father Gabot stiffened and was silent a moment. 'You're the man I met at the well earlier.'

'Correct. I'm not here to make trouble. Just hand over the boy and I'll be on my way.'

The priest crossed his arms. 'What do you want with the boy?'

Leksi stepped up to light a candle. 'I am taking him to his mother.'

The priest nodded. 'So it was her. They said she might come for him, but I told them no. A whore does not attach to their offspring the same way a mother in a union blessed by God's will does.'

'Do you know her story?'

'I know enough.'

'Do you know her father sold her at age *fifteen*? That she did not want to go?'

'She should have turned to God instead of away from him.'

Leksi bowed his head and whispered a quick prayer. Drawing his sword, he reached the priest in a few large steps. 'And there ends your sermon. Where is he?'

Father Gabot stared wide-eyed at the sword in his hand. 'You dare draw your weapon in God's house.'

'It has become clear to me that we're not going to see eye-to-eye on this particular matter.' He glanced over his shoulder towards the altar. 'Besides, I just had a chat with God. He knows I act for the good of the boy.'

The priest scowled at him. 'I have been trying to cleanse the child of her sins since his birth. If she really loved him, she would let me save him.'

'Why are you still talking?' Leksi raised his sword and brought the tip to the priest's neck. 'Take me to him.'

'You will burn in Hell for this.'

'Excellent, we can continue our discussion there.'

Father Gabot's face reddened. 'You are too late.'

'What do you mean?'

The priest swallowed against the blade. 'I asked him to repeat their conversation. He knows better than to lie. *Xander*. That was the name she said she would give him. A strange coincidence, don't you think?'

Petra had failed to mention that part of their conversation. 'It's the name she gave him at birth, so I would say it's quite fitting.' Leksi took another step towards him. 'I'm not messing around here. Where is he?'

Father Gabot shook his head. 'Like I said, you are too late.'

Leksi narrowed his eyes and increased the pressure of the sword. 'If you have harmed him in any way—'

'King Nilos's men took him. *Actual* soldiers,' he added, glancing down at Leksi's gold tunic. 'They left for Masville Castle an hour ago.'

The knight leaned in. 'How do I know you're telling me the truth?'

The priest looked genuinely offended by the question. 'Because I am a man of God.'

Leksi withdrew his sword, but his eyes remained on him for a moment longer. 'God must be shaking his head right now.' With that, he turned and strode from the church.

CHAPTER 23

*P*etra did her best impersonation of patience, waiting in the exact spot he had told her to, still and quiet. Leaning against a tree, she watched the sun on its journey west. It moved quicker than she would have liked, eventually reaching the horizon. She stopped watching then, staring into her lap. The prospect of losing light terrified her for so many reasons.

What have I done? King Nilos would show no mercy to the man who had kept her from him. Leksi would be executed, but probably tortured first to extract any information that might benefit them. Not by the king, of course; he never got his hands dirty. He had an army of men for that, including Prince Felipe, who did much of his less honourable work.

Insects chirped as though shouting at her. 'Get up,' they screamed. 'You promised him you would walk west.'

'It is not dark yet,' she replied to them, her forehead resting on her knees and eyes closed.

Press, press, press.

She focused on the pain in her fingers, and it helped for a while, but eventually, she was forced to open her eyes and blink into the darkness. Suppressing a sob, she pushed herself to her feet and looked around. He needed her to do this. If she could make it to Lord Belen's manor, someone would send for Tyron. He would know what to do. She could trust him.

Bending, she picked up the flask and blanket Leksi had left her, just in case. Perhaps he had known all along he could not succeed. She hugged the items to her chest as she made her way to the road, checking both directions before heading west. That was what he had told her to do, so that was what she did.

As she walked, she could not help but glance over her shoulder. Perhaps he had gotten lost, or Xander was refusing to go with him. Or maybe he was dead and her son taken once more.

She recalled the feel of Xander's small hand spread over hers, wondering if he had felt the outpouring of love.

The sound of hooves made her turn. She stared into the dark, waiting for the galloping horse to appear in front of her. She should have moved off the road, hidden herself, been smart, but hope anchored her feet to the ground. The horse came into sight, and she tried to focus on its rider. The animal charged towards her. When she realised it was not going to stop, she leapt out of its way.

Then she recognised Leksi, holding Xander in front of him.

'Leksi!' she called, running after the horse.

The mare slowed to a canter, to a trot, and finally stopped. He did not jump down, did not run to her. He did not even turn in the saddle to look in her direction. It was Xander who peered around the knight's arm, looking suitably terrified. She was out of breath by the time she reached them.

'Leksi,' she said again, then saw the arrow protruding from his back. 'Oh God,' she breathed.

'Take Xander,' he said.

She opened her arms and Xander leaned towards them.

'Are you all right?' she asked the boy, checking him for injury. He did not reply. She placed him on the ground and crouched down, holding his arms. 'I promise you I will explain everything soon, but first I need to take care of Sir Leksi. Do you think you can help me?'

The smallest of nods from him.

Petra stood just as Leksi slid from the saddle. She grabbed him, eyes on the arrow sprouting from his shoulder, then to the spread of blood on his side. So many questions, but only one of them urgent. 'What do you need me to do?'

He glanced behind them. 'We need to get off the road.'

She dragged his arm over her shoulders. That weight alone almost buckled her knees, but there was no way she would fall down while he needed her. 'Xander, can you please bring the horse?'

He stared blankly, clearly not connecting with the name she had used.

'It's all right,' Leksi reassured him. 'Be a good lad.'

Xander walked over to the horse and took the reins, guiding it some distance from the road because there was no tree cover nearby, only bare paddocks. Leksi eventually sank to the ground, taking Petra with him. She freed herself from his arm and kneeled beside him.

'First, I need you to take the arrow out,' Leksi said.

Petra nodded, outwardly calm while panicking inside. Standing over him, she took hold of the arrow with both hands. 'Any tricks I should know about?'

'Just do it quickly,' he said between clenched teeth.

She thought she might throw up. 'Do you need something to bite down on?'

He shook his head.

She turned to check on Xander, who still had not said a word. He was clutching the reins, eyes fixed on the arrow. 'Do you know what would be really helpful? If you could watch the road and let us know if you see any people or horses. Do you think you can do that?'

He nodded and turned to face the road. Petra drew in a breath and looked down at her hands. *Quickly*. With a sharp tug, the wooden arrow came free. Leksi's face contorted for a moment, but he did not make a sound.

'Good,' he said when he could finally speak again. 'Now help me out of these clothes.'

She moved as fast as she could, trying not to hurt him. When she peeled his shirt off, her hand went over her mouth. There was an oozing gash on his side. Pulling herself together, she pressed his bloodied shirt against the wound to stop the bleeding.

'Sword,' Leksi said, looking up at her. 'It always looks worse than it is. I'll be fine.'

He was not fine. He was pale and bleeding, and still he found it in him to comfort her. It was supposed to be the other way around.

She gave him a weak smile. 'Of course you will be fine.' Her eyes went to the shirt. So much blood.

Dear God.

'Keep pressure on it,' he said.

She nodded. That sounded simple enough. So why were her hands shaking so violently? She kept them pressed over the wound, terrified he would bleed out while she tried to figure out a way to secure it.

Xander appeared next to her carrying the towel from her saddlebag and a flask of water. 'I know how to comfort the dying,' he said, handing her the towel. 'Father Gabot takes me with him. Says it will keep me on a moral path.'

Petra blinked away his words. She would not let Leksi die.

Removing the shirt, she pressed the folded towel over the wound and watched as Xander gave Leksi a drink of water. When he was done, he took the soiled shirt from her, seemingly unfazed by the blood, and began wrapping it around the knight's shoulder, underarm and neck. Thankfully, Petra's hands finally stilled enough for her to secure it with the towel firmly in place beneath it.

'Get my tunic from the bag,' Leksi said. 'I'm not going home wearing gold.'

She ran to fetch it and helped him put it on while Xander continued to offer small sips of water.

'You need to drink lots when you lose blood,' he said in his small voice. 'That's what the physician told a woman before she died.'

Leksi patted his arm. 'I'm lucky you were here.'

Petra crouched in front of Xander. 'You are an incredible boy. Do you know that?' By the look on his face, she doubted he had ever received a kind word in his life.

'Sir Leksi says you're my mother,' he replied. 'Is that true?'

She took in his guarded expression. 'Yes.'

'It's a sin to lie.'

She wanted to hug him, reassure him, but she was a stranger in his eyes. 'I would not lie to you. I love you.'

'Father Gabot says my mother is dead.'

She gave a small shrug. 'Perhaps Father Gabot was misinformed, because I am very much alive.'

He studied her for the longest time before speaking. 'There are soldiers coming for you.'

Her eyes went to Leksi for confirmation. His dark expression told her that was true. 'What happened?'

'Seems they were expecting me.'

'There were guards in the trees,' Xander added. 'Sir Leksi killed them.'

'All except one, apparently,' the knight said, glancing at his wound. 'He'll be back, and he won't come alone.'

Petra's heart raced as she realised the danger they were in. They would kill Leksi and take her son.

She would not let them.

Turning back to Xander, she said, 'Do you think you can help me get Sir Leksi onto his horse? Then when we reach the manor, you can ask me as many questions as you like, and I promise to answer every one truthfully. Would that be all right?'

He studied her face before nodding.

Leksi pushed himself to his feet, swaying for a moment.

'You and Xander get on the horse,' he said.

'Absolutely not,' she replied, holding him steady. 'You and Xander will go on the horse.' They looked at one another. 'I can do this. Please.'

Leksi reluctantly nodded before half climbing, half falling onto the horse. Petra helped Xander up behind him.

'You need to hold on to the saddle,' she said before walking to the front of the horse and taking the reins. She tried to look confident as she walked in front of the animal, the one that was at least twelve times her weight. She gave the reins a gentle tug, and the horse began to follow her.

Her eyes went to Leksi, and she found him watching her.

'Are you all right?' he asked.

She managed a smile. 'You just remain upright and try to keep your laughter to a minimum.' She could not make out his mouth in the dark, but she hoped he was smiling. Turning back, she tried not to stumble on the uneven ground.

'Take the road,' he said. 'It's too hazardous out here in the dark.'

She led the horse back to the road. 'How far to Wripis?'

'At this speed? Around six hours.'

She closed her eyes. She could walk six hours for them. That was what you did for the people you loved—you walked until you fell down.

The first two hours passed quickly, Petra stopping only when Xander began nodding off. She was worried he would fall from the horse, so she placed him in front of Leksi, who cradled him with his good arm. As she stepped back, she let the image of the two of them cement in her mind. In that moment, standing on the side of a road in Corneo, she had everything she could possibly want.

'We need to keep moving,' Leksi said.

She returned to the front of the horse, and as she took the reins, light flashed in her peripheral vision. She turned and her heart stopped beating when she recognised the warm glow of torches in the distance.

'We need to get off the road,' Leksi told her. 'Now.'

Was it just her imagination, or did his voice sound weaker? The man slouched on the horse, cradling her sleeping son, would not be able to save them this time.

Her gaze returned to the torches, which shone a little brighter in the distance. She tugged on the bridle, pulling the horse off the road. They would not fight—they would hide.

But just as she stepped onto the thistle-covered grass, a familiar noise reached her, turning her blood cold.

Barking.

She froze, her breathing shallow. She turned to look at Leksi, and even in the dark, she could see his hopeless expression. 'Dogs?'

'They're hunting us,' he replied quietly. 'We can't outrun dogs.'

A ringing noise started in her ears, and she closed her eyes against it. Her mind raced, playing out what was about to happen. Leksi would die trying to defend them. Xander would disappear—again. Maybe they would return him to the priest, who would punish him for her new sins.

No, she would not let that happen.

She gathered the reins and placed them in his good hand, the one holding her son as though he were made of glass. Pressing her forehead to his leg, she said, 'Go. I will make sure the dogs follow me.'

'Don't be ridiculous. I'm not leaving you here,' Leksi stated, trying to sit a little straighter in the saddle.

There was strength in his voice, but she knew it would not last. She raised her eyes to him, her expression pleading. 'There is no time to argue. Please, take Xander and go.'

Dogs barked excitedly in the distance, and they both turned their heads to look. They were getting closer.

'Go,' she urged, her voice more insistent. 'Please. He will kill you. The two of you can make it if you go now.'

Leksi was shaking his head, but she could see him thinking it through.

'They'll catch you,' he said.

'I know.'

'They'll take you back to him, and he'll never let you go.'

She blinked and tears spilled down her cheeks. 'Promise me you will keep him safe.'

He shook his head again, glancing in the direction of the men. 'Shit.' His good hand clenched and unclenched. 'All right. Do exactly as I say. Grab something from the bag that belongs to you.'

She reached for the bag, fumbling with the strap until it opened, then rifled through it. 'A shoe?'

He turned to look at it. 'That will do. Rub it between your hands so it smells like you and my blood.'

She began working her messy hands over the detailed leather.

'Go back to the road and wait for the men. When they're close, drop the shoe and run north as fast as you can. Once the dogs have the scent, they'll follow you. Make sure they see you before you run, or they may follow the horse. Understand?'

She nodded, eyes on her beautiful sleeping son.

'It won't take them long to catch you, but it should give us enough of a head start.'

She stepped forwards and kissed his leg before reaching up to touch Xander's face. She wanted to wake him, say goodbye, but there was no time, and she knew it would be easier for Leksi if he remained asleep.

She stepped back from the horse, hugging the bloodied shoe to her. 'Go.'

They stared at one another in the dark for a moment.

'This is not over,' Leksi said. 'Don't let that bastard break you.' He faced forwards and pulled Xander closer before giving his horse a sharp kick, leaving her behind.

She watched them for a moment, willing them to go faster. Her chest squeezed, and when she tried to draw a breath, the pain was unbearable. It was the yelping of dogs that kept her upright. She could tell by their excitement that they were close. It was time to move.

Stepping onto the road, she waited as the torches continued moving towards her. Realising it would raise suspicion if she was just standing there waiting, she turned and jogged in the other direction. The dogs' excitement seemed to grow the closer they got.

'Over there!' someone shouted.

She immediately dropped the shoe and left the road, the running helping to clear her mind. With her feet pounding against the earth, she moved north in a straight line. Given how dark it was, she should have fallen or tripped, but nothing slowed her. When met with a fence, she squeezed through the rails with no thought as to what it was keeping in or out.

The men shouted, and she stopped for a moment to gauge the distance between them. Lights flickered, dogs whined. Slowly, the light shifted towards her, and the thunder of hooves grew louder.

Panting, she turned and ran.

CHAPTER 24

*T*hree mounted guards closed in around Petra, and the running hounds pulled against their restraints, snarling and growling just a few feet from her. She staggered back from them and slammed into a firm body, turning with a gasp and peering up at a fourth guard. The torch in his hand cast flickering light across his scowling face.

'Where are the others?' he asked, his tone impatient.

'I do not know. We got separated.'

The guard shook his head and looked up at the other men. 'She was leading us north. Two of you take the dogs south. They won't have gotten far.'

Her eyes sank shut for a moment, praying she had given them enough of a head start. The guard dragged her towards the horses, and with one swift motion he lifted her and plonked her in the saddle. Taking a length of rope, he tied her hands to one of the stirrup leathers.

'Is that really necessary?'

He snatched up the reins and turned the horse. 'You're lucky I'm not making you run behind me.'

She gripped the front of the saddle as he led her back to

the road. 'Where are you taking me?' she asked, already knowing the answer.

'Masville,' said the mounted guard behind her. 'King Nilos is eager to see you.'

She had known how it would all play out in the end. But as long as Leksi and Xander made it to the manor, it would all be worth it.

They travelled as a party of three, one soldier on horseback, the other on foot. The dogs had left with the other guards, and she hoped the fact that they had not caught up to them was a good sign.

They headed directly south, arriving in Ituco just before dawn. Petra hoped they would stop for a bit, but it was more of a pause. The men relieved themselves and passed a flask between them before offering it her. She drank the bitter water and handed it back.

A few hours later, they arrived in Chelia, but they did not stop at all. They walked along the main road, ignoring the gazes of passers-by who watched her like a criminal.

Just before noon, Masville Castle came into view, a bleak sight despite the high sun. The image made her nauseous, and for a moment, she thought she might actually be sick. She breathed deeply through her nose. Soon she would be brought before King Nilos; she had no idea what to expect from the man she had betrayed in so many ways.

Before she knew it, they were standing at the entrance of the castle. The click and screech of the portcullis rising made her skin crawl. The exhausted guards walked through without a word to anyone, waiting for the next gate to open. Petra jumped as the other one banged shut behind her. Through they went, right up to the front step of the castle. Petra's eyes went to the windows above, where she expected to see Nilos watching her, but the angle of the sun made it impossible to see.

Guards came forwards to take the horses while her escorts pulled her down and led her indoors. They were not too rough with her, no doubt aware that King Nilos would not take kindly to them putting their hands on her. Only he was allowed to do that.

She kept her head high as they marched her along the corridor towards the throne room. Her palms were sweating and her heart raced as the large doors swung open in front of her. There was no announcement, no instructions. In a few strides, she was standing in the centre of the room and soon abandoned. She watched her escorts flee, closing the doors behind them.

It took a moment for her eyes to adjust to the darkened room, but she knew he was in there with her because every hair on her body stood on end. She heard footsteps behind her, and she closed her eyes for a moment. Soon she would need to be brave.

'My queen has returned,' Nilos whispered.

Her eyes snapped open, and she drew a breath. 'Your Majesty.'

He stepped around her, coming to a stop directly in front. The first thing she noticed was his scent, familiar and bordering on repulsive. Her throat closed momentarily, but she forced herself to meet his gaze, and they stared at one another without saying a word. The sight of him unsettled her. His beard was long with patches of grey, and there was a strange light in his eyes. She could tell by his hollow cheeks that he had lost weight. There were new lines on his forehead, and she wondered if her disappearance had done all that to him.

'Did you really think you could leave me?'

What did he want to hear? And what lies was she prepared to say? 'I panicked.'

He reached out and grabbed her by the throat. 'You ran!' He lifted her to meet his face.

She held onto his arm and tried to remain calm. She would need to be smart if she wished to stay alive, because he was quickly crossing into dangerous territory. Her vision blurred.

'All that time apart,' she gasped. 'I do not want to fight.' His grip loosened slightly. 'I am back now. I am here.' It was not enough to make him let go. 'I am still yours,' she added. The words burned her mouth.

He let go and stepped back as though they had burned him also. She collapsed to the floor, her hands going to her neck as she drew greedy breaths, keeping her eyes down.

'To my *enemy* you turn in your hour of need.' He was pacing now. 'Have you not lived like a queen here?'

'Yes,' she whispered, then coughed.

'I had men sweeping the kingdom, searching for you. Then I learned you had crossed the border. Still I sent men. I was prepared to go to war to get you back.'

She closed her eyes. 'It was selfish. I see that now.'

'Selfish?' He closed the distance between them and pulled her to her feet by her wrist. '*Selfish?*' he shouted in her face. 'Come with me.'

He dragged her across the room towards the door and yanked it open, startling the guards on the other side. Without slowing, he continued down the corridor, his hand like a shackle on hers. She knew better than to pull away. If she was going to survive the next few days, she would need to submit to him.

She glanced down at her purple hand. He was holding her so tightly no blood was getting through. 'Where are we going?'

He spun, his face inches from hers. 'You do not get to ask questions!'

She stared down at her numb hand. 'I understand. I apologise, Your Majesty.'

He turned and continued towards the stairs, which he descended two at a time. She did her best not to fall, but she had not slept for more than a few hours in days, and her coordination was suffering.

They went down another passageway and then through a door that led to the eastern grounds. The king stepped off the path, pulling her across the freshly cut grass towards the wall.

Oh God.

'Your Majesty—'

His grip tightened. 'Do not speak unless I ask you a question.'

Tears surfaced, and she fought hard to contain them. Guards stared down at them from on top of the wall, and servants paused to watch them pass. Finally they came to a stop, and she winced when he yanked on her arm.

'Tell me what you see,' he said.

Confused, she looked around and then past him. She gasped at the sight, and her other hand went over her mouth.

'What do you see?' He dragged her closer to the wall. 'Tell me.'

She could not speak, only stare. Hanging from the wall were two corpses. It took her a moment to recognise the faces because birds had been feeding on them. A sob rose in her throat, and she could not contain it.

'Well?' he pushed.

She removed the shaking hand from her mouth. 'I see two dead bodies.'

He was staring intently at her. 'Who are they?'

She looked away from them, but another tug on her arm made her look back. 'The girl's name is Velma. She is a laundry maid.'

'*Was* a laundry maid. Now she is food for the crows. And the other?'

She stared up at the young boy, the one Velma said she was going to marry. Tears ran down Petra's cheeks. 'His name was Hugon. He delivered straw to the castle.'

'Now they are both dead.'

She pressed the palm of her hand to her forehead. 'You did not have to kill them. They knew nothing.'

The king turned to look at the bodies. 'In the end, it was the kind thing to do. They would never have walked again, or worked. They would have been nothing but a burden on their families.'

Petra forced her eyes up to the wounds on their knees and the strange angle of their legs.

'Spiked wooden blocks are placed behind and in front of the knee,' Nilos explained. 'Usually a good method for extracting information, though it proved somewhat fruitless in this instance.'

She turned to him. 'You... you *tortured* them?'

He took a step towards her. 'You asked them to betray their king. *You* tortured them.'

He released his grip on her wrist and she stepped back before turning to be sick on the grass. Her entire body was sweating. When she was done, she wiped her mouth with the back of her hand and turned to him.

'All right,' she said, her tone resigned. 'What now? What do you want me to do?'

He still had that crazed look in his eyes as he came towards her. Reaching up, he ran a finger down her cheek, neck and collarbone. 'You left me.'

She struggled to hold his gaze. 'Well I am back now. I am right here.'

His hand fell away. 'I could barely function with you gone. My sons thought I had gone mad.'

Another wave of nausea.

'Felipe told me I was being reckless, that I would lose my throne if I did not stop. He has barely spoken two words to me since I sent men into Syrasan. But you know why I did, do you not?'

'You wanted me back,' she whispered.

He shook his head. 'No, I *needed* you back. You took the air from my lungs the day you left.' He stared at her as though waiting for her to say something. 'And now I must find a way to forgive you, and you must find a way to earn back my trust.'

She was silent.

'You can start by telling me where the boy is.'

So they had not caught them. That meant Leksi was alive, or at least alive when he arrived. She tried not to let her relief show. She could not think about them, not while King Nilos's eyes burned through her. 'I have no way of knowing.'

'You should have let him alone.'

She drew a breath for courage. 'Father Gabot was not fit to raise him.'

His eyes were fixed on hers. 'Tell me you did not leave this life, leave me, for that bastard child.'

She flinched. 'He is my son. He is *your* son.' Her eyes pleaded with him. 'He deserves to be with people who will love him.'

The king's mouth pressed into a thin line. 'That boy has been a thorn in my side since his birth. The day he was born was the day I lost you.'

You never had me, she wanted to scream. Her hands were curled into fists, and she made an effort to relax them.

'You think he is better off in the hands of our enemy?' he asked when she did not reply.

His enemies, not hers. She had no doubt he was better off in Leksi's hands. Nothing the king said could make her second-guess her decision. 'I did what I thought was best at the time.'

He shook his head. 'When I find him, perhaps I will teach you a lesson that will last a lifetime,' Nilos said. He glanced at the bodies on the wall. 'It was Prince Tyron who helped you, was it not? His men protected you, and now they protect the boy.' He stared. 'The question is why?'

She held his gaze. 'The princess is a mother who understands what it means to be separated from your child. I threw myself at her mercy. She did not care that I was Corneon or that Xander is your son.'

'You are a fool, and you should pray I get him back before King Pandarus gets his hands on him.'

She shook her head. 'I could not let him grow up thinking he has to pay for my sins.'

He leaned closer. 'You have put a target on his back.' Looking her up and down, he added, 'Go clean yourself up. I will send for you later.'

CHAPTER 25

*A*ll eyes were on Leksi as he lay on his stomach in the crowded bedchamber, the physician leaning over him, tending to his wounds. Everyone was squashed into the stuffy room, looking between him and the frightened boy sitting at his side. Leksi knew he was the closest thing he had to a trusted adult at that moment.

'It's all right,' he reassured Xander.

The boy looked down at him. 'Are you going to die?'

'Not today,' Leksi replied with a wink.

Aldara stepped up to the bed and crouched in front of Xander. With a warm smile, she said, 'I bet you are hungry. Would you like to come with me and get some food?' She offered him her hand.

The boy glanced at Leksi, who gave him an encouraging nod. He hesitantly took the princess's hand and was led from the room.

Once they had gone, King Pandarus pushed off the wall he had been leaning against and ran a hand down his face.

'Just so I am clear with regards to the mess we are in, we

217

have gone from having the Corneon king's mistress to now having the bastard child they share?'

Tyron drew a long breath, his hands resting on his hips. 'He has what he really wants. The boy is just a pawn.'

Pandarus waved him off. 'So you keep telling me, but am I to assume he will come looking for the boy next?'

'He doesn't care about Xander,' Leksi said, wincing as the physician poured liquid on the wound. He had made it to Lord Belen's manor without too much difficulty, aside from nearly fainting a few times. Upon his arrival, he had let one of the men tend the wound, requested a fresh horse, and taken Xander straight to Archdale. Now he just needed to convince his king to let the boy remain in Syrasan.

'You are lucky the guards at the gates even let you in,' the king said, crossing his arms. 'I would have let you bleed out on the other side of the wall. It was Tyron who insisted I open the gate, despite the fact that you directly disobeyed orders.' Tyron went to speak and he raised a hand to silence him. 'If either of you tries to tell me Syrasan's most highly skilled knight was outsmarted by an unarmed woman who fled on foot, I will lock you in the tower myself.'

Tyron put his hands up in mock defence.

'I will not risk my men for this noble cause of yours,' Pandarus continued. 'I do not care if she aided your escape from Masville. That boy goes back at the first sign of trouble.' He took a step towards Leksi, pointing at him. 'And any further insubordination from you, and I will hand you over as well, let King Nilos sort you out.' Turning, he headed for the door. 'The child cannot stay here. I will not have my enemy's bastard living under my roof.' He opened the door and exited without bothering to close it behind him.

The physician finished tending Leksi's wound, looked between the two men, packed his bag and silently left the room.

Leksi turned his head to meet Tyron's disappointed gaze.

'He was not joking, you know. I practically had to beg to get that gate opened for you. What happened?'

Where to begin? He did not have it in him to lie to the man who was the closest thing he had to family. So he told him everything—excluding, of course, the part where he had broken his promise and slept with the mentor under his protection.

When he had finished talking, he waited for Tyron to say something. The prince's gaze seemed to go right through him.

'Oh no,' Tyron said after a long silence. 'Tell me you did not sleep with the king's mistress.'

Leksi hesitated a fraction too long before answering. Tyron exhaled loudly, then walked over to sit on the bed. He leaned his elbows on his knees and stared down at his boots.

'I have always believed who you invite into your bed is your business, but you have been overstepping some rather big boundaries of late. First Lord Belen's daughter—'

'That was different.'

'How?'

'It was just a bit of fun.'

'Lord Belen will be pleased to hear that.' Tyron looked at him. 'This is a new low for you. You were supposed to protect her, not take advantage.'

The words stung. Leksi propped himself up on his good arm. 'I didn't force myself on her, if that's what you're implying.'

'I never said that—'

'You just described my actions as *low*.'

'All right, careless, then.' Tyron stood. 'My fault though. I should have sent someone else.'

'You mean someone you trust?'

Tyron shook his head. 'I trust you, just not when it comes

to women.' He gave a small smile, no doubt hoping to lessen the blow of his words.

They rarely fought, and it was uncomfortable for both of them, but Leksi was not going to have the previous few months reduced to lack of impulse control. 'I'll leave with the boy as soon as I'm able.' His tone was cold. 'Take him somewhere safe.'

A smile tugged at Tyron's mouth. 'You know nothing of caring for a child.'

'So send a governess with me.'

'Why? So you can bed her?'

With his fists clenched, Leksi moved to sit up, wincing as he did so.

The smile left Tyron's face. 'What is the matter with you?' he asked, frowning.

What was the matter? He had ridden away and left her behind, knowing she would be caught. He had failed. And now he was going to make damn sure nothing happened to Xander.

He said none of those things aloud, instead shaking his head and opening his hands. 'I'm tired. I need rest.' He looked up at Tyron. 'Can I trust that Xander will still be here when I wake?'

The prince watched him for a moment. 'Why would you ask me that?'

'That is why Pandarus asked Petra to be brought here, is it not? So he could hand her over?'

Tyron's eyes darkened. 'There were Corneon soldiers swarming the kingdom. I wanted you to bring her here to regroup and figure out a plan.' He paused. 'I was also worried about you.'

Leksi drew his eyebrows together. 'Why?'

'Because your father died, and for some reason you chose

not to tell me.' He sighed. 'I was worried for good reason, it seems. What were you thinking, taking her into Corneo without permission? Or even a sensible plan, for that matter? There are easier ways to impress a woman.'

'You think I did all that to impress a woman?'

'I don't know anymore. Perhaps your grief impaired your judgement.'

Leksi waved him off. 'You know me well enough to know I wouldn't waste grief on that man.'

Tyron watched him. 'Actually, I think I know you a little better than that.'

Leksi slowly lay back down on the bed. 'I'm beginning to think you don't know me at all.'

The prince sighed. 'I cannot tell if this is your grief speaking or if you are just embarrassed by recent events. We are on the same side here.' He was quiet for a moment. 'Let's speak after you have slept. I know what lack of sleep can do to a man's mind.'

Leksi closed his eyes. 'Is there any way we can get an update on Petra's whereabouts?'

'We both know the king has her by now. But I will see what I can find out.'

Leksi hung his good arm over his face to try and ease the pounding in his head. 'Thank you.' The last thing he heard was footsteps headed for the door before sleep took him.

Leksi woke to blazing eastern light streaming through the windows. That meant he had slept for an entire day and night.

He propped himself up on one elbow and looked around the room. Charis was asleep in a chair next to him. Leksi picked up his pillow and threw it at his squire. Charis startled awake and sat up straight in the chair, his gaze darting about in confusion before finally settling on Leksi.

'My lord!' he said, scrambling to his side. 'Thank God you're alive.'

Leksi swung his legs over the edge of the bed and glanced at his bandaged shoulder, which continued to throb. 'Of course I'm alive. When did you get here?'

'Last night. Lord Yuri and Lady Hali brought me.'

'They're here?'

The squire nodded. 'Lady Hali is in the bailey with Petra's son. She's teaching him to play chess.'

Her name stung him. He needed to go see Xander. He would probably be overwhelmed by strangers gushing over him.

As he stood, Tyron's words returned to him. *What do you know about caring for a child?* He would soon find out.

'Help me change,' Leksi said.

Charis sprang into action, fetching clothes and filling a basin with water. When Leksi had finished dressing, they headed outside, where he found Hali and Aldara seated on a blanket with all the children, including the king's. He watched Xander for a moment before wandering over to join them.

Aldara stood when she saw him approaching.

'How are you feeling?' she asked.

'Fine, thank you.'

'Sir Leksi,' Hali said, running her fingers over Xander's hair before standing. She spoke in a low voice. 'How many lives do you have?'

'A few, it seems.'

Hali let out a breath. 'What an incredible woman Petra is, returning to that sadistic man so her son could have the life she wanted for him.'

Why did every mention of her name feel like his wounds were being reopened? He watched Xander, saying nothing.

'She figured a way out once before. Perhaps she will do it again,' Hali added.

Aldara looked down at the children. 'King Nilos will not be letting her out of his sight any time soon. If he genuinely loved her, I could envision an end to her sentence, but from what I witnessed during my time at Masville, the king's feelings stem from a very unhealthy place.'

He really wished they would stop talking.

'I think the fact that he sent armed men into Syrasan supports your theory. He sounds like a madman.'

Leksi took an involuntary step back from them, and both women looked at him in surprise.

'Are you all right?' Aldara asked.

'Of course he's not all right,' Hali said. 'Our knight took quite a shine to the mentor. You should've seen the two of them together.'

Leksi took another step back. 'Where's Tyron?' he asked, looking at Aldara. 'I need to speak with him.'

'He will be along shortly,' she replied. 'We were thinking the two of you could return east with us. You would remain his guardian, of course. I believe that is what Petra wanted.'

There was that name again. He looked down. 'Tyron agreed to that?'

'Of course.'

Before she could say anything else, Tyron came striding across the lawn towards them. Leksi watched him approach, unsure what to expect from the conversation.

'How are you feeling?' Tyron asked.

'Fine.'

'Has the physician seen you this morning?'

'Not yet. Any news?'

Tyron nodded. 'Some. King Nilos has sent additional men

to the West, no doubt searching for the boy. Lord Belen suspects they are preparing to breach the border. It is not safe to take Xander to Wripis.'

'I agree,' Leksi said.

Xander got to his feet and wandered over to stand with Leksi. 'When will my mother be here?'

All eyes went to him as Leksi crouched beside him.

'She really wanted to be here with you, but King Nilos needs her at Masville right now.'

He appeared disappointed. 'What about Father Gabot? Is he coming?'

Leksi swallowed. 'No. Father Gabot is not the right person to care for you.'

'I don't mind. Will you take me home?'

'What if Sir Leksi took care of you?' Hali asked in her most uplifting tone.

Xander turned to her. 'Is he my father?'

Leksi cleared his throat. 'No, but I'm your guardian until your mother decides otherwise.'

Curious eyes returned to him. 'But you love her?'

An enormous question asked in front of a very attentive audience. He was rarely at a loss for words, but none of his usually witty deflection came to him.

'I saw her crying. She didn't want to say goodbye to you.'

Leksi stared into the boy's wise, inquisitive eyes. Sharp and intelligent, just like his mother's. 'I thought you were asleep. Why didn't you say something?'

'Because she was already crying.'

Leksi cleared his throat. 'Would you like to stay with me for a while?'

'Where?'

Leksi looked up at Tyron. 'I could take him to the coast, back to the house.'

'We would be nearby to help,' Hali offered.

Tyron glanced at Aldara before looking down at Xander. 'Would you like to go see the ocean with Sir Leksi?'

Xander thought for a moment. 'Will my mother know where to find us when she's done?'

A sniff from Hali, and Tyron's arm went around his wife. Princess Zelia chose that moment to upturn the chess table onto the blanket, squealing with delight as she did so. The other children complained, but no one moved.

'Yes,' Leksi said with a nod. 'She knows where to go, but it'll probably just be us for some time.'

His expression said he was still not completely sold on the idea. 'Is there a church at the ocean? We'll need to pray—a lot.'

'Veanor has one of the most beautiful churches in the kingdom,' Hali said.

'Is that true?' Xander asked, eyes never leaving Leksi.

He had no idea. He had been inside every drinking house and tavern in the village, but he had never stepped foot inside the church. 'I've heard good things.'

Xander nodded. 'All right.'

Aldara left to tend the children who had begun screaming at one another, and Tyron placed a hand on Leksi's shoulder. 'It's settled, then. Just tell me what you need.'

There was warmth in the gesture, but Leksi found himself pulling away as he stood. 'I think we'll be just fine for now.' He smiled down at Xander. 'The sooner we leave, the sooner I can teach you to swim.' He took hold of the boy's shoulders and turned him away from the group.

'Leksi,' Tyron called to his back.

He turned.

'I will organise for a physician to visit each day and tend that wound.'

Leksi nodded. 'Thank you.'

He walked away with a heavy feeling sitting low in his gut. Something had broken inside of him.

Did he love her? That was what the boy wanted to know.

The answer was a soul-crushing yes.

CHAPTER 26

*L*eksi had just finished with the physician when there was a knock at his door.

'Enter,' he called, not looking up from the bag he was packing. It would only be Charis or Tyron.

Another knock. He stilled and frowned at the door before making his way over to it. When he opened it, his eyebrows rose in surprise. Standing there alone was Tyron's sister, Queen Cora. He leaned his good shoulder against the door-frame, watching as she assessed him. Her hands were folded neatly in front of her, and she looked every bit the queen in her sheer lace dress and gold crown. Her eyes finally met his.

'You are supposed to bow before the Queen of Zoelin,' she said, her tone even.

His mouth twitched. 'My apologies, Your Majesty.' He stepped back from the door and bowed. 'I heard you were visiting, but I didn't realise you were still here. Your husband must be missing you by now.'

'He copes rather well in my absence.'

He nodded. 'You look different.'

'How so?' she asked, raising her chin a little higher.

He studied her face. 'A little defeated, perhaps. How is married life?'

'Exactly how I imagined it to be—very fulfilling.'

'I see you kept your dry sense of humour.'

She held up her right hand. A pattern of ink wound her middle finger and spread over the back of her hand. 'Plus I have the pleasure of being stabbed with needles and painted like a cheap piece of canvas.'

He tried not to laugh. 'Your husband honours you with his marks.'

She rolled her eyes. 'He likes to watch, and he enjoys it far too much.'

Leksi smiled. 'And I bet you stare him down the entire time.'

'You know me well.'

He glanced over his shoulder. 'I would invite you in, but that would hardly be appropriate.

'Not with *your* reputation, no.'

His gaze returned to her. 'What can I do for you, Queen Cora of Zoelin?'

She looked past him, as though checking if anyone else was in there with him. 'I hear you have possession of King Nilos's illegitimate son.'

'What of it?'

Her head tilted. 'Why?'

'His mother asked that I take care of him.' She was watching him with a more serious expression than he was used to.

'You seem an odd choice of guardian.'

'She trusts me.'

There was silence as she processed his comment. 'I see. She is in love with you.'

He shifted against the door. 'Why would you assume that?'

One shoulder lifted in a shrug. 'Most women fall in love with you eventually.' She looked away for a moment. 'That still does not answer my question of why you agreed. I have known you most of your life, and you generally flee from responsibilities unrelated to war. I imagine there are far more suitable guardians up to it.'

'*I* am up to it.'

She eyed him. 'Why is everyone falling over themselves for this woman? Is she some sort of witch?'

He shook his head. 'I'm surprised you haven't met given how much time you spend with your new friends.'

'I would not remember if I had. They are all the same to me—expensive dresses and loose morals.'

Leksi looked down, his face void of any humour.

'Perhaps I saw her once during our last trip to Corneo. I thought it unusual that the king would have the castle's mentor at his side. It was even more unusual the way his eyes followed her every move. That form of lust is a disease, and it will be his undoing.'

Leksi swallowed. He was trying not to think about her back at that place, under the king's control once again. It did things to his mind.

An image flashed of her lying in the mud, clutching her stomach as she laughed. That was how he wanted to remember her, but fear never left him. He knew the only way she would survive would be to retreat so far within herself, there would be no chance of ever recovering the woman he had fallen in love with.

'There's no denying her beauty' was all he could say.

Cora watched him for a moment and then tutted. 'I suspect she might be the first woman who has ever truly gotten to you, Sir Leksi. Am I right?'

Again, no words came. Where were the inappropriate jokes and smutty humour when he needed them?

'Oh, dear,' Cora said. 'It seems we are *both* a little defeated.'

Cora had always been good at reading people, and he felt utterly exposed in that moment. 'Is there something specific you wanted, Your Majesty?'

Her eyes searched the corridor before replying. 'I suggest you do not push Tyron away. He is your best asset at the moment. I would hate to see you lose your life or be locked up for treason.'

He searched her for sincerity. 'I appreciate your concern.'

She swallowed. 'Take it from me, there is nothing more dangerous than an angry king.'

She seemed vulnerable in that moment, a rare sight.

'I'm very sorry if I've treated you poorly over the years. Despite your vile nature, you probably don't deserve my endless taunting.'

'You dare call the Queen of Zoelin vile?' Her eyes shined at him. 'You better hope my husband does not hear of your disrespect. His temper is worse than mine.'

'Which is exactly why I didn't invite you into my room.'

She straightened and tucked her inked hand beneath her unmarked one. 'It was good to see you, Sir Leksi.' She bowed her head.

'And you, Your Majesty.' He bowed low. 'Say hello to your husband for me.'

She went to leave and then stopped. 'I am on my way to Chelia, where I am to accompany my husband to the flag tournament.'

Leksi's breath caught. 'You're going to Corneo?'

She nodded. 'As you are aware, Zoelin is neutral with regards to any squabbles between Syrasan and Corneo.'

He got her meaning. 'Of course.'

'And my husband does not need additional reasons to distrust me.'

'I understand.' He knew King Jayr well enough to know any secrets he exposed would not end well for her.

Her eyes moved over his face. 'I often write to my family, updating them on my news. Naturally, every letter is read by someone before it leaves Onuric Castle, so I am always careful about the information I include.' Her fingers moved over the ink on her hand. 'I know my brother will be happy to share any news he believes might be of interest to you in the coming months.'

Leksi held onto the doorframe, demonstrating his understanding with a single nod.

'Good day, Sir Leksi,' she said before floating off down the corridor.

'Safe travels, Your Majesty,' he called after her.

CHAPTER 27

*P*etra thought she was prepared for her old life. She thought she would sink back into her role, like putting on worn boots that had moulded to fit your feet over the years.

What she was not prepared for was change.

'*You* are the new mentor?' she asked Nyla for the second time.

The former Companion nodded, trying to appear more confident than she likely felt at that moment. Nyla had belonged to Prince Kyril, who would now select another at the tournament. Two years with the same Companion was almost a record at Masville.

While Nyla was more than capable of performing the role, it begged the question of why King Nilos had chosen to replace Petra when he was so determined to get her back. She was not surprised to hear he had sold his own Companion in her absence. It had been a disaster from the onset.

'I am more than capable of mentoring,' Nyla said a little defensively.

'I agree.'

'I have been in the role a few months now.'

Petra looked around the room. 'So you were given the role of mentor, with no one to mentor?'

Nyla smiled her best Companion smile. Or was it her best mentor smile?

'That all changes today,' she said.

Petra was still in her robe. She had just taken her second bath since arriving. Bath, sleep, bath. At some point she would need to eat.

She looked around the dressing room, spotting the impractical gown laid out on the chair for her. She wished she could put on one of the plain cotton dresses she had worn in Veanor. Of course, Leksi would have loved the sheer fabric. For him, she would wear it. She could almost picture his face as he looked her up and down.

'What changes today?' she asked absently, trying to pick up the conversation again.

'The flag tournament is tomorrow, and both princes will be selecting new Companions.'

Petra's head throbbed. 'Wonderful. And the king?' she asked dryly.

Nyla lifted the dress and held it up so Petra could see it properly. It was blue silk with jewels sewn along the plunging neckline. 'King Nilos picked it out himself. You will be accompanying him to the tournament.'

Petra stared at the gown, imagining the king's hungry gaze on her. 'He wants me to attend the tournament?' She looked to Nyla. 'I only returned yesterday, and now he expects me to play Companion for the day?'

Nyla swallowed. 'Not for the day.'

It took Petra a moment to register her meaning, or perhaps her mind was blocking the sentiment. 'I see.' She locked her knees so they would not buckle beneath her. 'The king is not getting a Companion, because... he already has one.'

Nyla tried to smile. 'You understand. It just never works out with the others. His first choice has always been *you*.'

It was meant as a compliment, but Petra had to turn away from the words. 'It does not work with me either. Perhaps you have both forgotten that. I will just end up pregnant.'

'We are starting you on the herbs today.'

Petra fought the urge to put her hands over her ears. 'They do not work on me. That is why I have a five-year-old son.'

Nyla remained composed, like a good mentor. 'We will find a way to make this work.'

It took Petra a moment to get control of her emotions, her throat tight and her ears starting to ring. 'He has already taken nine years of my life. No other Companion has suffered as long as I have.'

'It is an honour—'

'Stop speaking before I pick up that chair and throw it at you.'

Nyla paled. 'What on earth has happened to you? You must remember your place.'

This was not her place. Her place was at the edge of the world in a run-down house they had turned into a home. Her place was near cleansing water, ocean spray and salty air, with Leksi and the tiny boy he had carried across the border. It was so painfully clear.

'I know my place' was all she said. She stared at the dress for a moment, thinking, then removed her robe.

Nyla's eyes widened in surprise. 'Oh. You want to try it on?'

She wanted to set it alight. 'Yes,' she lied. 'And I need you to paint my face and fix my hair.'

Nyla looked a little unsure. 'Why?'

'Because I am going to speak with the king.' She watched the conflict play out on Nyla's face.

'You cannot just go to him. You know how this works. If you need to communicate something, you do so via me.'

Petra's face was blank. 'If you think he would prefer to speak with you, then by all means. You may discuss the terms of the arrangement on my behalf.'

Nyla opened her mouth, then closed it again. She glanced at the door. 'This is not a negotiation,' she said with little conviction.

'If the king wants me as his Companion, then I have something I want in return.'

Sighing, Nyla said, 'If you go in making demands, you will only do more harm.'

'If he wants me as his Companion, he will agree.'

Nyla crossed her arms in front of her. 'If he wants you as his Companion, it will be so. Nothing has changed in your absence. He will do as he has always done.'

She was wrong. Everything had changed. Petra had grown up. 'The king has never truly had me.'

Silence.

'Would you prefer to have the conversation on my behalf?' Petra asked.

Nyla's arms fell to her sides. 'I really hope you know what you are doing.'

~

Petra entered the king's bedchamber knowing she would have to give the performance of her life. He had just finished dressing, and an empty tray sat on the table next to the bed, indicating he had not been up long.

He froze when he laid eyes on her, his gaze travelling shamelessly down her body. Despite a difficult few days, she was still displaying all the benefits of her time in Veanor. Her curves were rounder, her face full, and her skin bronzed. She let him look for as long as he needed in order for his resentment and anger to dissolve, even going so far as to turn, slowly, so he could admire her from all angles.

'My queen,' he said, his voice already thick with lust.

'Do you like the dress?'

He shook his head. 'You are going to need to cover yourself for the walk back to your quarters to stop me losing my mind imagining the guards' eyes on you.'

'As you wish, Your Majesty.'

He frowned, as though suddenly suspicious. 'What are you doing here in my bedchamber, dressed like that?'

'Nyla tells me you wish to have me as your Companion once more?'

He nodded. 'We belong together.'

She watched him for a moment, trying to read him. 'I worry…' She broke off and looked down.

He took a step towards her. 'Worry about what?'

Her eyes returned to him. 'That I might not be worthy of your affections. I have made some mistakes these past few months.' His eyes softened. 'I worry you will not be able to forgive me.'

He came to her then, gripping her shoulders, his thumbs kneading her skin.

'Will we be able to move past the mess?' she asked, the words bitter in her mouth. It took all her strength not to pull from his grip. His hands were too smooth, and it made her think of Leksi's callused ones.

'Enough,' Nilos said. 'You are my everything. That is why I tore the kingdom apart looking for you.'

She watched him through painted lashes, aware of the effect she was having on him. He cupped her chin, and rather than stiffen, she closed her eyes and turned into his touch.

He groaned and pulled her close. Then instead of going limp beneath his grip, she placed her hands on his chest, preparing herself for what would come next. His mouth crashed into hers and she parted her lips, despite the screams of protest inside her.

When she could not take it anymore, she pulled back and looked at him. 'You really want me as your Companion?'

'Yes,' he breathed. His grip tightened on her as he moved to kiss her again.

She placed a hand to his chest to stop him. 'I need something from you.'

He was breathing hard. 'Anything.'

Her expression turned serious. 'I want you to call off the search for Xander.' She mustered her remaining courage. 'I want you to leave him alone.' She felt him start to withdraw and she leaned in. 'If I can just be free of it all, I can open my heart to you again.' Her hands wound around his neck, repulsed by the feel of his coarse skin. 'Will you do that for me, my king?' She leaned towards his hungry mouth, waiting for his reply.

His hands went to her waist, tugging on her hips. 'And then you will be mine? Body and soul?' He all but moaned the words.

'Yes,' she murmured, closing her eyes so he would not see the repulsion in them.

'And you will never leave me again?' He licked her painted lips and she winced inwardly.

'If you give me your word and free up that space in my mind, I could be yours until death.'

He took a handful of her skirt and begun tugging her towards the bed.

'You must give me your word,' she said.

He stopped and looked at her. 'As you wish, my queen.'

She searched his eyes, trying to see if he was speaking the

truth. She could not tell. 'You would not lie to your queen, would you?'

His legs trembled, clearly enjoying this version of her. 'Please,' he said hoarsely. 'Let me have you.'

She stepped closer to him and brushed her hips against his. 'I am afraid we will need to wait a few weeks for the herbs to work.'

His red face collapsed. 'God, give me strength,' he groaned.

'The last thing we want is a pregnancy.' He dragged a hand down his face as she took a step back. 'Until tomorrow, Your Majesty.' She curtsied low, eyes never leaving his.

Only once the door was closed behind her did she breathe again. She wiped at her mouth as the guard watched on. One way or the other, the king would have her, so it might as well be on her terms.

Straightening, she walked off down the corridor in the direction of the Companions' quarters.

She was going to need another bath.

CHAPTER 28

*T*he wagon swung gently as Petra stared out the open window at the families making their way to the tournament on foot. Mothers carried young babies strapped to them, and the fathers carried smaller children on their shoulders when their legs had finally given up. They stopped to bow or curtsy as they watched the wagon pass them.

Petra smiled weakly through the window. The families lining the road would have likely skipped their morning meal to keep what little food they had for the event, but at least they were together.

A hand moved on Petra's thigh, and she glanced down at it, a cold sensation filling her. The king usually rode on horseback, but upon learning that his wife would not be attending due to yet another headache, Nilos had insisted they travel together. His hand had not left her all morning.

'Have I told you how lovely you look?' he said, watching her.

Every five minutes since beginning the journey. She turned to

239

him, mustering a smile. 'Yes, you have mentioned it once or twice.'

He squeezed her leg. 'Can you feel it?'

His fat hand like an anchor on her leg? Yes, she could feel it. 'Feel what?'

'Hope,' he said. 'A chance at the future we imagined before.'

It was an incomplete sentence, missing the *'before Xander was born'* part. She was certainly not going to bring the boy up. Any mention of him would jeopardise her plan. They had a deal. If he left Xander alone, let him stay with the guardian she had chosen, then she would be the Companion he so desperately wanted.

She hoped the lie would get easier.

'Until death,' she had promised.

He continued to watch her, and she continued to meet his gaze. That was how it would be from now on.

A woman approached the wagon, pulling Petra from her thoughts. She ran alongside the carriage, asking for food. Eyes bulged from the pinched face. It was easy to forget what the starving looked like when you lived in a castle.

'Just close the curtain,' the king said, looking out the other window.

Had there been any food to give, Petra would have handed it over.

'Have you a coin to give instead?' she asked, turning to him with a sweet smile.

He exhaled, as though the suggestion alone was hard work, then retrieved a coin pouch from inside his tunic. He handed her a small silver coin, enough to buy a few potatoes but not the meat she desperately needed. Petra leaned out the window and dropped it into her outstretched hand.

'God bless you,' the woman called as the wagon pulled away from her.

'They are like rodents,' Nilos said. 'You watch, now they will all come running with their hands out.' He knocked the wall of the wagon with one knuckle and the horses sped up.

Petra had not been to a flag tournament in years, and she was surprised at how much expense had been poured into the event when people were starving throughout the kingdom. The berfroises were dressed in lavish fabric, and tables were laden with food and wine. Of course, it was all for the noble guests. The common people arrived with a poor man's version of a picnic, watching the untouched food from afar.

The wagon stopped directly in front of the berfrois. The princes had arrived ahead of them and were moving among the guests, wearing gold tunics and expensive swords. Their gazes flicked to the crowd, where fathers were already shamelessly parading their daughters in front of the berfroises.

Petra frowned when she spotted King Jayr. He was hard to miss, sitting a full head higher than the other guests, his inked skin a stark contrast to the noblemen of Corneo.

'You did not mention King Jayr would be attending,' she said, fitting her mask over her face.

Nilos leaned forwards. 'Did I not? He is here with his wife.'

Petra searched for the queen among the guests. Despite her feathered mask, she was easily identifiable thanks to her crown and striking beauty. The men snuck glances while her husband kept a trained eye on her, clearly aware of the attention she drew.

Petra leaned back as the door opened, remembering what Hali had told her. She wondered if the queen had managed to let go of her feelings for Leksi. A man like King Jayr would not tolerate his wife's attention wandering elsewhere.

It seemed she had a few things in common with the queen.

Petra stepped down from the wagon and waited to take the king's arm. They made their way up the steps of the berfrois towards the fake smiles and forced conversation. Her red mask did not protect her from the judgemental glances of the noble women, but she tried to focus on whichever guest Nilos was flaunting her in front of, smiling warmly and saying all the right things.

Eventually they reached King Jayr. The men standing with him bowed and excused themselves.

'Good day, Your Majesty,' she said in Zoelin. She knew he was comfortable speaking in their language, but good etiquette was to begin the conversation in his language and then follow his lead. 'How was your journey?'

'Uneventful,' he replied in Corneon.

Petra glanced at the queen, who was now making her way over to them. 'I hear there are some excellent horses being displayed today.'

The king offered a hand to his wife as she stepped up next to him. She took it briefly before letting go.

'Your Majesty,' Petra said, curtsying before the queen.

Cora gave her a small nod before turning her attention to King Nilos. 'I was very sorry to hear your wife is not feeling well. A shame she has to miss the fun.'

Nilos cleared his throat. 'Unfortunately, she is prone to long spells in bed.'

'How dreadful,' Cora replied, almost sounding genuine.

'Lucky for you, Corneo has no shortage of beautiful women to accessorise with,' Jayr said.

Nilos gave a courteous laugh. 'Quite true.'

Neither woman joined in the laughter.

'I hear you have been visiting with your family in Syrasan,' Nilos said to Cora.

The cuffs on her wrists shifted, making a chiming noise. 'Yes, I had a rather extended stay at Archdale.'

Petra's pulse quickened. She knew Leksi would have gone to the castle if he were well enough for the journey. Of course, she could not ask after him. Companions were not supposed to converse with female guests at all, and the question would only raise suspicions.

'It seems she would rather be there than at Onuric with me,' Jayr added.

'I suppose you miss your family,' Nilos said.

Cora smiled politely. 'My mother has grown rather accustomed to having me around. The separation is hardest on her.'

'My queen likes her freedom,' Jayr commented, watching his wife.

'I trust your family are in good health,' Nilos said, feigning interest.

'Quite,' Cora replied. 'The family continues to grow.' She glanced at Petra. 'There seems to be a new child every time I visit.'

The timing of the glance made Petra wonder if perhaps the last part had been added for her benefit, but she could not imagine the queen passing on any information. It was well-known that she despised Companions of all varieties.

'And yet I hear Masville Castle is the place to be of late,' Jayr said, a smirk on his face. 'A dead Companion, a runaway mentor, and servants hanging from its walls.'

Nilos tried to laugh the comment off. 'Do not believe everything you hear.'

Cora threaded her hand through her husband's arm. '*This* is Masville's mentor, is it not?' she asked, nodding at Petra.

Nilos placed his free hand over Petra's. 'She is more like a queen.'

There was a brief silence before Cora said, 'Lucky your wife is not around to hear you say such a thing.'

Petra fought the urge to pull herself free and step away from him. 'I believe King Nilos meant it as a compliment.'

'I think every king has entertained the idea of multiple queens,' Jayr said.

'My husband is joking, of course,' Cora said, her expression sweet. 'He can barely handle the one he has.'

A horn sounded, signalling the start of the event and saving them all from the awkward conversation.

'Come,' Nilos said, gesturing to the adjoining berfrois. 'I will show you to your seats.'

'First, I shall need some wine,' Cora told him, withdrawing her arm.

Jayr leaned close to her ear. 'Just remember there is nowhere for you to sleep it off.'

The queen stiffened.

'I can fetch you some refreshments, Your Majesty,' Petra said. 'If you take a seat, I will bring them to you.'

Cora waved her off. 'I would prefer to pour my own wine.' She glanced at her husband. 'I will be right along.'

Jayr bowed to his wife before following after King Nilos. Cora and Petra stood staring at one another for a moment.

'This way,' Petra said, gesturing for her to go ahead.

Cora sauntered off in the direction of the table at the back of the berfrois. Most of the guests had already filled their cups and were either seated or standing to the side, ready for the first rider to enter the field.

The women stopped in front of the table, and Cora lifted each jar of wine, gently swirling and smelling them.

'Your son was at Archdale,' Cora said, her eyes on the table.

Petra stopped breathing. 'Was?' She barely got the word out.

'There are Corneon soldiers preparing to cross the border, so they have taken him east.'

Petra's mind raced. So many questions, and just a few seconds to ask them.

'King Nilos called off the search yesterday.'

Cora poured red wine into a cup, filling it much higher than was polite for a lady of her standing. 'Did he tell you that?'

'Yes.'

The queen glanced at her before bringing the cup to her mouth and taking a long sip. 'Does he seem like an honest man to you?' She tutted. 'It seems the most educated women in the kingdom still require educating.'

She would deal with King Nilos later. 'Is he all right?'

Cora took another drink. 'I assume so. I do not make a habit of liaising with the strays.' She topped her cup up and turned to leave. 'I think I can find my own way back.'

As she went to leave, Petra whispered, 'I was enquiring after Sir Leksi.'

Cora stopped.

'Did he...' She struggled to get the words out. 'Does he live?'

The queen took a long drink before replying. 'It will take more than an arrow or sword to kill that man.'

Petra let out the breath she had been holding but could do nothing to stop the shaking in her hands as relief washed over her. 'Thank God.'

Cora studied her for a moment. 'Now you better return to your king and play queen.'

Petra drew a slow breath to gain control of herself. Then, looking at Cora, she raised her chin. 'After you, Your Majesty.'

They walked to their seats, applause breaking out around them as the first rider finished. They stepped into the royal berfrois and Cora took the vacant seat beside her husband.

Petra looked around for the king and, not finding him, turned to the adjacent berfrois.

'He is speaking with the priest,' King Jayr said, eyes on the field.

Petra's eyes went to him. 'Which priest?'

He turned his head to her, his expression suggesting he neither knew nor cared.

She smiled. 'Thank you. I am sure he will be along shortly.'

She took a seat but could not shake the uneasy feeling rising inside her. She discreetly searched for him amid the spectators, finally spotting him with two guards near the stables. He was talking to someone, and her eyes widened when she recognised Father Gabot. The sight made her nervous, her concern validated when she noticed Nilos's rigid posture.

She turned back, trying to watch the field. Her hands even came together in a clap when the next rider entered, but her eyes kept returning to the king, and that time, she found him looking back at her. She swallowed, struggling to read his face from that distance.

Nilos leaned towards the guard on his left, giving him instructions, and then the guards marched off in the direction of the berfrois. Her heart pounded a little harder in her chest, and her fingers gripped the arms of her chair. Closer they came, and she had the distinct feeling they were coming for her.

She faced the field, aware of the men crossing her vision and then climbing the steps. She blinked and turned her head to watch them approach. Their gazes were fixed on her, and she tried to imagine what on earth Father Gabot could have said that would make the king send guards to collect her rather than simply coming to her himself.

The men stopped next to her chair. 'Come with us,' the one closest instructed.

She did not move. 'Come with you where?' She was surprised by the calm in her voice given how she felt inside.

Without responding, one guard grabbed her arm, pulling her from the chair.

'Take your hands off me,' she said, trying to yank free.

'The king has ordered you back to Masville,' said the man. 'Under guard.'

She turned, searching for the king in the spot she had found him earlier, but he was no longer there. 'Where is he?'

Silence as they tugged her away.

'Never a dull moment,' King Jayr said, smirking to his wife.

Cora was not looking at him. She was staring at Petra, her usually cold expression dissolving into something resembling concern. But she said nothing, did nothing. They just looked at one another for a moment before Petra was led away.

All eyes were on her as she was marched from the berfrois, a guard holding each arm as if she would try to flee at any moment. How far did they think she would get if they let go of her? The entire thing was absurd and unnecessary, yet her stomach roiled with each step in the direction of the waiting wagon. It was not the royal wagon, but an unmarked one.

She looked around, but for who? Leksi was not there. Her knight could no longer come to her rescue. She had made sure of that. All she had were the memories of him—his dark, smiling eyes, clever jokes and infectious smirk. His eternally warm hands and the feel of his hard chest and firm grip. Gone was the comfort. She was no longer safe and untouchable.

The guards practically lifted her into the wagon before

shutting the door. She turned and watched through the window as they mounted their horses, preparing to ride alongside her.

'Move out,' called one of the men, and the wagon lurched forwards, forcing her to take a seat.

Her hands went over her face, but she did not cry. She could fix this. She just needed to get in front of the king and find out what had sent his fear spiralling.

She dropped her hands to her thighs, damp palms pressing on expensive silk. A guard trotted next to the window, blocking her view of the outside world. She felt claustrophobic. It was too much like a prison.

She closed her eyes, letting her mind escape for a moment. She let it wander where it needed to go—to the ocean, to the vegetable garden she had nurtured every day, to the clean seaside air, to a sleeping Xander curled in Leksi's arms.

Press, press, press.

Yes, she would fix this.

CHAPTER 29

*P*etra knew something was very wrong when she was taken to a guest bedchamber instead of her own quarters. The guard may not have locked the door, but she knew he waited on the other side, occasionally hearing the shuffle of his feet.

Four hours she waited, pacing the room, before finally collapsing into the chair by the window.

Press, press, press.

It was almost dark outside when the door finally opened and the king stepped inside. She sensed his fierce mood before he said a word. Slowly, she stood from the chair, hands folded in front of her, deciding to let him speak first. Whatever information Father Gabot had shared with him did not bode well for her.

Nilos closed the door behind him, pausing for a moment with his back to her. When he finally turned, he made no move towards her. She remained where she was, safely on the other side of the room. Curtsying, she rose to meet his gaze with a neutral expression. 'Your Majesty.'

His fingers twitched as he studied her, as though trying to

decide if she were guilty before laying out his accusations. 'I spoke with Father Gabot today,' he began. 'I wanted to hear his version of the events that unfolded, to find out how you slipped through his fingers. I almost lost you a second time.' He sniffed and glanced at the bed. 'His saving grace was that he had the good sense to take precautions, despite your rather convincing act.'

There was bitterness in his tone. It was eerie the way he stared at her without blinking.

He walked forwards, stopping next to the bedpost. 'I would like to hear from your mouth about the events of that day, how it all played out.'

She clasped her hands tighter to stop from pressing her nails. After just a few days at Masville, her fingertips were bruised, her cuticles raw. 'It was not some spectacular plan, as you have probably figured out.'

'I believe I have most of the pieces now. Father Gabot was *very* helpful in filling in some of the blanks.'

'I understand you lost some men that day. I am sorry it came to that. It was not our intention for anyone to die.'

'*Our* intention?'

She swallowed. Had she said 'our'? 'I was under guard, as you know.'

His eyes flashed. 'He was not just any guard, was he?'

She shook her head. 'No, he was a knight following orders.'

'Whose orders?'

She did not like where this conversation was going. 'I believe he takes orders from Prince Tyron.'

He nodded thoughtfully. 'So Prince Tyron ordered this knight of yours to extract your son? For that task, he sent just one knight?'

She faltered. Of course Prince Tyron would never have ordered such a thing. He had ordered her to Archdale, and she had refused to go. Leksi had thought the plan was complete madness, but he had done it anyway. He had done it for her, and had almost lost his life in the process.

'I thought on my feet, if I am honest. I was desperate to see Xander.'

'You mean desperate to get him out of Corneo.'

She held his gaze. 'I did not arrive with the intention of taking him. It was only when I saw how he was living, how he was being treated, that I acted impulsively.'

'*You* acted? It was your knight who acted, was it not?'

There was that dangerous light in his eyes again.

'He returned, alone, sword in hand, and threatened a man of God,' Nilos continued. 'Upon hearing the boy had been taken away, he did not return to you empty-handed but rather pursued him, killing fifteen of my men in the process.'

Fifteen. It was no wonder he had ended up with an arrow in his back. 'I am sorry about your men, as I said already. It was never my intention—'

He held up a hand to silence her. 'No, you said it was never *our* intention.' His face twitched. 'I must say, I am amazed that such a well-trained knight would risk his life and reputation to appease the whims of one foreign woman.'

A cold realisation hit her. He knew. Or at the very least he suspected something between them. 'I was very fortunate that he understood the difficulty of my situation.'

His eyes never left hers. 'What was the name of this noble knight?'

Her mind raced. Withholding information from Nilos would only make her appear guilty, but she did not want to put a target on Leksi's back. 'You can understand my hesitance to share it. The man has my son.'

'Our son,' the king said. 'The man has *our son.*'

The muscles in her shoulders tightened. 'Forgive me, but a few days ago, you described him as "a thorn in your side".'

The king took a step towards her. 'It seems I have a new thorn in my side—a knight.'

She shook her head dismissively. 'What are you talking about?'

'Sir Leksi, is it not?'

A cold wave passed through her, followed by heat that burned her cheeks.

The king nodded, as though her reaction confirmed everything.

'That makes sense. He is Prince Tyron's right-hand man. He is also one of the few men I know who can ride into an ambush and come out alive.'

'Yes. He is a strong fighter.' She had to say something.

'Tell me,' Nilos continued, walking over to her, 'about your visit to Paton. I want to hear all about it.'

Again, she did not trust his tone. 'As I have already said, we had no great plan. We sat on the hill, ate some food and watched the church, hoping he would appear.'

Nilos nodded, a smile on his face. 'Lovely. I can really see the imagery, imagine the excitement.'

She frowned. 'It was more nerves than anything. I had not seen Xander in five years.'

'Making the moment all the more beautiful. Please, continue.'

She drew a breath. 'He finally came out of the church, heading to the well for water. Father Gabot had him scrubbing the floor of the church.'

'A noble task for an orphaned boy.'

She bit the inside of her cheek, determined to remain calm. 'I was not certain it was him, so I followed. It did not take me long to confirm who he was.'

'And then Father Gabot arrived, and you told him you were on your way to the flag tournament.'

'Yes.'

'With your husband.'

Her breath hitched. 'I knew a priest would frown upon an unmarried couple travelling unchaperoned.'

Another nod. 'He would assume the worst.'

'Yes.' She concentrated on keeping volume in her voice. 'We left soon after without a fuss.'

The king folded his arms and thought for a moment. 'I met him once.'

'Who?' she asked, already knowing the answer.

He raised his eyes to her. 'Your knight. It was a few years back, but I remember him.'

Her mouth was so dry. 'A loyal friend to the prince.'

He stared at the ground between them. 'And a good-looking man. He has a way with women. The Companions watched him whenever he was in the room, and the maids fell over themselves to serve him.'

What on earth was she supposed to say to that? 'I am sure he is not the first war hero to win hearts.'

'He has quite a reputation.'

'He was every bit the gentleman in my presence, so I cannot speak of it.'

'Was he?' Nilos reached out and ran his thumb over her painted lips. 'What about when he kissed you?'

She frowned, not about to walk into that trap. 'You are mistaken.'

'Are you telling me he never kissed you?' His hand fell away.

'No,' she said plainly. She was hardly going to share those details with a man prone to jealous rage.

He stared at her. 'Not even at the well? In front of Father Gabot?'

Her expression fell as she realised what he was referring to. Leksi had kissed her at the well while trying to extract her. He had wanted to ensure their married act was convincing. 'I can barely recall. Perhaps he did. We were posing as a married couple, after all.'

'You do not remember?'

'Your Majesty, I was seeing my son for the first time in years. I doubt I noticed anything other than Xander.'

'Father Gabot is a man of God. Do you think he would lie?'

She opened her hands and tried to relax her shoulders. 'All right, let us assume there was a kiss. In those circumstances, it meant nothing.'

His fingers curled and uncurled. 'Nothing?' He paused. 'He put his *mouth* on you.'

She held his gaze, thankful he did not know about all the other places Leksi's mouth had travelled. 'So we could leave the village without raising suspicion.'

'You are not his to kiss.' He was wrong, of course. She was his alone. 'What else did he do to you?'

She let out an exasperated breath. 'Nothing.'

'All those months together—alone, perhaps. Did he put his hands on you too?'

Yes, every inch of me, she wanted to scream. *He washed every trace of you away.*

'I already told you he was very respectful.'

His eyebrows rose. 'The man is a notorious womaniser.'

'I am not entirely sure what you want to hear.' She held out her hands, almost pleading. 'I can only tell you what I know of him.'

He looked out the window, his jaw working. 'I want to know how he touched you.'

'Sir Leksi was under orders—'

He stepped closer so his face was inches from hers. 'Did he put his hands on you!' It came out like a roar.

She jumped. Feet shuffled on the other side of the door.

Composing herself, she replied, 'No, Your Majesty.' She

was still, her heart racing because she had no idea what he would do next.

'I could practically smell him on you the day you returned.' His voice was quiet now.

She really wanted to step back from him.

'Do you know what Father Gabot told me?' He did not wait for her to answer. 'The reason he hesitated before sending word to the guards is because the man accompanying you kissed you with such familiarity, he thought you were genuinely in love.'

At some point during that sentence, she stopped breathing. 'He saw only what we wanted him to see.'

He took her face with both hands, squeezing. 'There is no *we*!'

'No,' she whispered, suddenly afraid he would snap her jaw. 'There is only *us*. You and me.'

He loosened his grip, but he did not let her go. He brought his lips to hers, a possessive, violent kiss. She held his wrists, confused as to whether she should kiss him back or push him away. Finally he pulled back, the paint from her lips colouring his own. He looked like a mad jester.

'I will kill you before I let another man touch you again.' His wild eyes bore into hers. 'Do you understand?'

A nod. 'I am yours until death. Remember?' She tried not to choke on the words. 'I belong to you.'

His hand covered her face, pushing her away. She staggered backwards but remained upright.

'You left me!' he shouted, hands clenched like an angry child.

'I came back.'

He began to pace, his face red. 'No, *I* brought you back.'

'Because you love me. I see that now.' She was desperate to contain the situation.

He did not look at her. 'You are a liar and a whore.'

She took a step back from his words, realising the conversation could not be turned around. There was nothing she could say, no right answers. This was how it would always be with him—pushing and pulling.

'Are you at least going to *try* to deny it?' he asked.

She felt so tired suddenly. 'What is the point?'

He stopped walking, dark eyes flashing at her. 'I see it so plainly now. Of course you fell in love with him. Why else would you trust a man like that with your son? That is why you came to me, begging I leave them be. You are not just protecting the boy, but him also.' His teeth seemed to creak as he ground them. 'Tell me I am wrong.'

Tears rolled down her cheeks. There was no winning the argument, so she remained silent. He stared at her, as though daring her to speak.

'You will stay here,' he said, his voice calmer now.

Her eyes widened. 'Do you mean here in this room?'

He turned on his heel and headed for the door.

'Your Majesty,' she called to him. 'For how long?'

He opened the door and faced the guard waiting outside. 'I want someone watching her at all times. No one in or out without my knowledge.'

The guard glanced at her before replying, 'Yes, Your Majesty.'

Petra took a few hurried steps towards the door. 'Nilos, please!' The door swung shut. 'It will never work this way.'

The sound of a key turning in the lock made her stop. She clutched her stomach and looked around the bare room.

'Don't let that bastard break you.'

CHAPTER 30

'Every boy must know how to ride well,' Leksi said to Xander. He was standing beside his horse in the yard, keeping hold of the bridle while Xander gathered the reins.

'What about girls?' asked the boy.

'And girls too.'

'Does my mother ride well?'

She knew how to hold on. Leksi fiddled with a strap on the bridle. 'Ladies who live in castles travel in wagons.' He reached up, adjusting the boy's grip on the reins. 'Your mother, while very brave, does not like to ride alone.'

'Why?'

Leksi squinted up at him. 'Between us, I think she might be afraid of horses.'

'Did she fall off one?'

'Not that I'm aware of.'

Xander thought for a moment. 'Is she afraid of cats too?'

Leksi marvelled at the workings of his mind. 'Not sure about cats. Ready?'

Xander nodded.

'Big squeeze with your legs. Keep those heels down.' He led the horse in a circle for a few minutes. Then, once Xander seemed confident, he let go of the bridle and went to stand in the middle of the yard. 'You're a natural.'

The boy glanced in his direction. 'You didn't come to church this morning.'

Leksi had been rather hungover that morning. 'I was feeling a little under the weather, but Lady Hali is always more than happy to take you.'

'She doesn't like to be called Lady Hali. She says it sounds stuffy.'

Leksi nodded. 'Fair point.'

Xander fell silent for a moment. 'Will you come with me tomorrow? To church?'

The thought of attending every morning was too much. 'God and I are better suited to weekly visitations. Besides, you pray enough for both of us.'

Xander frowned at him. 'I don't think God listens to my prayers, but he might listen to yours.'

Leksi studied the boy. 'Why do you think God isn't listening?'

'It's been so many days.'

Leksi's gaze dropped to his feet. Xander was waiting for his mother, no doubt eager to get to know her.

The boy faced forwards again. 'How many days has it been?'

'Three weeks,' Leksi replied. 'Twenty-one days.' And just one piece of news. She had been at the tournament, on the king's arm, apparently back in his good graces, according to what Cora had said in her letter to Tyron. It was a casual mention, disguised as gossip for the benefit of her controlling husband.

'How much longer 'til she comes?' Xander asked.

He shook his head. 'I'm afraid I don't know.' They were

trying to get eyes and ears inside the castle, but no one was prepared to risk their life for it.

He walked over to the horse and it stopped. 'What I do know is that if there was any way she could be here right now, she would be. She's been waiting five years to spend time with you.'

'Is she a prisoner?'

Leksi blinked, and the muscles in his shoulders tensed and released. 'She's not locked in a dungeon, if that's what you're asking.' But no one really knew anything for certain. No one knew how long she would remain in the king's good graces.

'Maybe she's waiting for us to come get her,' Xander said

Leksi patted the boy's leg, unable to meet his gaze. 'Trust me, if I could, I would.'

Xander thought for a moment. 'Why don't you ask Father Gabot to get her? He knows the king.'

'I don't think Father Gabot will be doing me a favour anytime soon.' He forced his eyes up and took in the boy's disappointed face. 'Three weeks might feel like a really long time, but it's not.' He was not sure if he was saying that for the boy's sake or his own. Waiting for news of her was the cruellest form of torture. 'I'm starving. Shall we go see what Charis has cooked up?'

Xander nodded. 'What do I need to do?'

Leksi lifted him from the horse and set him on the ground. 'What do you mean?'

'To get food? What chores?'

Leksi crouched in front of him, holding his arms. 'We've been over this, remember? We fill our bellies first, and then we have energy to work.' Xander wore the same guarded expression Petra had in those early days. The resemblance was frightening. 'Now, you hungry?'

Xander nodded.

Leksi gave his arms a squeeze before standing. 'Excellent. Let's go.'

~

Three weeks became eight. Eight weeks with no news of her.

Eight weeks.

Tyron had returned east with his family, resumed his life and duties there. He wrote to Leksi regularly, enquiring after the two of them. Leksi's replies were brief and on point. If he was honest, he was terrified his pain would leak onto the page and betray him, that he might actually show cracks for the first time in his life. He had always been strong and resilient, and people expected him to remain solid and unemotional in those situations. So why did his stomach turn and his throat burn whenever he watched the boy pray next to his bed?

He knew something had changed in him when he decided to stop numbing his pain with cheap wine. It was not only the disapproving looks from Hali whenever she visited, her eyes resting briefly on the empty bottles. The final decision was made the night Xander showed up at his bedside in the middle of the night, while he was still drunk.

'What is it?' he asked when he was tapped awake by a small shadow. Sitting up, dizzy from drink, he listened for the sound of horses outside while searching in the dark for his sword.

'Can I sleep with you?' Xander asked.

Leksi stilled and looked down at the scared boy, remembering when his own mother had died. He used to wait for his father to pass out from drink and then climb into bed with him, sneaking out in the morning before he woke. Before long, he began staying overnight at Archdale, where he had slept on the floor of Tyron's bedchamber. The queen had turned a blind eye when she learned of the reason why, and as the boys got older, she had eventually organised his own bedchamber at the castle.

Shuffling over, Leksi patted the bed next to him. 'Can't sleep?'

Xander shook his head, climbed in, and was out within moments. The thought of being the drunk father figure Xander would remember later in life was enough to sober him up. When he did eventually see Petra again, he wanted to be able to look her in the eyes and tell her he did the best he could.

~

'I'm going to drown,' Xander said, scrawny limbs wrapping Leksi below the water's surface.

'What did I tell you? When I'm here, you're safe.' Leksi immediately thought of Petra when he said it. He had told her the same thing, and then he had left her behind to be hunted by dogs. 'First you must learn how to float.'

Peeling Xander's legs from his middle, he turned the boy and leaned him back so his head rested on Leksi's shoulder. He had the same silky hair as his mother.

'What happens when a wave comes?'

'You'll fly over it.'

The boy's eyes widened. 'How?'

'Like this.' Holding him under the arms, Leksi lifted him high in the air. Xander squealed as a wave crashed around them, then laughed when Leksi spat a fountain of water high into the air before lowering him back into the sea. 'All right, now I need you nice and loose in the water. That's it. Now push your hips up and spread your arms out.'

'Don't let go.'

'Only when the next wave comes, so I can see how much

you've learned.' He laughed when he saw Xander's frightened expression. 'I'm joking, I'm joking.'

Xander floated for a few moments before being hoisted into the air once more. More laughter.

'I think you're ready to swim to Galen,' Leksi said, turning the boy to him. Legs wrapped him once more.

'Galen! You need a ship to get to Galen.'

'Men who can't float might need a ship, but not you.'

A wave splashed over them, and Xander wiped water from his grinning face. What a difference just a few months had made.

'My lord!'

Leksi turned to the shore, where he found Charis waving his arms to get his attention. Another wave crashed over them, making it difficult to hear what he was shouting, but the expression on his face was enough to make Leksi toss Xander onto his back and return to the shore.

As he waded in, Charis ran into the water towards them.

'Horses!' he shouted. 'At least fifty of them!'

Leksi jogged the final few paces to close the distance between them. He heard it then, the sound of hooves approaching. 'Get the boat and take Xander around the point, out of sight.'

'I want to stay with you,' Xander said.

'I need you to go with Charis.' Leksi handed the clinging child over. 'I need you to do exactly as Charis says.' He looked at his squire. 'If anything should happen, take him to the manor as soon as it's safe.'

Charis nodded before running off towards the rocks to fetch the boat. Leksi shoved his legs into his trousers, his wet braies immediately soaking them. He did not bother with his shirt or shoes, just took off at a sprint towards the house, hoping to reach his weapons before the men reached him. He glanced in the direction of the approaching horses as he ran.

The riders wore plain clothes, but he knew by the arrows pointed in his direction that it was not a friendly visit.

Hiss.

An arrow passed behind him just as he reached the house.

Tugging open the door, he went straight for his sword, securing it around his hips before snatching up his bow and quiver. He needed to take down as many as he could before they reached him.

He stepped outside, using the door as a shield, and began shooting. One, two, three. He kept reloading the bow. Four, five, six. Nothing wrong with his aim, but there was no way he could kill them all before they reached him. Seven, eight, nine, ten, eleven, twelve. An arrow grazed his arm, and he stepped behind the door as ten more rained down on him. The horses split into two groups, no doubt intending to surround the house. He stepped out one more time and released another five arrows. Not enough. By his guess, there were at least another thirty riders, who were now leaping from the horses and drawing their swords as they charged towards him. With a flick of his wrist, an arrow fell into place. He released three in a row, taking down the closest men before dropping his bow and drawing his sword.

Steel crashed and screeched, and Leksi moved and twisted to avoid the blades coming at him. He found his rhythm, his home now a battlefield where blood sprayed the walls and bodies fell at his front step.

The sound of glass smashing in one of the bedrooms made him turn and look. They were coming behind him now, and his position was no longer optimal for fighting as his back was exposed. He shifted away from the door, swinging ruthlessly to move past the ten or so men still in front of him. He felt the sting of a blade across his arm, but he did not even look at it.

Another window smashed, at the front of the house, and

an arrow appeared, pointed in his direction. He grabbed one of the soldiers by the arm and pulled the man in front of him like a shield, bashing the weapon from his hand just as the arrow hit. The man collapsed at his feet, and Leksi looked around, panting. Men came from the other side of the house on foot, swords drawn. Another arrow was already pointed at him from the window, and a bitter realisation hit him at that moment.

He was going to die.

CHAPTER 31

*T*he window faced west, and for some reason, that helped. Maybe it was because Xander was west. And Leksi.

Petra sat curled in a ball beneath the glass, one hand outstretched, turning it in the light. She watched her skin change colour until the sun disappeared, marking the end of another day. The shadows grew darker, but she did not move from her spot on the floor. Running a finger along the bruise on her neck, she remembered her last encounter with the king. He had scared even himself that time; she had seen it in his face. He held all the power, and the boundaries were blurring.

For weeks she had been locked inside that bedchamber. Her only visitors were the king and the maid who brought her food and emptied the chamber pot. The young girl never said a word, never even raised her eyes to Petra. She knew what was happening, knew she was playing a part in her destruction. Nilos came every day, sometimes more than once. He would lie on the bed with her, stroking her hair and running his fingers down the bare skin of her arms, needing to forgive but being unable to.

'Let me out,' she would say to the wall.

He would watch her in the dark, thinking. 'Not yet.'

His answer was always the same. 'When?'

'When you are cleansed of him.'

What did that even mean? Was he waiting for a confession? Waiting for her to open her wrist and bleed him out? It would not work.

At some point the air thinned, the nights cooled and the mornings brought frost. The warm season was coming to an end, taking the colour from her cheeks with it. Every day she woke to find another piece of herself missing. Perhaps that was his plan. When there was nothing left, would he consider it a victory?

She stopped putting on the dresses he sent each morning. It was pointless. Who was she dressing up for? Him? Well, she just did not care enough to go to the effort. Instead, she remained in her nightdress with her hair out and unbrushed.

Food arrived three times every day and sat mostly untouched on the tray. She was not hungry. She drank the water though, if only to reassure herself that she intended to survive.

'You are not taking care of yourself,' the king scolded during one of his visits.

She was seated in the chair, fingers splayed on the arms as she watched him across the room. 'I am not hungry.'

'You are not trying.'

She stared at him, eyes hollow. She was too tired to try. He wanted something from her, the piece of herself she had given to Leksi, but it was not hers to give.

'The maid says you are sleeping on the floor.'

That was true. She only used the bed when he was there, a heavy arm suffocating her while he slept. She always stayed awake, wondering how long it would take her to starve to death.

'I am at a loss how to fix you,' he said. There was concern in his voice, but not enough to let her out of the room. He walked over and crouched in front of her. She was forced to look at him.

'There are some nights I think I can still smell him on you,' he whispered.

She pushed her matted hair from her face, tucking it behind her ears. *You are mad*, she wanted to scream. But the fight had left her. He could do as he pleased. She turned away from him.

He might have been insane, but so was she.

'You laid with him, did you not?'

She shook her head. It seemed like the right response.

'Perhaps he forced himself on you,' he continued. 'Could not take no for an answer?'

Was that what he needed to hear? That she had never wanted another man? She would not give him that. 'No. Leksi would never do that.'

Nilos's forehead creased as he watched her. 'I cannot bear to see you this way. If I could trust you with a mirror, you would understand why.'

She pulled her legs up, hugging them. Her fingers pressed her bleeding cuticles. She did not care about hiding it anymore.

'I have some news to share with you. News that will help you, help *us*.'

'Are you letting me out of here?'

He sat with his back against the wall and his legs stretched out in front of him. 'Come,' he said, gesturing with one hand. 'Lay your head in my lap.'

She thought about it, crawling over to him and lying down so he could stroke her hair and feel better about himself. That would have been the smart thing to do—submit.

'Tell me the news,' she said. 'That is why you came here.'

His expression hardened. 'I have been gathering information,' he began. 'And I have located Sir Leksi.'

Her eyes went to him. 'Why are you looking for him?'

'With him gone, we stand a chance.' He leaned forwards, gripping her bare calf. 'You are still my queen. I am not giving up on you.'

Her hands tingled and her mind buzzed. Perhaps she should have eaten the food, because she could not think suddenly. 'What do you mean, "with him gone"?' She searched his eyes. 'You promised to let them be.'

He looked annoyed, as though he had expected her to light up at the news of his betrayal. 'That was before.'

She shook her head. 'What have you done?' Her eyes welled up.

'The boy will not be harmed. I already have a family lined up, one you would approve of.'

She just kept shaking her head. He was taking away the only comfort she had left in the world. 'What family? I told you to leave him be.'

'You know I could not let that man live. He has taken too much from us.'

No, he had given her everything.

'What are you saying?' She sat forwards, gripping the chair until every finger throbbed. 'Did you kill him?'

His look of surprise dissolved into a scowl. 'Everything I do, I do for us.'

Another shake of her head, rejecting his words. Leksi could not die. He was Syrasan's best knight, a killing machine on any battlefield. 'You are lying.'

He stood, his tall frame looming over her. 'He was easy

enough to find. He returned to the same house, the one my men had visited before.'

There was no air left in the room. 'Your men died. I was there. I saw them die.'

'Not all.'

She tried to think. He was right, one had survived and fled before Leksi returned to the house.

'My men crossed into Syrasan yesterday.'

She looked up at him, eyes filled with hate. 'Prince Tyron is not stupid. He knows what you are. He would never have let your men pass, never leave his friends vulnerable.'

He leaned down. 'Prince Tyron knows nothing of it. My men entered from the North, from Zoelin.'

Her hands went over her ears and she tipped forwards, her chest pressing on her thighs. She thought she might be sick.

'I did it for us,' he said.

At that, she shot out of her seat. He took a quick step back. 'No, you did it for yourself. You did it because you are jealous and sick.' She ran to the door and tried to open it. Realising it was locked, she pounded it with her fist. 'Let me out of here.'

The king watched her from across the room. 'For *him* you grieve?'

Yes—for him, her son, and herself. It was a giant pool of pain. 'I cannot even look at you.' She slapped the door with both hands. 'Let me out!'

He walked over to her slowly. 'You just need more time. You will see clearly soon enough. Do not waste your grief on that man.'

She spun around. 'That man?' Her chest heaved, her voice broken. 'I *loved* him. I gave myself to him willingly.'

The king pressed his lips into a thin line. 'You want to hurt me? Is that it?'

Shaking her head, she said, 'I do not care enough to hurt you.' She took a step towards him. 'You are nothing to me but a prison guard, a monster. I could never love you. Every day, I hate you a little more than I thought possible.'

In two strides, he reached her, gripping her throat. 'Shut up.'

Tears spilled down her face, pooling in his fingers. She stared unblinking at him, her arms limp at her sides. She was not going to fight him. He could watch the life drain from her and carry the image with him for the rest of his miserable life. 'Do it,' she spat, barely getting the words out.

He released her as though she had burned him, and she collapsed at his feet, gasping and coughing. The door swung open and the guard appeared, looking between them, his hand on his sword as he took in the scene.

'We are fine,' Nilos said, his eyes on Petra. He crouched to her, eyes full of remorse. 'Let me see your neck.'

She scooted away from him until her back hit the table where a tray of food sat. She could not speak, but her expression made it very clear that he was not to put a hand on her.

Nilos looked completely lost for a moment, then looked around the room, stood and stepped up to the tray on the table, dipping his finger into the soup. 'I will have some more food brought up. This is cold.'

She watched him warily, her hands on her neck as she continued to draw greedy lungfuls of air. Nilos walked to the door, and the guard stepped out of his way. He disappeared through it, and then she heard his footsteps fade down the corridor. The guard stared down at her for a moment, looking bewildered and conflicted as to what he should do.

Let me out, she wanted to say. But she was too weak to run, and she had no one to run to. Grief swelled in her, and she felt like she had been kicked in the stomach. She lay down on the ground with her hands over her face, unable to hold her pain in any longer. Sobs tore through her, racking her body.

Leksi.

She kicked the table as hard as she could, and the guard jumped back as cold soup sprayed the wall. The tray landed with a clang on the floor, and the empty bowl rolled for some time before rattling to a stop. She turned to the wall and curled herself into a ball. After a while, she heard the guard exit the room and the familiar sound of the door locking.

'Don't let that bastard break you.'

Too late. She was completely broken.

CHAPTER 32

*H*e was outnumbered, and they were pressing in on him. Occasionally he got lucky, his blade meeting flesh, but it would not be enough. He leapt backwards as another arrow was released, sailing straight into the face of a soldier running from the other direction. The fact that they had shot one of their own would have amused him at any other time, but he was too busy trying to dodge death to appreciate the irony.

Another soldier lunged, and Leksi's elbow hit the outside wall of the house as he blocked the blow. He was trapped. There was nowhere for him to go. His only option was to fight his way out, and he knew his odds of surviving were dismal at best.

The archer in the window leaned out to navigate the tricky angle, and Leksi wondered what the chances were that he would miss again. Not great odds at that proximity. He would need to block the arrow with his sword. He had done it before, but he had not been surrounded by men trying to kill him at the time.

He pushed the closest man back with his foot and pressed

himself flat against the wall, hoping the arrow would miss. It did, buying him a few more seconds of life, but then they were on him again.

As he fought back, he braced for the inevitable arrow. Instead, he heard a groan and turned to watch the archer fall out of the window. At first he thought Charis might have come back to help, but then he remembered the squire did not have a bow with him. More men cried out before collapsing to the ground, clutching their wounds. The remaining soldiers glanced nervously behind them, no doubt searching for the shooter. Leksi took advantage of their distraction and cut down the men closest to him.

Three horses skidded to a halt on the other side of the soldiers, Tyron dismounting and drawing his sword. The two men with him followed, weapons ready.

More Corneon soldiers burst from the house, having realised there was no one inside. Soon, only a handful of them remained alive, and those soldiers were no match for the four of them. Within minutes they lay bleeding next to their comrades. Only then did Leksi glance down at the cut on his arm, assessing the damage. It would need a few stitches, but he would live.

He bent to hold his knees, panting and sweating. Tyron looked around at the bodies while his men went to finish off anyone still alive. No one wanted to listen to them groaning and writhing in the dirt.

'You did fairly well with these odds,' Tyron said.

Leksi straightened and wiped his forehead with the back of his hand. 'I won't pretend I wasn't quietly shitting my pants for a moment there.' He nodded at Tyron. 'Impeccable timing.'

One of the soldiers at Tyron's feet let out a faint groan. The prince thrust his sword through the man's side.

'I'm going to hazard a guess that King Nilos wants his son back,' Leksi said.

Tyron wiped the blade of his weapon and returned it to its sheath. 'I am not convinced he does. I think they were here for you.'

Leksi frowned. 'Me? Why?' But even as he spoke the words, the answer formed in his mind. There was only one reason the mad king would send a small army to kill him—he knew something.

Tyron looked past him to the house. 'Where is Xander?'

'With Charis, in the water.'

Tyron nodded. 'Better he stays there while we clean up.'

Leksi stared at the bloodied corpses. 'Agreed.'

It took almost an hour for the four of them to drag the bodies to the edge of the property for burning. Then they collected all the weapons and piled them behind the house, out of sight. Their attackers' horses were unsaddled and either put in the small yard or tethered to its fence.

Tyron instructed his men to clean up the blood as best they could while they went to fetch Charis and Xander. To avoid having to explain the blood-soaked earth in front of the house, Leksi announced to the anxious boy that they were going to cook mutton over a fire on the beach. He hoped the smoke would disguise the sixty corpses burning in a fire at the back of the property.

If Xander suspected anything, he did not let on, not even when Charis stitched up Leksi's arm. But he clung to the knight, making it impossible for him to talk privately with Tyron.

'Charis, why don't you take Xander down to the water to build a sandcastle,' Leksi said.

The squire nodded and came to collect the boy from his lap.

'Are you going to come with us?' Xander asked.

Leksi smiled. 'I'll be along in a minute.'

The two men watched as Charis and the boy headed down to the water. Once they were alone, Tyron turned to Leksi.

'He's really attached himself to you.'

Leksi continued to watch Xander. 'The feeling's mutual.'

'I am pleased, and I am sorry for suggesting you were not up to the task.'

Leksi looked at him. 'It was probably a fair assumption.'

Tyron gave a small smile. 'I have been worried about you. You have barely said two words in your letters.'

Leksi picked up a stick and stoked the fire. The flames burned a little brighter. 'What's there to say? I thought you might've heard something by now. It's been months.'

Tyron's expression turned serious. 'We have not been able to get ears or eyes into Masville. The king has everyone fearing for their lives. Lucky for us, Cora has a remarkable network of spies.'

'That doesn't surprise me at all. Though it's probably not much help given how closely she's watched by her husband.'

Tyron stared into the fire. 'There are rumours. Substantial enough that I thought it best to tell you in person.'

Leksi straightened, a feeling of dread rising in him. 'Oh?'

The prince hesitated. 'Aldara has this crazy idea that you might be in love with Petra.' He kept his eyes on the fire. When Leksi did not deny it, he added, 'And I am inclined to think she is right.'

Leksi watched the flames. There was no point lying. They knew each other far too well for that. 'Is that the rumour you're referring to?'

'I wish it were.'

Leksi drew a breath. 'Why do I get the feeling you're preparing me for some rather bad news?'

'You are not going to like what I am about to tell you,' the prince said, sounding apologetic.

Another breath for courage. 'All right. Let's hear it.'

CHAPTER 33

*X*ander sat on the top step of the manor, his head in his hands and a scowl on his face. 'How many days will you be gone?'

Leksi was beside him, looking out over the immaculate grounds. It was early morning and the sun was at an uncomfortable angle, yet somehow it was easier to stare into the blinding light than to look down at Xander. 'I don't know exactly, but I'll be back as soon as I can.'

Xander was silent for a moment. 'What if you don't come back?'

Leksi looked down at his hands. The separation was hard on him also, but he could not hide away in Veanor after learning Petra was suffering at the hands of the king. He was going to get her out of there.

He moved to crouch in front of Xander, taking hold of his arms. 'Do you see Prince Tyron seated on his horse behind me?'

Xander looked past him to where Tyron was waiting patiently, watching them. He nodded.

'Well, he's an excellent bodyguard, and he'll be coming with me. It's his job to make sure I get back here to you.'

Xander studied Tyron for a moment before looking back at Leksi. 'I thought it was your job to keep *him* safe?'

'It is. We take care of each other.'

Xander appeared sceptical. 'You said you're a stronger fighter than him. Shouldn't you take someone better?'

Leksi glanced over his shoulder to see if Tyron had heard that last comment. Judging by the way he was shaking his head, and the faint smile on his face, he guessed he had.

He turned back to Xander. 'And I stand by that statement,' he said, loudly enough for Tyron to hear. 'But since it's impossible to find someone who matches my skill, the prince will have to do.'

Xander thought for a moment before finally nodding. 'But you will come back? With my mother?'

He could not make that promise. Thankfully Hali, who had no doubt been eavesdropping, walked over and placed a hand on Xander's shoulder. 'Time to say goodbye.'

Leksi stood and looked at her. 'Thank you for doing this.'

'No need to thank me. We always love having him. We have so many fun things planned that I suspect the time is just going to fly by.'

'What about my riding lessons?' Xander asked.

Leksi gave his head a pat. 'Lord Yuri is an excellent rider.'

'He also mentioned something about needing a sparring partner,' Hali said, looking down at the boy. 'Do you think you're ready to handle a sword?'

Xander looked up at Leksi to gauge his reaction.

'Lord Yuri is an excellent swordsman too. You'll be ready for battle in no time.' He brushed a thumb down Xander's cheek. 'Behave.' He went to turn away, but the boy hugged him about the hips, holding tightly. Leksi wanted to reassure him, to promise he would be back, but he had decided to do whatever was necessary to get Petra out of Masville—and that came with enormous risk.

'Let's go visit the dogs out back,' Hali said, taking him gently by the shoulders.

Xander reluctantly let go and turned his watery eyes up to Leksi. 'I'll pray for you.'

Leksi felt the same choking sensation he had experienced the last time he had seen Petra. He was hopeless at goodbyes. He should have told her he loved her.

He swept his thumb down Xander's nose. 'Thank you.' Turning away, a hard lump lodged in his throat, he descended the steps towards his waiting horse. Thankfully, Tyron knew better than to ask if he was all right.

They rode east with the prince's men in tow, arriving at Lord Belen's manor in Wripis in the middle of the night. Their exhausted mounts were taken to the stables, and Tyron and Leksi made their way down to the small house where the prince and his family lived most of the year. It was quiet and dark when they stepped inside, not the usual chaos Leksi had come to expect from the household. Everyone was no doubt asleep.

'If you want to go see Aldara and the litter, I'll tend the fire.'

Tyron came to stand in front of the dying embers. 'They are not here. I sent them to Roysten before I came to you.'

Leksi knew his friend did not want his family anywhere near danger. First sniff of trouble and Tyron had sent them away. Leksi tossed a log onto the fire and watched the flames grow. 'When are they due back?'

'I will collect them when it is safe.'

'You think King Nilos will try to breach the border?'

'I think he wants you dead at any cost, and I am not going to let that happen.'

Leksi swallowed. 'I know I haven't been completely

upfront with you of late, and I know you question some of my recent decisions.'

'Yes, because I did not understand your motives.'

'But now you do?'

'I believe so.' Tyron paused. 'It seems Sir Leksi finally met his match.'

The knight glanced at him. 'It seems I'm not immune to love after all.'

Tyron laughed and clapped a hand on his back. 'It is not an illness.'

'A sentence, then.'

The prince shook his head. 'So how do you plan on getting Petra out of Masville Castle with the mad king on your heel?'

He released a long breath. 'I'll think of something.'

'It's going to be an interesting fight.' Tyron paused. 'I'm going to have to tell Pandarus what happened in Veanor.'

'He'll probably have me handed over.'

'I am sure he would like nothing more, but the crown owes you a little more than that.'

Leksi's smile fell away. 'You know I'm not waiting around for his approval.'

Tyron's expression was resigned. 'I know.'

'And you know you can't come with me to Corneo, right?'

Tyron exhaled. 'Your fight is my fight. That is how it has always been.'

'I might be the most hated man by that family at present, but you're most definitely a close second. Prince Felipe will kill you on sight if you step foot into Corneo.'

Tyron watched the flames for a moment. 'If you think I am going to sit back while you ride off to die, you are wrong.' He rubbed his forehead. 'Get some sleep. We will talk in the morning.'

Leksi did not want to waste time sleeping. 'I can go right now, drag some men from their tents if I need to.'

'Then what? Scale the castle walls and kill every person in sight until you find her?' Tyron shook his head. 'You need fresh men, a fresh mind, and a plan if you are to have any chance of succeeding.'

All of those things took time, which he did not have. He had promised to protect her. 'I should've gone back for her sooner.'

'It was not possible then, and I am not convinced it is possible now.'

'I need to get her out of there before he kills her or...' He could not finish.

Tyron narrowed his eyes. 'Or what?'

Leksi just shook his head, remembering her words the day they had met.

'There might be a way,' Tyron said, 'but let's be clever about this. How many times did you bring me back to Archdale when Aldara was imprisoned in Zoelin?'

Silence.

'You need to act carefully or you will only endanger her further.'

Tyron was right, of course. He prided himself on being practical, but his good sense seemed to go out the window when it came to Petra. He would kill the entire Corneon army and their king if that was what it took to free her from that man.

'You're a good friend.'

The prince shrugged. 'You are blood as far as I am concerned.' He stepped past Leksi and headed for the stairs. 'You had better be here in the morning.'

～

Leksi woke to the sound of horses and muffled voices. Sliding out of bed, he stepped into his trousers before making his way downstairs. He found the front door open and Tyron standing outside talking with someone—not a soldier by the looks of him, but a common man. Leksi waited in the doorway, watching the exchange. A letter was handed over, and Tyron opened and read it. After a minute, he looked up and thanked the man before sending him on his way and turning back to the house.

'Good or bad news?' Leksi called.

Tyron walked up the narrow path towards him, looking conflicted. If he was having trouble deciding, it was probably bad.

When the prince reached him, he held out the letter. Leksi took it, glancing first at the bottom to see who it was from. Lord Belen.

'He is sending her to Onuric Castle in Zoelin,' Tyron said before Leksi had the chance to finish reading.

'Petra?' He scanned the rest of the letter.

A nod. 'She is being transported today.'

Leksi stared at the words on the page, trying to get inside King Nilos's head. 'That doesn't make any sense.' He read it one more time to ensure he had understood the message properly. When he was done, he folded the paper and handed it back to Tyron. 'How did Lord Belen find out?'

Tyron looked out at the garden. 'It seems the king has made no secret of the fact.'

Leksi ran his hands over his face. 'He cannot stand to be away from her. Why would he send her to Onuric?'

'Maybe he wants to teach her a lesson.'

'Hali describes Onuric as a prison for Companions.' He thought for a moment. 'Does the fool think she'll return from that place more in love with him?'

Tyron shrugged. 'It will be a rather harsh existence for

her there. Perhaps he is trying to show her there are worse places to be than in his bed.'

'She's been locked up for months and suddenly he decides to hand her over to King Jayr?' He paused. 'Does that sound logical to you?'

'Are you really expecting King Nilos to make logical decisions at this point in time? The man is not fit to rule.'

Leksi stared out into the grey light. 'I think he wants me to know. He must have figured out by now that his men failed. Perhaps he's trying to lure me out.'

Tyron gave a silent nod. 'What are you going to do?'

He looked at the prince. 'Follow the breadcrumbs, of course. What else can I do?'

'If you are right, they will be expecting you.'

He pushed off the doorframe. 'Best not disappoint them, then. How many men can I have?'

'You mean to breach the border without permission from your king?'

'Yes.'

Tyron exhaled. 'Well, I will go with you.'

Leksi thought on this for a moment. 'There will be hell to pay afterwards. Pandarus won't be pleased.'

Tyron turned and headed inside. 'As opposed to all those times I am in his good graces?'

'Fair point,' Leksi said, following after him.

The prince shook his head. 'If we make it out alive—'

'If? Since when does the fierce Prince Tyron of Syrasan go into battle throwing around words like *if*?'

'Since we decided to knowingly walk into a trap set by a king who wishes us both dead.'

Leksi reached up and patted his shoulder. 'Better armour up.'

CHAPTER 34

*P*etra paced the length of the room, bare feet padding the smooth floor. Her feet left prints that evaporated by the time her next foot was planted, and she found it calming to watch.

Lately she had possessed a strange sort of energy, though it came in waves. Some days she would walk the room, stopping only when her legs gave out, and other days just the thought of getting off the ground was too much.

Those days were dangerous because her mind ran free. Sometimes she imagined her own death, King Nilos entering the room and finding her corpse. Thinking of his grief brought a strange satisfaction. Other times, she imagined *his* death. On very bad days she visualised being the one to kill him. She could picture herself crushing his bones with her bare hands. She liked to imagine the guard rushing in—too late. Perhaps he would hit her in the head with the hilt of his sword, or drive the blade through her stomach. She wondered what it would feel like to die that way.

She stopped walking and focused on the trees outside the window. It helped ground her sick mind. She knew what she had become. At some point she had stopped fighting it and started indulging it. There was no coming back from the darkness now. The only thing she knew for certain was that she could not be saved.

A knock came at the door, and she turned to stare at it. No one ever knocked; they just walked in, avoiding eye contact for fear of catching her misfortune.

Her fingers stretched and curled as the door opened. Perhaps it was King Nilos coming to fulfil her prophecy. She had not seen him since he had broken the news of Leksi's death. She had not slept either, so her mind was particularly dark.

To her surprise, Nyla stepped into the room, looking around before spotting her by the window. There was no hiding the mentor's… surprise? Horror? She collected herself before taking a few more steps into the room, her smile uncomfortable.

'Hello, Petra.' Her tone was patronising.

'What are you doing here?'

The mentor turned and signalled to someone outside, and a maid peeked hesitantly around the doorway before entering. Nyla turned back with an even bigger smile. 'I am here to pretty you up. I am confident I will have you feeling like your old self again in no time.'

There was no *old self*, just her possessed remains.

More people entered, servants carrying pails of steaming water, towels, brushes, garments. A cloak. *What could I possibly need a cloak for?* She watched as they placed the items on the floor and bed, frowning at the absence of linen. Had they not heard? You could make a rope and hang yourself with bedsheets.

'Am I going somewhere?' Her eyes were still fixed on the cloak. 'Outside?' She was not hopeful, only confused.

Nyla's smile failed her for a moment. 'Actually, I do not

know. I was only instructed to get you ready.'

She should have felt hopeful. She should have felt something. Anywhere was better than being stuck in that room.

'All right.'

It did not matter to her. In here, out there—same prison, different scenery. So she let the women do as they pleased, not caring that the guard remained in the room with them. The maids did their best to form a body curtain around her, but they need not have worried. No man would look at her in her current state. She was a breathing skeleton wrapped in skin. She was also insane.

They scrubbed her skin, face, hair, and teeth. They cut her fingernails, saying nothing of the bleeding cuticles and purple flesh. They brushed her hair, patiently working through the knots. It might have hurt in another life.

Nyla let out a small gasp when she spotted the marks on her neck. Petra turned to take in her expression. They must have been bad, because mentors saw bruises all the time.

'We could try to cover it with paint,' Nyla offered.

Petra looked out the window. 'Do not bother. If you try to cover every mark, you will be here all day.'

Nyla nodded and picked up the scented oil, rubbing it over Petra's dry skin, pausing whenever she came across a new bruise. After they had dressed her, Nyla stood in front of her, brush poised to paint her face. Her gaze stopped on the large, yellow bruise above Petra's eye. What was that from again? Ah, yes. The king had pushed her off the bed because she refused to answer one of his questions. She had succeeded too well at blocking out the persistent sound of his voice.

'Is it painful to touch?' Nyla asked, biting her bottom lip.

Was it? She did not think so. 'No.'

Nyla looked sceptical. Perhaps it was worse than Petra had realised.

'I think we will just add a little colour to your lips instead.'

Petra did not reply, just stood still and let Nyla do what she needed to. She did not wish to make trouble for the mentor.

Servants left with the dirty water and clothes, and one returned with a tray of food. Nyla picked up the bread and held it out for her, and Petra stared down at it like it was poison.

'I am not hungry.'

Nyla frowned. 'You need to eat something.'

She picked up the water and drank it. It turned her empty stomach cold and nauseous.

'That is not food,' Nyla pointed out.

Petra reluctantly took the bread but did not eat it.

Nyla waited.

Petra waited.

Eventually, Nyla looked around the room and said, 'I believe my work here is done.' She gestured for the maids to clear the room and glanced again at the bread in Petra's hand. 'Please eat. You are frightfully thin.'

And bruised. And alone.

'I do not suppose you have heard any news of my son?'

Nyla glanced at the guard over her shoulder. Even if she did, she would never risk telling her. 'I am certain the king is handling the matter.'

'I am certain he is not,' Petra replied, not caring if the guard heard. 'But thank you for the lovely bath.'

Nyla's cheeks coloured, but she simply gave one more smile before heading for the door. The guard followed her out, and the door clicked closed.

Petra tossed the bread onto the tray and sat on the edge of the bed. *Now what?* She stared down at her cloak and the short, laced boots they had brought her.

It was almost half an hour later when the key turned in

the door and it swung open. Apparently they were done knocking.

She was more than a little surprised when Prince Felipe stepped through, wearing his usual look of disapproval. She stood, but she did not curtsy. He came to a stop in front of her, a hand resting on his hip as he looked her up and down.

'My, how the mighty have fallen.' He paused. 'It seems my father has finally come to his senses. He has asked that I escort you to Onuric Castle.'

Her expression did not change. Onuric was every Companion's worst nightmare. Young women were lured there under the pretence of a better life, their unsuspecting parents believing the lies fed to them. But the truth was some of those girls were worse off than her.

'Are we leaving now?'

He studied her, seemingly taken aback. 'Have you no objections?'

'They have done me no good so far.'

Felipe sniffed. 'Let us hope this is the end of this insanity.'

There was no end to it. She was his until death.

'This kingdom needs a king, and you have poisoned his mind long enough.'

She glanced at the door. 'Where is he?'

'Staying well away, no doubt fearing he will be put under your spell once more.'

Her gaze returned to him. 'This was his idea? To send me to Onuric?'

The prince nodded. 'And if I have my way, you will not be returning any time soon.'

She did not believe that for a second. He would never send her away. He would see her dead before being separated from her, before handing her over to another man. 'What am I to do at Onuric?'

He shrugged. 'Whatever they tell you.'

Still, her expression did not change. 'I see. He wishes to teach me a lesson.'

Felipe gestured at the bruise above her eye. 'Well, it seems the last one did not stick.'

She was not buying any of it. King Nilos had an agenda.

'After you,' Felipe said, nodding towards the door.

She knew he would be thoroughly enjoying himself. He had never liked her, because she saw through him. She saw through them all.

Walking to the door, she was unsurprised to find four guards waiting in the corridor. Leaving the room did not bring the relief she might have expected. Perhaps it was because she was immediately surrounded by the guards, who then marched her all the way to the front entrance of the castle.

When she stepped outside, she took her first breath of fresh air in months. Her eyes went to the six waiting horses, one for each of them. There was no handsome knight waiting with his hand outstretched, ready to pull her up behind him.

She closed her eyes at the image of Leksi, grinning at her from atop his horse.

'Something the matter?' Felipe asked.

She opened her eyes. 'No,' she said, walking over to the horse. If she could not ride behind Leksi, she would ride alone. A guard stepped forwards to help her mount, and then she gathered the reins, the way she had seen Leksi do a thousand times. She was surprised to discover she was not scared. Perhaps because she had faced every fear already.

Another group of guards approached on horseback, and Felipe turned to them.

'Keep out of sight. I am not expecting trouble, but I am not taking any chances either. My father is collecting enemies in the North.' His eyes went to Petra. 'Do I need to bind your hands, or are you going to behave?'

'If it will make you feel safer to have me restrained, by all means.' She just did not have it in her to care.

Her eyes returned to the door to her left. For some reason, she was expecting to see King Nilos standing there. She could always feel his eyes on her, the small hairs on her body prickling.

What are you up to?

'Move out,' Felipe ordered.

Her horse walked forwards without her doing a thing, and she saw it was tethered to the prince's mount.

The portcullis rose in front of them, and once again she found herself leaving the castle. She was a prisoner moving between prisons, never in control of her own life, never sure if the next man would be any better than the last.

King Jayr was no saint—she knew that much.

As the portcullis lowered behind her, she glanced over her shoulder, eyes going straight to the window above the entrance. There he was, his shape so familiar. She was too far away to see his face, but she stared straight at the spot she imagined his eyes would be.

I am not afraid of monsters anymore.

He remained there, watching her. She pictured his contorted face and twitching hands.

The portcullis lowered between them, and she faced forwards again, only to find Felipe watching her.

'Take a long look,' he said, 'because I am going to make sure you never see inside Masville's walls ever again.'

She stared at him with the same blank expression. 'That is the best news I have received in months.'

He turned away from her, and they left the castle.

CHAPTER 35

*A*bout three hours into their journey, Petra glimpsed the dense forest of Corneo's west. Memories scraped at her mind, memories she would have preferred to suppress. But there they were, the trees they had ridden through, with her cheek pressed to Leksi's warm back. She had been invincible. She had laughed beneath those branches while rain and wind whipped her face, hair, and body. Not the kind of laughter that stroked the egos of men, but the kind one could not hold in. It had torn through her body until everything ached with it. When she had finally calmed enough to look at Leksi, she had seen how much he needed to witness that moment, what he had been trying to bring to the surface for months. She had seen his complete adoration, the kind that made one's pulse slow.

'*Would you like me to build you a shelter?*' he had asked.

He had been her shelter since the moment he found her shivering on the forest floor.

Half an hour later, they rode beneath those very trees, careful to stay on their side of the border to avoid running into any Syrasan guards. It was unusually hot for that time of year. The sun sat high in the sky, scorching everything it touched. Petra removed her cloak, and the men took advantage of the shade the trees provided. Water was passed around, and as she was handing the flask back to Felipe, she noticed a change in his expression, as though he were listening for something. A few moments later, he stopped his horse and held up a hand. The guards also stopped, their eyes searching the surrounding trees. It was hardly surprising that King Nilos had enemies in every corner of the kingdom.

A bird took flight overhead and the prince drew his sword. The other men followed his lead, two reaching for their bows, one pointed east and the other west. They swung them slowly, covering all directions. Petra should have been afraid. Whatever exchange took place, she would be caught in the crossfire. But she was past fear. She felt only a numb sort of resignation.

An arrow passed her head, landing in the neck of the bowman closest to her. She turned to watch him fall to the ground. His horse sidestepped into hers, and she gripped the pommel of the saddle to keep from falling. While she accepted her fate, being trampled by a horse seemed like a bad way to go.

'Find them!' Felipe barked.

Petra held her breath, expecting an arrow to hit her at any moment. The other bowman began releasing arrows, but Petra could tell he was shooting blind.

Hiss.

An arrow pierced the guard's neck, and he cried out before falling from his horse. She closed her eyes against the image. Whoever was shooting at them knew what they were doing. Instinctively, a hand went to her neck and she held her breath.

'Ready your bows!' Felipe shouted.

She forced her eyes open and watched the men fumbling

with their weapons. Before they had a chance to load their bows, a horse emerged from the trees to their right.

'I suggest you lower your weapons,' came a familiar voice.

Petra whipped her head around to look, then froze, not trusting her own sight.

Leksi.

He appeared through the trees, an arrow aimed at Felipe. *I am hallucinating, my mind deceiving me. That is what happens when you are locked in a room with your grief for too long.* Yet she did not look away, too frightened to even blink for fear he would disappear.

He was not looking at her, his eyes trained on Felipe.

'Sir Leksi,' Felipe said, shaking his head. 'Should have guessed it was you.'

Another horse stepped into view from the other direction. It was Prince Tyron, bow in hand and aimed at Felipe's men.

Her gaze returned to Leksi, expecting him to be gone, but the ghost remained. She sucked in a breath, remembering the guards following out of sight. 'There are six more men—'

Before she could even finish the sentence, an arrow flew over Leksi's shoulder, just missing his face. He swung his bow, eyes sharp as he searched the trees. Tyron spotted him first and took aim. A moment later, a cry rang out around them.

More arrows flew, some narrowly missing Petra when her horse's front legs lifted off the ground.

'Get down!' Leksi called to her, still searching for the other shooters.

Tyron's horse pivoted, and he released a few more arrows. A pained cry seeped through the trees. Luckily, the Corneon soldiers were not so accurate.

By that stage, the guards closest to her were feeling brave and attempted to draw their bows. As though sensing their actions, Leksi swung in the saddle and released two consecutive arrows, striking them through the neck.

Felipe reached for Petra's horse and yanked the gelding closer. Taking hold of her arm, he pressed the blade of his sword to her neck. 'Enough!'

Leksi aimed his bow at the prince, the string taut beneath his fingers. Petra knew if he killed the Crown Prince of Corneo, they would hunt him to the ends of the earth. She shook her head, the cold blade piercing her skin with the movement.

'Leksi, no!' Tyron called.

The knight hesitated just long enough for the tables to turn in Felipe's favour. The remaining soldiers emerged from the trees, weapons aimed at the two men.

'Finally, some calm,' Felipe said, keeping his sword in place. 'You can drop your weapons now, gentlemen,' he added, looking between them.

'If it's all the same to you,' Leksi said, 'I'd prefer to keep mine pointed at your face.'

Felipe looked at him. 'The infamous knight. I actually sympathise with you. Every now and then, a woman comes along and makes us look foolish in front of our enemies.' He nodded towards Petra. 'Isn't that right, Prince Tyron?'

'You have never needed a woman for that,' Tyron replied, his bow swinging between the men surrounding them.

'This one has done a really thorough job on my father,' Felipe said, shifting his sword.

Petra winced as the blade pressed into her neck, but she did not make a noise.

'Lower your sword,' Leksi demanded, his voice like gravel.

Felipe glanced at him. 'Why? You cannot shoot me. Even your prince, the man who wants me dead more than anyone else, knows that.'

'You know,' Leksi began, 'I had heard rumours that you owned a sword. I suppose I shouldn't be surprised that it's used only on women.'

Anger flashed in Felipe's eyes. 'Need I remind you that there are two arrows pointed at you.'

Leksi glanced both ways at the two guards. 'I've seen your soldiers shoot a few times in my life. They'll likely miss, and by the time they reload, Prince Tyron will have killed them both.'

Felipe laughed, an odd, vicious sort of noise. 'Your prince is faring no better than you.'

'I am not too worried,' Tyron said. 'I suspect your men will let me live for the same reasons I let you live—twice now. If either of us dies today, it will start a war bigger than we have seen in our lifetime.'

The men eyed one another for a moment, and Petra saw Felipe's throat move as he swallowed down that realisation. 'What is it with this woman? She has men falling to their knees. I know for a fact that you have no shortage of pretty women in Syrasan.' He paused. 'I had one myself once.'

Tyron did not react, likely prepared for whatever taunts Felipe would throw at him.

'You may kill the knight,' Felipe continued. 'I will pay Prince Tyron the same courtesy he showed me.' He narrowed his gaze. 'You may return home after watching your friend die.'

'No,' Petra said, stiffening beneath his sword.

Felipe's gaze returned to her. 'Perhaps I will kill you first.'

Felipe moved his hand so the tip of his sword was pressed into Petra's throat. She swallowed against the sharp edge, and a drizzle of blood ran down her throat onto her chest.

'Stop,' Leksi said, his confidence waning. His bow went taut, but something caught his eye in the distance. The guard closest to Tyron turned his head also, just as an enormous spear came hurtling through the air, piercing him through the side of his stomach where his armour was vulnerable. The horses stirred, and moments later more spears flashed through the trees, taking down every Corneon guard.

Felipe lowered his sword and watched, wide-eyed, as ten inked men emerged from the trees on their muscled horses. He looked around at his men on the ground, clutching their wounds. There was no hiding the panic on his face.

Leksi glanced at Tyron, then turned as the horses divided down the middle, creating a path. Queen Cora rode down the centre, seated on a black horse, the skirt of her tangerine dress cascading down the animal's rump. She pulled up the mare and narrowed her eyes on Prince Felipe.

'Forgive the rather dramatic arrival, but I get a little edgy when people point weapons at my family.' She looked between the three men. 'If this were a feast, I would happily settle myself at the high table and watch the conflict, but this is not fun for me.' She turned to Tyron. 'I knew you would follow Leksi on this foolish quest.'

Tyron nodded a greeting at his sister. 'I never thought I would say this, but I am really pleased to see you.'

'I really hope you appreciate the effort I went through to be here today.'

Leksi's bow was still pointed at Felipe. 'Time to drop your sword. Prince Tyron might not want to go to war over your death, but if that blade touches her skin again, I will kill you without hesitation.' He walked his horse towards them. 'Weapon down,' he said, louder that time.

Felipe's face was contorted with anger. Everyone knew he was a sore loser.

He glared at Petra before letting his sword drop to the ground.

Leksi watched as the air returned to her lungs. She turned to look at him.

'He told me you were dead.'

He continued towards her. 'King Nilos will have to send more than sixty men to kill me.' His teeth pressed together when he noticed the bruise above her eyes and the marks on her neck.

'What lies are you speaking?' Felipe asked, eyes following Leksi.

The knight looked at him. 'Did your father not tell you he sent men into Syrasan to hunt me?'

Judging by the prince's face, the answer was no. 'My father did no such thing,' he shot back.

'I am guessing there is much your father has not told you,' Cora said, rejoining the conversation. 'Like the fact that he has sent you on a fool's mission.'

That was news to Leksi, who stopped his horse to listen.

'What are you talking about?' Felipe asked.

She exhaled. 'I am talking about the fact that you are on your way to Onuric without my husband's knowledge. He does not like broken things.' She glanced at Petra when she said that. 'Everyone knows your mentor is just a few days from death and incompetent of training anyone.'

Leksi glanced at Tyron, who looked equally as surprised by the revelation.

'Ridiculous,' Felipe said. 'Why would he tell me to take his whore to Onuric only to be turned away?'

Without missing a beat, she replied. 'Because he never intended for you to make it that far. His only intention was to draw Lord Leksi out, because his last attempt to kill him failed.'

Prince Felipe shook his head. 'You expect me to believe

our men breached the western border and rode into Syrasan for the purpose of killing one man?'

Yet even as the prince spoke the words, Leksi saw the doubt in his face.

'Your father is not fit to rule,' Tyron said.

Felipe looked stricken as he pieced the new information together. When Leksi glanced at Petra, he noticed her face was suddenly paler than a few moments ago. She was trembling in the saddle. He pushed his horse forwards, wanting to get to her in case she was about to faint.

She met his gaze, eyes blazing.

'You need to run—now.' Looking around, she added, 'All of you!'

Leksi reached for her, ready to pull her from the saddle and put her safely behind him, where she belonged. But to his surprise, she leaned out of his reach. He put his hands up slowly, showing he meant no harm.

'Run!' she screamed.

When no one moved, Petra pressed her palms against her eyes. 'Don't you see?' she said before looking up. 'He would not send a handful of men to kill you after sixty failed.' Her eyes pleaded with him. '*Run,*' she whispered through gritted teeth.

He stared at her, and something in her expression told him this was not fear speaking, but a deeper perspective he did not have.

'Leksi,' Tyron called.

He turned.

'Listen.'

He could not hear it at first, but then he did. A faint vibration rumbled around them. It was a sound he recognised— the sound of battle.

'What is that noise?' Cora asked.

Leksi turned his horse so he was in front of Petra and

pointed his weapon at the trees, knowing it would not be enough.

'Protect your queen!' Tyron shouted to the Zoelin guards.

The men formed a circle around Cora and drew their swords.

Leksi snuck a glance at Felipe to gauge his reaction. He looked just as confused as the rest of them.

'I am so sorry,' said a broken Petra. 'He needs you dead in order to forgive me.'

'Easy,' Leksi said when his horse shuffled nervously beneath him. He looked over his shoulder at her just as a line of horses appeared on the horizon. 'Forgive you for what?'

Her eyes were dark pools of pain. 'For loving you.'

CHAPTER 36

*L*eksi estimated there were around four hundred men.

Dear God.

King Nilos had brought an army, which suggested he *really* wanted Leksi dead. The Zoelin guards would not fight to defend them, only their queen, which meant his odds of getting out of the forest alive were impossible. Add Petra's protection to the equation, and it would not end well.

The men formed rows of fifty, bows in hand ready for orders. Leksi looked over at Tyron, who was standing in front of his sister, also doing the math.

'It seems the power has once again shifted,' Felipe said, acting like it was part of a plan he knew something about. Having dropped his sword on the ground, he retrieved his bow and loaded it to reinforce the point.

Leksi ignored him and watched the men on the other side of the opening, his own bow poised.

'If you hand me over, he might let you live,' Petra said unconvincingly.

'There is not a chance in hell that I'm handing you over to that man for my sake.'

'Leksi, please. You do not know what he is capable of.'

He had seen the bruises. He knew exactly what that man was capable of.

His gaze moved down the line of soldiers stretching out before them, searching for the king. 'Perhaps your father got lost,' Leksi said to Felipe.

At that moment, there was a disruption in the line and King Nilos finally emerged—overdressed, overfed, and a sword at his side that had probably been made especially for the occasion. He stopped his horse halfway between his men and Leksi. His blazing eyes went straight to Petra and did not leave.

'Good afternoon, Your Majesty,' Tyron said. 'Is there a war on that we do not know about?'

The king dragged his eyes away to look at him. 'If you come into my kingdom, try to take what is mine, then you better be ready to fight.'

'Always up for a fair fight,' Leksi said. 'But this seems a bit much.'

Nilos glared at the knight. 'Just the man I wanted to see.' He looked suddenly pleased with himself. 'I knew you would come for her.'

'I wish I could say I knew you would bring an army of four hundred men, but I'd be lying.'

Nilos's face darkened. 'Did you really think you could put your hands on my queen and live?'

The man really was insane. 'Your *queen*? Corneo already has a queen. Perhaps you mean Companion. Or prisoner.' He snuck a glance at Felipe, who appeared embarrassed by his father's words.

'My love, my life,' Nilos said, one hand outstretched

towards Petra. 'Come to me. We cannot have you getting caught in the crossfire.'

Leksi turned, taking in her defeated expression.

'If I go with you, will you let them live?' Her voice barely carried the distance.

The king shook his head. 'It is for *you* that I do this, so you can finally be free of him.'

Leksi was torn between telling her to go with the king so she might live and telling her to stay where she was. With two swords, he might stand a chance. Though not a big chance. 'I might be missing the mark here, but I'm getting the distinct impression that she doesn't want to return to Masville with you.'

Nilos stared at him. 'I am really looking forward to killing you.'

'Oh? Then it looks like you brought your army for nothing.'

Nilos looked past him again. 'Petra, my queen. Come. Let us finally put this mess behind us.'

Leksi lowered his bow and turned to her, saying nothing. He would let her decide for herself. If she chose to go, he would not stand in her way. If she stayed, he would kill whoever necessary to keep her safe.

Staring at the king, Petra said. 'I will never be your queen. If you are asking me to choose a life with you, or certain death facing your army, I choose to stand with Leksi. I would choose him every time.'

Leksi released the breath he had been holding, feeling both relieved that she had taken a stand and terrified that he had just sentenced her to death. Clearing his throat, he said, 'I'll be honest with you. I may be in a little over my head this time.'

She reached for him, tipping forwards, eyes filled with

complete faith that he would catch her. He did. With one hand, he pulled her behind him. Her forehead rested on his back, and for the briefest moment, everything was right in the world.

'Tell me Xander is safe,' she said. 'That he is loved.'

Leksi looked at King Nilos as he spoke. 'He is safe. He is loved.'

He felt her exhale.

'Thank you,' she breathed.

'It seems your plan has some minor flaws,' Leksi called to the king. 'Like the fact that she would rather die than spend one more minute with you.'

The king's face glowed red, and his cheeks trembled.

'No one wants Petra to die,' Tyron said, taking a step forwards. 'Let her leave here safely with Queen Cora, and then you can have your war.'

King Nilos looked over at the queen, as though noticing her for the first time. Then his gaze returned to the delicate hands clutching Leksi's armour. 'No one leaves!'

Felipe walked his horse forwards a few paces. 'Father, you have been out in the sun too long. Let Queen Cora leave.'

Nilos's eyes were wide and almost as red as the rest of him. 'She is against us—a spy.'

The Zoelin guards might not have spoken their language, but judging by the way they readied their swords, they understood what was happening.

'Oh God,' Petra said. 'What have I done?'

'Your father is mad,' Leksi stated, turning to Felipe. 'You kill the queen, and King Jayr will crush you. His army will knock your castle to the ground and kill every member of your family. Corneo will cease to exist.'

'And they will have the full strength of the Syrasan army when they do it,' Tyron added.

Sweat gathered on Felipe's brow as he looked over at Tyron. 'Queen Cora is free to go, along with her guards.' He hesitated. 'And the Companion with her.' The words seemed to sour in his mouth.

'No,' Nilos said, hand going to his sword.

'And Prince Tyron,' Leksi added. 'It's me your father wants. Let everyone else leave unharmed.'

Tyron looped his bow over his shoulder and drew his sword. 'I fight alongside Leksi.' He looked back at Cora, who was watching the exchange from behind her guards. 'Sister, take the Companion with you.'

Petra's grip tightened on him. 'You will both be dead within minutes.'

'It's all right,' Leksi said, pressing his lips to the top of her head. 'Go with Cora. You can trust her.'

King Nilos drew his sword. 'Did you hear me? No one is going anywhere.' He raised his weapon above his head. 'Ready your bows!' he instructed his men.

'You will kill her,' Leksi shouted as the first row of soldiers raised their bows.

Tyron swung his horse around and called to his sister's guards. 'Get her out of here. Now!' He spoke Zoelin so there would be no confusion as to what was about to happen. The men had already raised their shields and were forming a protective wall around her.

'Nock!' Nilos shouted. Arrows were loaded.

He was really going to do it.

Leksi turned to Felipe. 'For the sake of your kingdom, stop him.'

The prince kicked his horse into a canter, still clutching his bow. 'Lay down your weapons,' he called to the men. 'Do not shoot!'

The soldier's bows wavered for a moment, and they looked between each other.

'Draw!' Nilos continued, as though his son had not spoken. Bows creaked.

But before the king had a chance to finish the command, Felipe raised his bow and shot an arrow at his father.

CHAPTER 37

The arrow struck the king's side, and he doubled over in the saddle. He managed to keep hold of his sword, while his free hand went to the arrow protruding from his hip. Petra's eyes locked on his, and she saw fear in them.

His horse shuffled sideways as an eerie silence fell over the forest. Felipe pulled his gelding up beside his father's and leapt from the saddle just in time to catch him as he tipped sideways. He lay the injured man on the ground.

'Traitor,' Nilos said, his face paling.

Felipe crouched next to him, eyes going to the wound. 'Killing the Queen of Zoelin would have been the end of Corneo. If you had just listened…'

Nilos's icy stare remained unchanged. 'Traitor,' he repeated.

Felipe stood, a look of disgust on his face. He turned to the waiting army and saw that some of the men were pointing their bows at him. It seemed their loyalties were divided.

'Do not aim your weapons at me.' He took a few

menacing steps in their direction. 'I just saved all of your lives, and those of your families. You want to go against the Syrasan and Zoelin armies? You think you would have stood a chance against them?'

Nilos was not even listening. He was searching for Petra. 'Where is my queen?' He reached in her direction, but she did not move. 'My queen.'

She heard the desperation in his voice as blood pooled beneath him. When she moved to dismount, Leksi caught her arm.

'What are you doing?'

Her eyes never left the king. 'I need to go to him.'

He hesitated before lowering her to the ground. 'You don't owe that man anything.'

She was already walking away, her legs surprisingly steady. Perhaps she drew strength from the king's disempowerment.

'My love,' he whispered when she came to a stop beside him. He reached for her, his bloodied fingers brushing her foot. She glanced at the blood on her shoe, captivated by the sight of it. The puddle beneath him grew because no one had tried to stop the bleeding, not even his own son. How many times had she imagined this moment? She had always thought she would be the one to do it and could not decide if she felt relieved or robbed.

'I am dying,' he said, sensing his end.

She looked down at the arrow, wondering if she had it in her to pull it free and apply pressure to the wound. He might live if she did.

Her gaze returned to his pale face. There was spit in his beard, and he looked every bit the mad king.

'He is not fit to rule,' Felipe said to no one in particular, his eyes on the ground. There was grief in his voice, yet he did not move to help his father.

Nilos gestured for her to come closer. 'Please.'

She obeyed, kneeling, her palms pressing against the ground either side of her. She felt the warmth of his blood between her fingers. Staring down at him, she waited to feel something, pity perhaps, but she was depleted of emotion. Her eyes went to her blood-painted hand, remembering the day she had been confronted by a dead Companion lying on the floor. It might have been labelled a suicide, but Petra knew who was really responsible.

'Tell me you love me,' Nilos said.

Her gaze darted to meet his. He coughed and twitched, life bleeding from him while she just sat there watching. She should have tried to save her king. They all should have.

'Tell me you love me,' he pleaded. 'Give me that.'

She leaned closer, the acidic smell of his blood over-whelming. 'Love you?' Her eyes moved over his grey face and pale lips. 'I cannot even *forgive* you.' She straightened. 'Even in death.' Pushing herself to her feet, she walked away, the king's pleas following her.

Leksi had dismounted and stood waiting for her. When she reached him, he laced his fingers through her bloodied ones. His other hand cradled her head, pulling her to him, his armour cool against her cheek. The king's strangled breathing reached them, and Petra closed her eyes as he drew his final breath. A horse whinnied, the only noise amid the deathly silence. No one moved.

Queen Cora was first to break the silence, pushing her horse through her barrier of guards to stand beside her brother. They looked at one another, siblings above all else.

'What a mess,' she said, turning to Felipe.

The prince raked his fingers through his hair as he stared down at his father. Tyron approached him on horseback, stopping a few feet away and looking out at the army of men. 'You are not dead yet, so that is a good sign.'

'Because every man here knows he was about to ruin us. I did what any good leader would do—I put my kingdom first.' Turning to the soldiers, he shouted, 'I will be ten times the king my father was.'

No one spoke.

'Your actions saved our lives,' Tyron said. 'If you walk away, I will attest to the fact that you acted in the best interest of the Corneon people, and that you were left with no choice but to shoot him.' He glanced at the dead king, whose head was turned in Petra's direction, one arm still outstretched. 'I will even say that you tried to save your father's life, as any son would his own father.'

They stared at one another, and then Felipe looked past him to Cora.

'Is that what you also witnessed, Your Majesty?'

She studied him for a moment before nodding. 'Yes.'

Felipe released a breath, then pointed at Petra. 'I never want to see that woman again. She is a curse on my household.'

Petra turned to face the glaring prince, his words hanging between them. Leksi kept hold of her, and she was fairly certain he was the only reason she was still standing.

'And keep your bastard child away from my throne,' Felipe added.

She had no intention of letting her son anywhere near it.

'Then we have an agreement,' Tyron said.

Felipe nodded. 'It seems we do.'

'Then best you take charge of your army, Your Majesty.' He bowed his head at the new king.

Petra turned back to Leksi. He was really letting her go.

Leksi hoisted her onto his horse before going to speak with Tyron. She watched as Prince Felipe approached his soldiers, addressing them as only a king would. They followed his orders to tend the dead, two men required to lift

King Nilos. They wrapped him in a flag of gold and hefted him onto his horse to be transported back to Masville for what would surely be an elaborate funeral.

She realised how few people would be saddened by the news of his death. Not his wife, not his children, not his people. A new king would bring fresh hope. He could win them over with food and promises of a brighter future. If he could just make it rain, he would be hailed a god.

When the task was complete, Felipe looked in their direction and, with a parting nod, led his army south.

The rest of them travelled east to Nuwien, then stood together at the intersection outside of the village, saying their goodbyes.

'Are you sure you don't want me to come with you?' Leksi offered. 'It's my mess, after all.'

Tyron shook his head. 'Best I deal with Pandarus.'

'They have developed a certain rapport that comes with years of sibling rivalry,' Cora explained. 'Pandarus will be less likely to behead his own brother.'

'What about you?' Leksi said. 'Your husband will be far from pleased when he hears of your escapades.'

'My husband will be none the wiser. I told him I was going to Archdale, and I am.'

'You trust your guards to keep your secrets?'

She flashed a wicked smile at him. 'Do you honestly think I would surround myself with men I did not trust?'

'Foolish of you to suggest such a thing,' Tyron said to Leksi, his tone dry.

'Thank you for your help, Your Majesty,' Leksi replied, bowing his head.

Cora pushed her horse forwards. 'Good luck with that one.' She gestured to Petra as her guards moved into place around her.

'Your Majesty.' Petra bowed her head.

'I will see you back in Wripis,' Tyron said. 'When you are ready.'

'Assuming Pandarus lets you leave.'

Tyron turned his horse. 'If he locks me up, I expect you to be first in line to rescue me.'

Leksi laughed and watched them until they were out of sight. Petra continued to stare at the empty road long after they had disappeared. She owed her life to those people.

Leksi's warm hand slid over her bloodstained one, his touch still familiar. Turning to her, he said, 'I'm taking you home.'

She raised her eyes to him and drew a shaky breath. 'Where is that?'

He frowned like she should know the answer. 'Where it's always been. With your son.'

CHAPTER 38

When the manor came into sight, Petra's hands went clammy and her heart raced. The last time she had seen him, it had all been a mess. She had not even had time to say goodbye. This time would be different: no one pursuing them, no façade, just hard truths and a long road of healing. What would he think of the woman presented as his mother? She was a stranger even to herself.

Before the horse had even come to a stop, the front door of the manor opened and Xander burst through it. He came at a run, round-faced and rosy-cheeked, an enormous grin splitting his face. She froze atop the horse, captivated by the sight of him. He was a stark contrast to the neglected boy she had met at the well months earlier.

Leksi dismounted and turned to help her down. The moment her feet touched the ground, he let go of her and jogged off in the direction of the steps.

'Leksi!' Xander squealed, leaping down the steps two at a time.

Petra just continued to watch, her heart almost bursting when Xander sprang into the knight's arms. Leksi laughed and hugged him tightly for a moment, and Petra's heart lodged in her throat. All those weeks she had been shut away from the rest of the world, suffocating, dying piece by piece, Xander had been living. She marvelled at their bond, expecting to feel a pang of envy but finding only gratitude.

Smiling, Leksi placed Xander back on the ground, crouching in front of him to comment on how big he had gotten.

'I saw you two days ago,' Xander said, beaming. *Beaming.* 'I thought it would be weeks.'

'So did I.'

Hali and Yuri had wandered out of the house. They stayed back, happy to watch the reunion from afar. Petra remained by the horse, in awe and a little afraid. Her hand went to the cut on her neck where a sword had rested the day prior. What would he make of it all?

'And look who I brought with me,' Leksi said, turning to her.

Xander's curious gaze was on her then. 'Why does she look different?'

So he did see it.

'Because she needs fattening up, like you did when you first arrived.'

Leksi stood, and Xander took his hand. 'Did the king not feed her?'

'Not enough, it seems.'

The boy studied her. 'She looks sad.'

Such a perceptive boy.

'Nothing a swim in the ocean and a lot of laughter can't fix,' Leksi replied.

She met his gaze. He sounded so confident, so sure there was something left to salvage. But soon he would realise that the woman he remembered had died in that room at Masville.

'Why don't we go say hello?' Leksi suggested.

She had intended to move, to go to them, but now she felt like an outsider, like she did not belong in their world.

They walked towards her, and Petra's eyes went to the small hand swallowed by Leksi's large callused one.

He was safe.

He was loved.

Now he watched her, seemingly unsure. She crouched, feeling too tall for him suddenly.

'Hello,' she said.

He chewed his lip and leaned closer to Leksi. 'Hello.'

She took in his smart clothes, which were covered in dog hair. 'Look how handsome you are.' Her eyes welled up as she spoke the words, but she did not cry.

He looked up at Leksi, then back at her. 'Do you like dogs?'

Her mouth twitched. An almost smile. A miracle. 'I can see *you* do.'

He looked down, brushing at his trousers. 'Hali let Muno sleep with me.'

'Muno?'

'Muno is a dog,' Leksi explained.

'She was supposed to guard the sheep,' Xander continued, 'but Lord Yuri says she's not very good at it.'

Petra nodded. 'I see. Perhaps she is good at something else, but no one has figured it out yet.'

Xander thought about that for a moment. 'She is good at being my friend.'

Warmth spread through her. 'Well, there you go.'

'Want to meet her?'

A close encounter with a dog was the last thing she felt like, but still she replied, 'I would love to meet her.'

She stood on shaky legs, determined not to ruin the moment by collapsing. They had travelled overnight, stopping frequently because her malnourished state had finally caught up with her. In fact, everything had caught up with her, the past few months hitting like a rock. But now Xander was inviting her in the only way he knew how, and she would not fall down.

The boy tugged on Leksi's hand.

'And you have definitely gotten stronger,' Leksi said, pulling his hand free and giving it a shake.

Another laugh from Xander.

Leksi wrapped an arm around her waist and brought his lips to her ear. 'I've got you,' he whispered.

She closed her eyes and swallowed back tears. While she could not say it, or show it, she loved the man.

Opening her eyes again, she looked down at Xander. 'All right. How big is this dog?'

'Huge!'

'And tied up?' she asked, hopeful.

'No such luck,' Leksi said, walking her towards the steps.

The previous months walked alongside her like a shadow, a dark stain on her soul. During that time, she had deprived herself of food and sleep, imagined her death, imagined the king's, shut down. Now the man responsible for her misery was dead, and somehow she was alive.

The realisation planted the smallest seed of hope. Perhaps with Leksi beside her, and a small boy whose smile radiated more warmth than the sun, she would not only survive, but live.

EPILOGUE

*S*ometimes Petra dreamed that she walked down to the ocean only to find it empty. No water, just parched sand stretching out like a desert, its sea creatures food for the crows. Waking with a start, she would creep from her bed and walk down the sandy slope, standing with her feet in the water and listening to the gentle roar coming off the waves, as though reassuring her that she had not been abandoned.

Five.

That was the number of years she had missed of Xander's life. Now he was six, and she had an entire year's worth of memories, small moments, laughter and gappy smiles to hold on to.

They began every morning the same: first mass, then a long play by the water. She never tired of watching Xander wade in the shallows, searching for shells and crabs. Muno was always close by, bounding alongside him, splashing cold water over anyone within ten feet of her.

That particular morning was no different.

'Naughty girl,' Petra gasped, brushing water off her dress.

She looked down at the dog who stared back at her with bright eyes, her tongue hanging from the side of her open mouth.

Xander was playing in the water nearby and looked up.

'You were wet anyway,' he said.

She glanced down to find the bottom of her dress soaked. The tide had come in and she had not even noticed. She often disappeared inside her head, sometimes losing hours. Xander never said anything. Perhaps he understood in his own six-year-old way. He was always there waiting when she returned from the dark nooks of her mind, boisterous and affectionate.

'Did you find any crabs?' she asked, gesturing to the pail in his hand.

'Three.'

A wave came in, catching the skirt of her dress. She did not step back from it, because every barefoot encounter with the water restored a small piece of her. 'Show me.'

He ran over to her, the crabs sloshing in the pail. She crouched, peering down at the clawed creatures. Muno trotted over and stuffed her enormous black snout into the pail. Petra went to push her away and lost balance, tipping backwards into the water. Muno licked her face as though it might somehow help the situation. Xander dropped the pail and rushed to help his mother.

'Now you're wet everywhere,' he said, trying to push the enormous dog away from her and failing.

That was what she got for letting Muno sleep with her son. The animal did not know her place. But as soon as the thought came, she pushed it away, scolding the mentor who occasionally surfaced. An enormous pink tongue came for her again, and she closed her eyes as she tried to get a grip on the dog. When she finally succeeded, she opened her eyes only to find Xander with his hands over his mouth, holding in laughter. He might not have shared Leksi's blood, but they shared the same sense of humour.

'Is that funny, is it?'

He nodded, keeping his hands in place.

'Then perhaps you will find *this* funny.' She scooped some water and threw it at him. He squealed and leapt back from her, laughter ringing out from him. Muno barked and bounded between them.

'Watch out for the crabs,' Xander called over his shoulder.

Her eyes went to the empty pail sitting on its side. Now it was her turn to squeal. She kicked her feet, imagining them crawling on her. A large wave came, splashing up her side. Another gasp, but that time followed by laughter—another piece of her restored.

'So this is what happens when I'm away?'

Leksi.

She turned her head, searching for him on the shore. He strolled towards her, a lazy grin on his face. She pushed herself up from the water and stumbled in her efforts to reach him quickly.

'Careful,' he called. 'Wouldn't want you to get wet.'

The moment her feet were on dry sand, she broke into a run. His smile widened as she flung herself at him, and he caught her without hesitation, not caring that his shirt and trousers were soaked in seconds. Before she could say anything, Muno bounded up to them, followed closely by a very excited Xander. Leksi kept hold of her with one arm while picking the boy up with the other. Even the dog got a brief pat.

'Looks like I'm just in time for a swim.'

It was all Xander needed to hear. He immediately wriggled out of Leksi's grip and sprinted back to the water, stripping off his shirt and trousers while he ran. Muno galloped after him, barking excitedly, sand and water spraying from her coat.

'I better make it a quick one,' Leksi said, glancing back at the house. 'We have company.'

'We do?' She followed his gaze as he placed her on the ground. 'Who?'

'Everyone.'

Her eyes widened at the sound of children. 'Aldara is here?'

'The whole family is here.'

She looked down at her soaked dress and sand-covered arms. 'I wish I had known that five minutes ago.'

He cupped her face and kissed her so deeply that she soon forgot about her dishevelled appearance.

'You look absolutely radiant,' he whispered into her mouth.

She pulled away so she could look at him. 'How long are you staying?

'A few days.'

She tried not to show her disappointment. It was not long enough. It was never long enough. 'I plan on making it very difficult for you to leave me.'

He ran a thumb over her cheek. 'You always do.' He moved his mouth to her ear. 'You might need to wait for our guests to leave though.'

She pushed on his chest, her cheeks burning.

'Are you coming in?' Xander called from the water.

Leksi tugged his shirt over his head, and Petra took in the sight of him, the silver scars painting lean muscle. She had to look away. The man was beautiful, a god, and she was lucky enough to call him her husband.

'Go on, then,' she said as he jogged away from her. 'I will tend to our guests, shall I?'

Leksi turned and walked backwards a few paces. 'You

might want to change your dress first, mentor.' He winked at her. 'Straight back, hands clasped in front of you. You remember how it's done?'

Petra shook her head. 'I have really missed your bad jokes.'

A grin from him. 'And sarcasm is unacceptable.'

Another shake of her head as she turned away, but she could not stop the smile that followed or the warm sensation that pulsed through her. It took her a moment to recognise it.

It was happiness—in its purest form.

That evening, Leksi sat with his arm draping the back of Petra's chair. Aldara had finally gotten Zelia to sleep, and Charis was playing chess with Xander and Mako in one of the bedrooms. Later, the royal family would travel back to the manor where there was plenty of room for everyone.

They were only mid-meal when Hali pushed her food away and leaned back in her chair, releasing a long groan as she did so. Her pregnant belly still touched the edge of the table despite her change in position. Aldara reached a hand out and placed it on top of her stomach.

'It will not be too much longer.' She gave Hali a knowing smile.

'There is literally no room for food in there.'

'Small, frequent meals are the key,' Aldara replied.

'Frequency is never Hali's problem,' Yuri said.

Hali shook her head at her husband. 'I would swat you if I could reach you, but just the thought of moving right now makes me tired.'

Petra laughed, and Leksi immediately turned his head to look. It was a sight he never tired of. She was a different woman to the one he had chased down a year earlier. Her once hollow eyes shone brightly, her cheeks round and full of colour. She was alive, brought back from the dead.

This was the woman he had glimpsed briefly all those months ago, the one King Nilos had suffocated. There were times where he still lost her to that life, brief moments when his voice did not reach her and the light would fade. But she always came back to him. Sure, she still turned the handles of the pots so they pointed in the same direction, but this version of her loved openly, and with her whole heart. She was no longer afraid to say it, to show it, to feel it. And he loved her back, more than he could ever put into words.

Tyron stood and everyone looked to him. He excused himself for a moment and returned with a roll of parchment secured with the king's seal. 'I have something for you,' he said, handing it to Leksi.

Leksi frowned at the seal. 'Has King Pandarus finally sentenced me to death?'

Everyone laughed.

'Something like that,' Tyron replied, a smile tugging at his mouth as he took his seat again.

Leksi broke the seal and read it. When he reached the bottom, he cleared his throat and then read it again.

'Well, do not keep us all in suspense,' Petra said. 'Am I to watch you hang or not?'

His gaze went to her. 'Look at what a bad influence I am. You're developing a rather wicked sense of humour.' He handed her the parchment. 'Looks like you will be addressing me as *my lord* from now on.'

She rolled her eyes. 'What are you talking about?' She read the letter, and her lips formed a small smile. When she looked up at him, he saw pride in her eyes.

Hali was holding a cup of wine with two hands, balancing it on her belly. She looked between them in confusion.

'Lord?' She turned to Tyron. 'I can only assume the document is forged, or His Majesty was drunk at the time of signing.'

'I assure you Pandarus did eventually agree,' Tyron said. 'It just took a year for him to sign it.'

Leksi laughed and caught Tyron's gaze across the table. 'Thank you. This is a great honour.'

'Of course, the title is not without perks.' The prince took Aldara's hand as he spoke. 'It comes with land.'

'Let me guess,' Leksi said. 'Somewhere near the Braul border, where even weeds refuse to grow?'

There was light laughter around the table.

'That was Pandarus's first suggestion,' Tyron said, 'but I finally convinced him to give you something further north.'

'Oh, fancy,' Hali said. 'Where? Please say Veanor.'

'Right here, actually. This house, this land.'

Petra's gaze went to her lap, and she brought a hand to her face. 'Sorry,' she whispered, becoming emotional.

Leksi reached out and brushed a finger down her cheek. 'I really hope those are happy tears, because given my current standing with the king, I'm not sure how fussy I can be.'

She smiled and wiped her eyes. 'Definitely happy tears.' She looked at him. 'Our piece of ocean.'

'This has been your home for some time,' Aldara said. 'Now it is just official.' She glanced at her husband. 'There is more.'

Everyone turned to Tyron, waiting for him to continue.

'A late wedding gift,' he said.

Leksi nodded as though agreeing with something. 'To be honest, we thought the money you gifted was a little light, but Petra insisted I not say anything.'

More laughter.

'A long time ago, I promised you a house in Wripis. It has finally been built. I do not like the idea of families being separated.' He looked at Petra. 'Whenever Leksi travels east, you and Xander can now join him.'

Leksi was all out of jokes. He glanced across at his crying wife, then stood. Walking around the table, he pulled Tyron to his feet and into a hug. 'Thank you, brother.'

Tyron patted his back before returning to his seat.

'Oh dear, now you have started Hali off,' Yuri said, smiling at his wife.

'She has the perfect excuse,' Aldara said, rubbing Hali's round belly.

Cups were filled, wine consumed, jokes made. It was an evening of friendship, of family, a reminder of what they had all fought so hard for.

Only when Hali's yawns became so incessant they could no longer be ignored did the party come to an end. Sleeping children were carried out in the arms of their parents and loaded into the wagon. Goodbyes were exchanged, and then Petra returned inside to tuck Xander into his bed while Leksi scolded Charis for falling asleep when he was supposed to be watching the children. The dog jumped onto Xander's bed, snuggling into the boy's side as he had done every night since they had been introduced.

Leksi leaned in the doorway, watching as Petra stroked Xander's hair before giving the dog a hesitant pat.

'He is safe. He is loved,' he whispered.

She turned to him, unaware that he had been watching them. Pushing off the bed, she went to him, wrapping her arms around his middle and kissing his chest. 'I love you.'

'I love you, *Lord Leksi*,' he said with a straight face. She laughed softly into his tunic, and he lifted her face to see it. Such beauty. 'Want to go for a swim?'

Her smile faded. 'Now? It is dark.'

He bent to kiss her. 'It's *perfect*.'

'We will not be able to see a thing in the water.'

When she took a step back from him, he caught her hand. 'What have I told you? When I'm here, you're safe.'

She studied his mischievous expression. 'Very well, *Lord Leksi*. I put myself in your very capable hands.'

He nodded approvingly. 'That's more like it.' Turning, he led her out of the house and down to the water.

She was safe.

She was loved.

ACKNOWLEDGMENTS

I would like to express my gratitude to the many people who contributed to this book. My biggest thanks goes to my readers. Without you guys, I wouldn't get to do what I love. Next, a huge thank you to my rock star husband who supports and encourages me even though my writing takes time away from him. I love you to bits. A big thank you to Joanna Walsh from Saltwater Writers for your ongoing feedback and support. A big shout-out to my beta readers, who each brought a unique perspective. Your insights were fabulous. Thank you to Kristin and the team at Hot Tree Editing for polishing the manuscript into something beautiful, and to my proofreader Rebecca Fletcher for catching everything I missed. A round of applause for MiblArt for this gorgeous cover. And finally, a huge thank you to my Launch Team for your encouragement, honest reviews, and being the final set of eyes on my work. You guys are amazing.

ALSO BY TANYA BIRD

You can find a complete list of published works at
tanyabird.com/books

Made in United States
Cleveland, OH
23 December 2024

12572081R00194